THE DRAGON'S
BOOK ONE:

Dragon's Egg

SR LANGLEY

Published by The House of SoRoL
100 Colne St.
Castleton
Rochdale
OL11 2UG

***

DRAGON'S EGG COPYRIGHT PAGE:

All characters are fictional. Any resemblance to persons living or dead is purely coincidental.

DRAGON'S EGG, DRAGON'S ERF and all original characters, events and settings © 2019 SR Langley (identified as the author of this work) All rights reserved. No part of this book may be reproduced in any form or by any electronic or mechanical means including information storage and retrieval systems without permission in writing from the author, except by a reviewer, who may quote brief passages in a review.

***

Conditions of Sale

This book is sold subject to the condition that it shall not, by way of trade or otherwise, be lent, resold, hired-out or otherwise re-circulated without the author's prior consent in any form of binding or cover other than that in which it is published and without similar condition including this condition being imposed on the subsequent purchaser.

***

Sign up for my Newsletter here: info@srlangley.com
Check out my Website here: https://www.srlangleywriter.com
(Receive further information about the worlds of Dragon's Erf… and lots, lots more!)

GIFTS

I give you demons, give you trolls,
I give you ancient magic scrolls,
I give you spells that make you king,
For those that like that kind of thing.

I give you colours, red and blue,
Of summer's green, and yellow too,
The hues of autumn, winter, spring,
For those that like that kind of thing.

I give you diamonds, pearls and jades,
I give you light that never fades,
And stars and moons and Saturn's ring,
For those that like that kind of thing.

I give you song and dance and play,
I give you speeches, words to say,
I give you words that soar and sing,
For those that like that kind of thing.

I give you thoughts, ideas and dreams,
I give you sighs; I give you screams,
I give you angels on the wing,
For those that like that kind of thing.

I give you all these things and more,
From my imagination's store,
From me to you, these things I bring,
For those that like that kind of thing.

(From ~ Jaxx - the Mad Jester of the North's ~
Book of Serious Jokes)

Table of Contents

PROLOGUE

Only twelve of the Royal Guard had survived. The smoking corpses of their fallen comrades lay scattered in discarded ruin amongst the rubble of the outer court. The once one hundred strong cohort of proud Warrior-dragons had been decimated.

Captain Strebor gave the command to fall back to defend the inner sanctum where their Lord, Divad Sivad, High King of the True-Dragons, sat curled and slumped on his royal couch-throne, awaiting with no great concern the unfolding of his supposedly fearsome fate.

The High King Sivad had lost too much already. Long gone was his and the True-Dragons' Golden Age. His slow slide into insanity and indifference had begun over a thousand years ago, when he had lost his wife and Soulmate, in the Battle of the Black Cavern. He could now no longer face the past, let alone the future. And the latest news of the loss of his only son and the present, de facto, ruling King of the True-Dragons, was too much to bear.

The slow death of his all-consuming apathy was now nearing completion.

The loyal One Hundred, however, had refused to desert their posts. They had now paid the ultimate price. The Fire-Worm Lords of the Core had surprised the Dragon Kingdom with their attack on the High King's Palace. The kingdom had been left much weakened with the new King-Regent, the Lord Nevets Yram, now reportedly lost on a mission to aid a distant Under-Erf Cavern-World.

"Form a ring around the High King!" Captain Strebor cried out urgently to his Warriors. "Let no Creature of the Core come near him. We will keep our oaths and defend the High King to our last flicker of red battle-flame!"

The Guards obediently surrounded the unseeing and uncaring High King; each Dragon Warrior facing resolutely outwards, ready for the next vicious onslaught.

As they waited, the teeming Minion Army of the Core filled the Inner Court from all directions. Every inch of the blue-marble flooring was now covered with the writhing, loathsome worms; the sickly-red and yellow, foot-long grubs, with wide, pincer-like maws and drooling, toxic fangs. The floor was a heaving sea of acid-spitting death.

"I know we are beyond all hope, our reserves of protective blue flame are now near-exhausted, but we still have our red battle-flame and we will stand and do our duty!" Strebor grimly telepathed, knowing indeed, that each of his twelve brothers would hold firm, no matter the odds against them.

***

Lord Morgrim surveyed the scene before him and shivered with pleasure at seeing his age-old foes outnumbered and all but vanquished. He had only agreed to this sudden assault on their deadliest enemy because now was the right time. Morgrim was extremely cunning. He had definite plans and this well-prepared raid upon the High King of the True-Dragons and his heirs fitted very neatly into the overall scheme of things. *His* scheme of things.

His twin brother and the current King of the Core, Morgrave, however, though far less cunning, was a lot more enthusiastic about killing True-Dragons. In fact, he was fanatical about it and had become more so with each passing century.

King Morgrave stood next to the more patient Morgrim. Morgrave was foaming at the mouth and grinning in gleeful anticipation at the demise of his most hated, ancient enemy, the High King Divad Sivad. And was unknowingly being mentally restrained from launching into the battle himself by the subtle telepathic control of his brother, Lord Morgrim.

"Come, my Brother, let us finish them all off, the so-called noble line of the Sivads must be ended and forever quenched in the fires of our almighty wrath! I have so sworn it!" King Morgrave hissed to Lord Morgrim eagerly. "It is that cursed line of Dragons, above all others, who have forever foiled our rightful domination over the Under-Erf and its wealth of Cavern-Worlds. Do you hear me, Morgrim? No matter the cost, the foul line of Sivad must be destroyed forever!"

King Morgrave quivered and coiled in agitated frustration as he bellowed his feelings of burning hatred to his royal twin, Lord Morgrim. However, in truth, Morgrim was listening only half-heartedly; His foolish brother's thoughts only echoing annoyingly in his head like an insect's constant and irritating buzz.

He has of late become increasingly given to these bothersome bouts of boiling bile and fuming fits of ferocious ire; Much like an erupting geyser, always ready to spurt its vile and vitriolic abuse, Morgrim quietly thought to himself, then answered his regal brother as soothingly as he could.

"Not quite yet, brother, not quite yet; we still have no word of the Dragon Queen, Sivam Sivad and her final Egg. Thus, we must apply some force and some intelligence now. So, patience, we will yet have our reward, but we must have all of the Sivads for that."

Lord Morgrim now turned his attention to Strebor, the Captain of the Dragon Guard and telepathed to him, oozing charm and confidence.

"Captain, you have fought bravely, but you are about to lose your life as well as the lives of all your valiant Dragon warriors, and what for? Nothing! Look at your High King; He is a broken, abject wreck, of no worth to you or me. Why throw your lives away on such a thing as that? Turn him and his offspring over to us now and I promise we will let you live."

Morgrim's powers of persuasion were infamous. All Dragons, both True and Un-True, had great powers of Mind, but Lord Morgrim's Arts of Mind Manipulation were second to none. The Captain lowered his head and looked behind him, glancing at his ancient High King. What he saw stung him to the quick.

For a mere moment, Strebor weakened and even considered the proffered course of capitulation and surrender. The uncomfortable truth was that Morgrim's words had rung true. The High King lay behind him unmoving and seemingly unknowing and totally indifferent to the terrible fate awaiting the remnants of his loyal Dragon Guard.

"Oh, yes, you filthy, winged-flies," hissed King Morgrave, now interjecting suddenly, "do as we demand and be our slaves, or you will die, do you hear me, you will die, horribly!" Unfortunately for Lord Morgrim, and his hope for a swift and more effortless resolution, this broke the spell he'd been carefully weaving.

The weary Captain quickly came to his senses, reared his weathered and battle-scarred head up and blasted out several gouts of red, dragon flame in irate defiance.

Then before Morgrim could take control, or Morgrave could blurt out anything more 'helpful,' a beetle-like Minion-Messenger came scuttling up to them both from the rear.

"My Lordships, I have been sent to inform you that the Dragon King, Nevets Yram, has been sighted and is returning with his Warrior Army. Reports say his strength is but half of what it was, but by the pace he is making he will be upon us this very day!"

"That stupid brute Nevets! He has somehow survived the ambush we set!" Morgrim hissed furiously, briefly losing control of his emotions. "He must have somehow discovered that the call for help from the Goblin's Cavern-World was a mere ruse to lure him away. He will now attempt to maintain the True-Dragon Kingship and ensure his son is hatched and so lives to be the Sivad heir. It is vital we find the Queen and destroy her and her Egg, no matter what!"

"Yesss!" King Morgrave spat back contemptuously in reply. "But we still have plenty of time to finish these Dragon scum off and their feeble High King too, and while we're here, I want us to kill everyone and everything we can find!"

"Oh, dear brother," Lord Morgrim sighed. "You forget, we are here, as you yourself so ardently desire, but to end the line of the Sivads forever. Yes, we have the High King now and long ago we dispatched his wife. And I'm sure the current King will soon be ours as his power is broken and his first son and daughter we have dealt with. It is only this nuisance of a Queen and her third Egg that survives and is any threat to us now."

"Your counsel is wise brother. Then I will search the Dragon Cavern-World and all of the Erf if I have to… until I find her and her troublesome, addled Egg. I will not be thwarted. You hear me, my oh so clever brother. I will see they all die. Every Sivad shall perish!"

With that, he broke Morgrim's mental hold and ordered his Minion hordes to attack.

***

"Conserve your blue flame as much as possible, fellow Dragon Guards. Protect the High King and do not falter. Live and Die by your Oath!" cried Strebor, as the squirming multitude of Minions wriggled towards them in a relentless, seething swarm.

Captain Strebor and his cohort of True Dragons now joined mind to mind, raising a pale, flickering, blue dome of repellent flame around themselves and their old, apathetic High King. Strebor well knew they had mere minutes to maintain such a protective shield.

There were just too many minion worms and too few Dragons.

He turned to face the High King, hoping for a miracle. In his prime, he had been unbeatable. He prayed to the Dragon Spirits the High King would somehow find his old self again and save the day.

Our High King once wielded the High Magic and had the Mind-Skill to better these brutal Core-beasts, he thought. If only that High King of yore, Divad Sivad was with us now, I could then die a proud True-Dragon!

But he saw that the one all-powerful and noble, High King, remained motionless and unmoved by all the chaos and destruction being wrought around him.

So, Captain Strebor turned and focused his attention back onto the advancing horde. Then there was no longer time to even think. The marauding mass of worms were upon them.

Strebor could see that the right flank of his circle of True Dragons was faltering and slowly being overwhelmed. Their blue dome of magical flame was flickering and weakening. Then two of the Dragon Guards on that side collapsed.

Within a hot heartbeat, a flood of hissing and spitting minion worms swarmed over the two Dragon's thrashing bodies.

There was nothing more that the valiant Captain of the Guard could do. One by one, each True-Dragon Warrior was similarly overwhelmed. Each was brought down and then rapidly became a lonely island of seething, acid-spitting worms. Each of their huge, battle-scarred bodies being ravaged by the deadly, mindless Worm-Minions only the Fire-Worm Lords of the Core controlled.

Their blue dome of protective flame had been extinguished. Strebor roared his final battle cry. He flailed around, scattering the voracious worms to the left and right.

But to no avail. Even his fiery strength was consumed by the vile swarm as they smothered his defiant form.

At the very last, the High King of the True Dragons, surrounded by nothing but charred corpses, raised his tired, old head and observed the carnage spread out before him. Then momentarily, something re-kindled within his chest. Some ancient memory of valour and pride; of royalty and responsibility, fleetingly reappeared. Some remnant of his old fire had found its way into his heart.

He majestically reared up over his dead comrades and charged.

For a moment, he was fully alive and a Warrior again. His mind a searing blast of pure hatred for these foul, evil Worms of the Core, who had wrought so much destruction upon his beloved Dragon Kingdom and his precious family.

But the brave and defiant surge came too late.

As he charged across the Courtyard, straight towards King Morgrave, he was brought down by a bludgeoning blow from Lord Morgrim's heavy, clubbed tail. Then the swarm of rampaging worm Minions was upon him, stinging and ripping him to bloody shreds.

Thus, the Last High King of the True-Dragons died.

"Now for Queen Sivam Sivad!" Cried Morgrave ecstatically. "You return to the Core with our new captives, Morgrim. For I will not return until I have killed the last Sivad! Come, my Minions, we will search the Palace and wherever else we need to… until we find her!"

***

"Oh, my foolhardy brother!" Morgrim rumbled quietly to himself. "Your rashness could mean the ruin of all my carefully laid plans. Now just what am I going to do with you?"

***

CHAPTER ONE.
HOME IS WHERE THE HURT IS.

It was ten o' clock in the morning, and Grannie's caravan was filling up with smoke.

"Oh Gran, not again, you know it's bad for you!"

Mary Maddam, Grannie Maddam's thirteen-year-old granddaughter, was still not used to her Grandmother's unhealthy, bad habits, especially her insistence on smoking her morning pipe of baccy.

"I do wish you'd give a body fair warning when you're going to smoke the place out!"

"Ain't nuffin' like a good lung-full of' raggedy shag to get yer tonsils tickled," Granny Maddam replied, sweetly smiling at her, as Mary gathered her snack box and flask into her shoulder bag, getting ready for her Saturday morning foray into the nearby woods.

"Raggedy 'ag, raggedy 'ag," cawed their colourful South American parrot, Jemima, in her badly rendered and raucous echo.

"An' you can keep yer beak shut, too," Mary muttered over her shoulder as she quickly exited the caravan. Jemima was always one to take Grannie's side, probably because it was Gran that actually fed and watered the talkative, old parrot, as well as the one who taught her all her very colourful language.

"Don't you's be getting into mischief in them woods now, you hear?" Grannie called after Mary, as wisps of tobacco smoke curled out of the open door into the cool morning air.

But Gran could see Mary was already gone and making her way jauntily through the trees. Grannie Maddam smiled, knowing that Mary's annoyance would quickly turn towards her usual cheerfulness at being out and about in the woods and the wind and the wild.

Grannie Maddam watched her go and heaved a wistful sigh. She sat comfortably in her cosy armchair, contentedly puffing on her pipe and stroking her rather plump tabby cat, Jericho, (whom she called 'Jerry' for short).

Lying next to her, on the little table by the chair, lay the crumpled letter she'd just received from the SPS, the Social Police Services.

She'd screwed it up angrily and then flung it down amongst all the assorted detritus of teacups, magazines, half-eaten biscuits, and other bric-a-brac strewn there. Grannie Maddam was not well suited to orderly housework. She tapped her pipe on the over-filled ashtray and looked down upon the letter now with disgust.

"Well, there's no needs fer a causin' a kerfuffle for the child now, is there?" she muttered to herself. "Those SPs are full o' their usual gobbledygook, sending their officious warnings, more like vicious yawnings, if yer asks me!" She scratched Jericho's ear and took another big, relaxing draw on her pipe, then reached down and picked the letter up once more.

There, it clearly and callously stated, in the SPS's usual bureaucratic monotone:

Dear Sir or Madam,

We have sent you repeated warnings regarding your legal standing, duties, and commitments in the proper upbringing of your Ward and Granddaughter, Miss Mary Maddam (age 13). The Social Police Service under the auspices of the Psychonomy, has noted that as yet, no heed has been paid to these warnings. So, we are herewith issuing this final, official warning letter to you.

You are hereby advised to adhere to the legal requirements as laid down by the Psychonomy of Inglande and the Greater Council for Under Lundun, regarding these aforesaid duties.

If your Ward continues to fail to attend her assigned school and regimen in the new term after the current summer break and/or fails to adhere to the correct dress codes of aforesaid institution, then your Legal Guardianship will be revoked and your Ward taken for placement in a facility for orphans and delinquents. Furthermore, you will be officially charged with all parenting violations that we now have on file.

An Officer of the Social Police Services will be attending your address on Monday the 10th August, at 10.30am, to officially inspect and ascertain your complete adherence and compliance. Please sign the enclosed copy of this letter in due acknowledgment of receipt of this warning.

We hope, forthwith, to find you fully complying with the Psychonomy's official, 'Parental Rules & Regulations.' Your failure to do so will result in immediate action, as outlined above.

Yours Dutifully,

Miss. Abigail T. Watt. Esq. Parenting Psychonomist. SP Class 3. (Under Lundun)

"Load of argle-bargle," she muttered again. But then frowned deeply. This was indeed a very worrying bit of argle-bargle. "Well, I'll 'ave to speak to the girl 'bout this. We'll 'ave to be doin' sumfin, but I'll let 'er 'ave 'er weekend free of worry fer now."

***

Mary, meanwhile, was making her way through the woods, blissfully ignorant of such mundane but mendacious matters.

Today was Saturday, and this was Mary's favourite time of the week, the weekend; when it was her and Gran and no one else; when her schooling and her chores had all been done, and she was free to roam wherever she wanted. But this Saturday, she had a particularly important job to do. She was off to find a good remedy to help cure her Gran's arthritis. As Gran was getting older, her aching joints seemed to be getting worse every year. She wanted to help her Gran get better. She was, after all, all the family she now had left.

I'll head down near the River Quaggy, sees if I can find some of that rare White-Willow Bark Grannie was telling me about the other day. Maybe I can get 'old of some Angelica an' Eyebright an' even some Heartsease there as well, she thought hopefully, as she made her way ever deeper into, what she knew as, the Good Wood.

Mary walked happily and directly on towards the tree-lined banks of the River Quaggy, completely oblivious of Grannie Maddam's worries, and heading for an adventure beyond her wildest dreams. She saw it was indeed a lovely day and the Good Wood felt friendly and familiar to her. This wasn't at all surprising really, as she had spent nearly all her childhood playing in, exploring and discovering its many natural treasures.

Mary knew a lot about plants, and she was learning more all the time. She loved the wild woods; she loved nature and all the things it was made from; all of the amazing variety and wonder of the living things in it. Her favourite place in the whole Erf was the Good Wood, which luckily for her began just behind her colourful caravan home.

But as she made her way, on this lovely, late summer's day, she tried to keep her mind on her mission and not be distracted by any other marvels of nature she might come across.

"I just wonder though," she mused to herself, "I just wonder what it's really like across the River Quaggy? I juss can't believe all them horror stories they tell us at school about it."

Mary made her way down the sloping trail she had used many times before, toward the winding river that bordered the south-eastern part of what was, in fact, a very large forest, known as the Great Forest of Lundun.

On the other side of the Quaggy stretched the dark and mysterious part of it which the locals in those parts called the 'Bad Wood.' And according to her sketchy geography lessons, this went as far as the old River Tymes. But what was on the North side of the River Tymes, was said to be even weirder and wickeder than anything on the Southern side.

"I bet if I dared crossin' the Quaggy though, I could find some real rare an' useful plants," an' I juss bet anything, I'd find some o' that White-Willow Bark over there too."

The Bad Wood was supposedly bad enough, but this morning, for reasons she couldn't even begin to understand, she was feeling even more curious than usual about the many dark mysteries that it was rumoured to contain.

"Trouble is, that's where the so-called 'bad' plants an' animals are all supposed to live," she sighed, as she trudged along. "An' people just never go across the River Quaggy now, coz its considered way too dangerous; They says that people disappear if they goes off into them there Bad Woods for too long!"

Even Grannie Maddam had warned Mary to always keep to the paths of the Good Wood, and never to go across the River Quaggy. The Bad Wood had a very bad reputation indeed!

"Some nasty critters an' even nastier plants," was all her Gran would say on the matter.

But Mary had heard all the scare stories before; it was just common knowledge as you grew up, there were still some wild areas across the Planet Erf, and even in the more civilized country of Inglande, that Man had yet to fully conquer. The Great Forest of Lundun and its south-eastern part, known as the 'Bad Wood,' was but one of them.

Grannie Maddam was of ancient gypsy stock and had taught Mary a lot about all the different plants that grew in the Good Wood. Mary remembered when she was just a wee little girl how her Gran had always taken her out to the Good Wood and told her all about the plants and the animals there. Mary had loved learning and finding out where the different sorts of herbs and flowers grew. She was what her Grannie had called "a Nat'ral Herb'list."

"But getting hold of some White-Willow Bark right now is my most important and pressing problem. This trip I'm determined to get some, no matter what," she thought emphatically.

But as she sauntered through the green freshness of the wood, she began to daydream and think about her much-missed mum. She could hardly believe that two whole years had gone by since her mum had become very ill and had been taken away by the Psychonomists.

She loved her Gran, but she still loved and missed her mum very much. She did her very best, though, to keep her feelings about losing her mum to herself, locked up, along with the broken bit of heart inside her; a sad and silent sort of secret.

As she walked along, she remembered hearing how her mum was something called a 'single-mum,' which she'd thought at the time a really strange idea.

"How could a mum be anything else, you only had one mum after all, didn't you?"

Then she'd heard that her mum had some sort of a 'syndromey' thing and so had to go away for "full-time care" in a special hospital.

Her Grandma had taken overlooking after her then, so now it was just her and her Gran, and of course Jemima the parrot and Jericho the cat, living all alone, but happily, in their colourful and cosy caravan by the edge of the Good Wood.

The long-awaited summer holidays had arrived, and Mary eagerly looked forward to many days of roaming the woods, without the interference of having to go to school. She knew that her missing lessons and 'bunking' off school caused her Gran a lot of trouble.

She also knew, as her legal guardian, her Gran had already been seen by the Social Police Service. Mary had 'accidentally' looked at a letter that Grannie had left lying about a month or so ago. The SPS had voiced their grave concerns that her Grannie Maddam may not in fact be suitable as Mary's Guardian.

The last thing Mary wanted was to be taken away and put in some horrid Psychonomy Institution and so lose her Gran as well as her mum.

But it wasn't in Mary's nature to dwell on such things for too long.

"Poor ol' Grannie, she does suffer from her bone aches and such like," Mary thought as she walked onward and strengthened her resolve to find the needed White Willow Bark.

"It's probably juss too much of her home-brew, herb-cordials, and all her smoking too," she added as an afterthought, shaking her head with a motherly sigh.

Mary's worry about her Gran's health and unorthodox ways and so-called 'bad habits' were of real concern to her. She did her very best to disguise this and keep cheerful though, but the truth was - Home was definitely where the Hurt was.

***

"And where do you think you're off to?" boomed Mr. Briggs from his ground floor study, just as Roger, his one and only son and heir, came creeping down the sweeping stairway, doing his level best to evade just such an encounter.

"I thought I'd go out for a b-b-bit, to do scientific field work, Father," Roger answered.

"Well, have you done your homework? Where are you now on the school class rankings? Are you still the top of your class, eh? Well, you'd better be, my boy. We can't have a Briggs slacking off now, can we?"

"Yes, S-s-sir; I mean n-n-no, F-f-father; I mean yes, I have d-d-done my homework… and yes, I'm still t-t-top of the class. At l-l-least I was - when we were l-l-last tested, Sir!"

"Harrumph! Well, let's keep it that way, eh? We have to show the world what the Briggs's are made of, eh? And I see you still have that silly stammer of yours. Just when are you going to grow up and get rid of it boy, eh? Pure affectation it is, I say, pure affectation!"

"Yes, F-f-father; I mean, s-s-sorry, Father. I'll try to get rid of it, I p-p-promise."

"Well, see that you do, my boy, see that you do! Don't you forget, I am now an elected Councillor of Inglande, serving on the Under Lundun Council."

"Yes, F-f-father. I mean, no Father."

"And that I'm standing for election as Prime Councillor this year. So, we all need to be smart and on the ball in the Briggs family right now, now don't we, Roger?"

"Yes, S-s-sir, of course. I'm sure the f-f-field work helps my school r-r-results too, Sir."

"Very good, very good; well carry on then, Roger, and no getting into any mischief, right?

"R-r-right Sir. Yes sir."

"Good. I don't want you getting mixed up with that rif-fraff that attends your state school. Really, if it wasn't for your mother keeping you tied to her apron strings, I'd have boarded you out years ago, no matter the Psychonomy's policies on such things."

"Yes, S-s-sir," agreed Roger meekly, as Mr Briggs indicated he was dismissed.

Then, just as he thought he was free, his mother came bustling in through the front door, carrying a hat box under one arm and a rolled-up newspaper under the other. And she wasn't in a good mood.

"Brian dear, will you kindly instruct the paper boy to desist from hurling your paper into our front porch? It's most uncouth and downright dangerous too. This newspaper thingy nearly had me right over. It would have totally ruined my new hat if I'd been tumbled over. It's really not on, Brian. Brian, do you hear me!"

"Yes dear, I mean no dear, of course, dear, err… not on at all dear." Mr Briggs replied, suddenly quite meek himself.

He dutifully took the paper Mrs Briggs rammed into his ribs, after depositing her precious hat box onto the hall stand.

Roger could see boldly blazoned across the newspaper's front page, the startling headline:

THE DAILY BEACON: - Saturday, August 8th. 1951.

'THE FUTURE IS SAFE! ATOMIC POWER WILL SOON BE OURS!!!

"Government Scientists have now scheduled a series of experiments over the next six months for the production of Atomic Power. The series of experiments will be overseen by a joint team of top scientists from Ameriga and Inglande, headed by Professor Kluxklu of…"

At this point, Roger's attention was pulled away from the paper as his mother stepped abruptly between him and his father. His father, seeing his opportunity, quietly shrank back into his study with the newspaper and closed the door.

Roger's rather shrill and excitable mother had now decided to directly address, what she considered, was her somewhat weak and ailing only child by giving him the doubtful benefit of her motherly attention.

"Now, now Roger, whatever are you up to? You know you mustn't go out without a scarf! And do you have enough hankies with you, dearest?" she demanded, in a burst of effusive and frantic fussing, pulling him to her ample bosom and taking a scarf from the nearby hat stand and wrapping it around his neck several times.

Roger grimaced and showed her his wodge of hankies in his pockets. "Very well, dear, now don't be late and do keep warm and away from any, er, well you know… bad people."

With that, Roger finally scuttled across the hall and out the front door as fast as he could.

"Free at last, and its Froghopper day!" he gasped with great relief as he hurried away from the large and austere Manor-house perched on the outskirts of upmarket Mottington.

Roger Briggs was what, in olden times (at least as far back as the last century when Queen Victoria was on the throne) was called a "swot." A swot is someone who likes to read books a lot and study and to do well at school and all that sort of thing.

And Roger did indeed love nothing more than reading, studying, experimenting and learning stuff! His favourite subjects all being scientific ones.

Now you may well ask, "Well, what's wrong with that, surely, they are all good things, aren't they? So, therefore, we should all be swots, right?"

And the answer to that of course is yes, you're quite right. However, the trouble with Roger was that he was **only** a swot. He thought he just had no time, and definitely no interest, for anything else but his books and his studies, as he was repeatedly taught at School, it was: 'Science and Law and Nothing More!'

The straight and simple truth though was he really believed that nobody had any time or any interest in him. He would tell you, if you asked him, that his most favourite subject of all was something called 'entomology.' This, however, was just the fancy word that he liked to use to either impress, or to put off other people from bugging him about it, 'entomology' of course merely being the important sounding name that so-called 'proper' scientists had for the Scientific Study of Insects.

What it came down to though, what Roger really liked most of all, was simply, 'bugs!'

On this particular Saturday morning, near the beginning of the school summer holidays, Roger had planned for a very special field expedition. He had escaped from the unwanted administrations of his over-zealous and too doting mother and was at long last on his way. His school satchel stuffed full of his 'things of scientific interest.'

And for this trip, he also had his trusty homemade 'bug-catcher.' This last item being but a simple net on a pole he'd made from some of his mum's net-curtains and a bamboo cane he'd 'borrowed' from one of his dad's garden sheds.

His dad really didn't bother with the Manor's gardens or the sheds any more these days, that was all left to the gardener, Bob, so Roger had found a shed that was a useful place to use as his own personal laboratory and private retreat.

However, the possession he most prized of all was his Flea Circus that he kept hidden in an old tobacco tin. This was a very big secret indeed. Nobody knew about his Flea Circus, absolutely nobody.

One day I will be famous from publishing my paper on Fleas, Roger thought, proudly, as he made his way steadily onwards, walking through the Good Wood.

Roger knew very well his parents and his teachers would just disapprove and so interfere, and all of his so-called class-mates at school would just tease and make fun of him. In fact, he would end up being bullied even more than he already was.

'The Holometabolous Life Cycle of the Common Flea', now how's that for a snappy title? he thought, lost in blissful reverie, as he contemplated his many future scientific discoveries.

Or, what about, 'Mystery of how Fleas actually jump at last resolved by a brilliant, young Entomologist! Research from Professor Roger Briggs of the University of Umbridge, at last sheds light on how Fleas can jump and reach speeds of up to two meters per second!'

Roger warmed with imagined pride and honour as he entered the Good Wood. He was on automatic now, scanning the vegetation all around him, earnestly looking for his desired scientific quarry. His eyes bent down to the leafy vegetation that bordered the Good Wood, scanning the hundreds of stalks for the one particular insect he most craved to discover and so completely oblivious of the wider world around him.

And I'll keep my Flea Circus a total secret so that no one bothers me about it. Then I'll be able to do all my researches and experiments and make my discoveries, and then they'll see! he thought to himself in his innocent daydream, as he continued searching.

When I get the Noble Prize and all the recognition for my exciting and unprecedented research into Ethno-entomology, * that will show them all, I'll be a real somebody then! Even more important than my Father!

(*Ethno-entomology, of course, as you and just about everyone else knows, simply being the study of the relationship between insects and people.)

Mr. Briggs, Roger's Father, was in fact, a very important man; well, at least he thought so. After all, he was a local Councillor, and also, Wellingford Wood-Mill's Senior Accountant.

He was also widely tipped to be the up-and-coming future Prime-Councillor for the whole of the United States of Britannia.

The timber company of Wellingford Wood-Mill was also where many of Roger's school colleagues' parents worked, but mostly in their lowlier employ, as laborers and lumbermen, as his Father called them.

Just imagine that! Roger smiled at his own inner vision. Me, Professor Roger Briggs. First Prize Winner and Noble Laureate and esteemed member of R.I.S.K; The Royal Institute of Scientific Knowledge. All from advancing the Knowledge of Mankind – By Bugs!

CHAPTER TWO.
THE BUG HUNT.

Roger at last came to the area of the Good Wood that he knew would be the most likely to provide specimens of his much sought-after quarry. For it was here, on this sunny summer's morning, that he had set forth with the specific purpose of finding a very tiny creature called a Froghopper. This being a very particular insect he needed for his steadily growing private museum collection.

It's time to do some serious comparative morphology, he thought to himself excitedly, as he took a firm grip on his trusty bug-catcher and magnifying glass.

This was the one activity that took him far away from the unhappy environs of his home, and especially from his over-strict and status-conscious parents.

As parents, Mr and Mrs Briggs, at best, just went through the motions of being parents. They didn't mean anything personal by this really. Their attitude to their one and only child was mostly one of mild interest and enforced toleration. To them, he was just like a pet and so just had to be put up with as something to be managed and kept clean and under control. Thus, Roger had learned not to get in their way and to not say very much at all.

Now though, all his concentration was centred on finding himself the elusive Froghopper.

"Let's see if I can get a hold of some Spittlebug Nymphs too, that would really make my day," he quietly mused to himself, "if I could get some of the adults along with some baby nymph specimens as well, that would be just wonderful!"

He had unconsciously begun to talk to himself, muttering his thoughts as he went along, bent over, head buried in bushes, studying them intently, all alone and in deep concentration.

Roger had studied up on the Froghopper and knew it was the greatest champion jumper of all the animal kingdom. The Common Froghopper could jump over seventy centimetres into the air; this being a much greater height even than a Flea could perform, although the tinier Froghopper was a relatively heavier creature.

Roger had been studying and training Fleas for some months but had recently branched out to the more impressive Froghopper. For its jump was so powerful that during the initial stages of its flight, a G force of over four hundred times Erf gravities was generated.

This was indeed an incredible phenomenon, considering that even the astronauts currently training to fly rockets to the edges of outer space experienced only G-forces five times Erf gravities! But he seriously doubted that a Froghopper could ever be trained, anyway.

"It's such a tiny, short-lived blighter though," Roger mumbled as he slowly moved about, head and shoulders buried deep in the bushes. And as the elusive Froghopper was only about ten millimetres long, Roger really did need his powerful magnifying glass to spot it.

"But I know how to find you, don't I, you heroic little Hoppers?" he wryly muttered, relishing the hunt.

And Roger did indeed know some very useful woodland lore to help him in his quest to find this particularly tiny bug. Namely, Cuckoo Spit!

Cuckoo Spit was the frothy white stuff that looked just like the gobs of spit that you'd see on some plants during the summer months. This white foam was secreted by the little larva, the tiny Nymph babies, that when hatched, would become fully grown Froghoppers.

Wherever there was Cuckoo Spit, there was bound to be a Froghopper. And Roger had now found one such clump of leaves, covered in foamy globs of the stuff and so knew that he was very close to bagging his much sought-after prey.

"That's the stuff, that's what I'm after; bet there's a few Froghopper Nymphs in that lot," he muttered, smiling to himself.

"Watcha got there, bug boy?"

Roger jumped a foot out of his skin!

"Yeah, watcha got there, eh? Watcha talkin' to yerself about, Bugsy?" cackled another of the gathering gang of jeering and dangerous-looking yobs.

"Yer gone cuckoo or sumfin?"

Roger had been bent over, half hidden in the bush, keenly concentrating on his search and been so intent on his task, he'd been oblivious to anything else in the world around him.

"Wh-wh-what d-d-do you want?" he stammered, looking around in sudden alarm.

(His being shy and having a stutter as well, especially when he was nervous or scared, didn't help matters at all.)

He saw a large, leering youth standing over him with a mocking sneer on his pudgy, dirty face. Roger recognized Sid the Squid, one of the local louts from the infamous Cold Arbor Gang, who plagued the streets of the Council Estate in nearby Eltingham. And there were several more he recognized too, from his school, who were quickly gathering around him.

There were about a dozen of them now, all sneering down at him as they maneuvered and surrounded the bush he'd been caught in the middle of. They must have been silently tracking him for quite some time; enjoying their very own, 'bug-hunt.'

"Come on then, Bug-baby, let's be 'avin' yer," called out another of the belligerent bullies, from just behind him.

Roger jumped again, confused, turning from one threatening dirty face to another as they gathered ever closer, ready to pounce on him at any moment.

"Been sneezin' yer snooty snot all over the woods, 'ave yer?" said a third, giggling and pointing downwards towards a large glob of the Cuckoo Spit.

This one he also recognized. This was the actual leader of the Cold Arbor Gang, known as Josh the Cosh. And a nastier and a meaner brute of a bully you'd never be likely to meet.

Roger looked from snarling face to snarling face. He was surrounded, his blood thumped in his temples, his heart was racing, and panic was bubbling in his throat. He was trapped!

Then, all at once, without thinking, he suddenly acted. He blindly charged past the fat boy, Sid the Squid, swiping his bug-catcher net swiftly and deftly over Sid's bulbous head.

He saw that there was only one thing he could possibly do.

Run!

***

Mary had gotten about halfway on her journey to the River Quaggy; The forbidden boundary that she wasn't allowed to cross; the clear dividing line between the Good Wood and Bad Wood. But it was there, close to the banks of the Quaggy she knew the rarest of herbs and flowers were to be found; including, of course, the much sought-after White-Willow Bark.

She'd long suspected that across the river, she'd find even stranger and more potent plants, but she'd never wanted to go against her Gran's wishes and so had always obeyed and kept to the south side of the river. Always. She knew her Gran was far wiser than her in such things.

Still, she couldn't help thinking that maybe, just maybe, one day the temptation would prove too much and that maybe, just maybe, that day could be today!

Mary was now quietly singing to herself as she walked along, picking the odd herb here and there as she went, but mainly intent on getting to the Quaggy's riverbank. The Good Wood was green and peaceful, with a soft, warm sun sprinkling lazily down through the leafy trees, spilling pools of light and shadow on the springy, flower-strewn turf at her feet. A few birds chirped and whistled, and the insects hummed in happy chorus all about her. Mother Nature was smiling on her and Mary was smiling back. Then without warning:

Crash!

A body suddenly hurtled toward her, straight through a thicket of brambles and ferns, his hands waving wildly about, clutching a satchel in one hand and a magnifying glass in the other. He'd come out of the blue, at breakneck speed, and had slammed right into her!

"Oh, my goo…!" was all she had time to say.

She'd fleetingly recognized the boy as Roger, a boy she knew from school, but who she'd never spoken to before. He'd always seemed so posh and aloof and… well, so preoccupied. Now her sudden introduction was proving to be a lot more painful than she'd have liked.

Roger had slammed straight into her, thumping her with a sudden and forceful wumphh!

She was badly winded and immediately bowled over onto the ground, with all her belongings scattered to the winds. She lay flat on her back, dazed and awkwardly entangled in a flattened dogwood bush, with Roger on top of her.

Luckily the bush had cushioned her fall. However, not so luckily for her, she'd done the same for Roger. He looked at her wide-eyed and dumbstruck, feeling dazed and dishevelled, with his round-lensed glasses hanging off of one ear.

"Awf, awf, awfully s-s-s-sorry!" Roger stammered to her, as he lay there, trying to recover his legs, his belongings, and his dented dignity. "B-b-beg your p-p-pardon. I didn't see you; I'm s-s-so… s-s-s-sorry!"

"Oh, shut up!" snapped Mary. "You sound like a cross between a wet dog and a dry snake! Just get off of me, will you? Where are my…?"

At that point, she became quiet, realizing that in all the confusion, she had totally failed to hear the loutish bullies now silently surrounding them. She saw Josh and his gang standing there, laughing and watching her embarrassing collision and consequent entanglement with Roger and the bush, with much sadistic amusement.

There were about a dozen of the thugs, all two or three years older than Roger and herself, leering menacingly down at the two of them, and with snarlingly pleased and evil grins on their dirty faces.

Their leader, the black-haired, black leather-jacketed thug, Josh, was the first to approach.

"Well, well, well, what do we 'ave 'ere then?" he said jeeringly.

He loomed over them and prodded Roger roughly in the ribs with a big black boot.

"If it isn't our good ol' friend Brainiac Briggs! Got yerself a girlfriend 'ave yer then, ol' Bug Boy?"

Roger remained silent and just lay there, clutching his satchel tightly while trying to get his glasses back on to his face.

Mary, meanwhile, was pushing him off of her and was still feeling very cross with him. She hadn't had time, as yet, to get to grips with the leering gang of bullies surrounding them.

"'Ere you go, missy," said Josh, extending a grubby hand to her, which she just ignored. She didn't like the look of this grinning gargoyle of a greasy haired youth at all.

"Let's 'elp you up an' dust yer down, shall we? We carn't 'av' these thoughtless thickos like ol' Brainiac Briggs 'ere, chargin' around an' knockin' over damsels in distress like you, darlin', now can we?" he persisted, oozing soothingly to her.

He then leaned over her, hands on hips and arms arrogantly akimbo. "You can call me Josh, Josh the Cosh, darlin'," he continued, "an' this 'ere's me gang." He then flung an arm out in an all-embracing arc, introducing said gang. "This one 'ere's Sid the Squid; 'ee likes squeezing things tight. Then 'ere's the Dawson twins, Digger an' Delver, coz they do like to pick at their 'orrible noses an' flick boogies everywhere. Disgusting, ain't they?" He smiled at her smarmily, then brusquely demanded, "Come on then darlin', let's be 'avin' yer upright, an' I'll introduce the rest o' these fine gentlemens to ya."

The rest of the gang just leered and chuckled in ignorant appreciation.

Mary was getting the idea that there was really something quite nasty and dangerous about these uncouth youths, and especially with this toothy and slyly grinning, black-jacketed Josh. She had heard of him and his gang, but like Roger, their paths had not directly crossed before.

He was now bending over her, hand extended, and acting the part of being her one, true, gallant knight in shining armour, coming courageously to her timely rescue.

"No thank you," she said primly pushing Roger off to one side and dusting herself down. "I'm quite all right and can take care of myself, so you can all just leave now and let me be, thank you very much," she finished firmly, getting to her feet and preparing to walk away.

"Oh no, I don't think so, missy, I really don't think so!" Josh chortled with an evil grin.

"I think we should be much more friendly; we'll 'av' ourselves some fun an' games first; now won't we, eh, lads?"

His like-minded gang chortled along, mindlessly agreeing with their leader's every word.

Mary now fully realized that she was in something of a tight spot. The hackles on the back of her neck were rising, and flushes of scarlet were beginning to appear in her cheeks. Yes, she was feeling scared, but what she was also starting to feel, even more than that, was angry. And this was not a good thing, because when Mary got angry, there was no telling what sort of damage and destruction might ensue.

However, Roger spoke up before Mary could say or do anything further.

"L-l-look here, Josh, you don't have to b-b-bother with her. It's me you're after, isn't it, not her? She's just a g-g-girl, after all. So why not just l-l-let her go, eh?"

Roger was desperately trying to think of something that would get Mary off the hook and, also possibly save his own bacon as well. He knew that they were always interested in getting money. Josh and his gang came from the same village that Roger came from. And in fact, most of their dads knew Roger's dad very well, because of him being the Chief Accountant at the local Wood-Mill, where their dads all worked. A fact which he well-knew made him even more of a prime target for their bullying, but maybe he could turn that fact to his advantage.

"How ab-b-bout I promise to p-p-pay you a ransom, Josh? If you l-l-let us go that is?"

Roger waited hopefully for Josh to respond in a positive way, banking on his being easily tempted by common greed and well knowing his dad was an important and wealthy man. However, greed wasn't the only vice in Josh's repertoire of the seventy-seven deadly sins.

But Roger could see Josh wasn't going to play along; he indeed had other vile vices and cruel games in mind. Ones that consisted of pain, torture, humiliation and violence. He just sneered and looked down at Roger as if he was nothing but a lowly bug, something small, and insignificant, there just to be squashed.

Josh shifted his smirking gaze back to Mary.

"I know what," he gleefully announced, "I've got a better idea. I think we'll plays us a game of Cowboys an' Injuns; a sort of hunt the injuns game!"

He looked back at Roger, meanly and meaningfully. "That'll be a much better idea, now don't you think so, Bodger, me little ol' bug boy, eh?"

These bullies really are just like those packs of Higheenas I've read about that live down in Darkest Afrikaa, Roger thought to himself, aghast.

He didn't know what else to think or say. So, he got to his feet and dusted himself down, and then he just stared at the ground and grew steadily more like a beetroot in complexion. He was scared, and he was embarrassed, but all mixed up, all together and at once.

"We'll be the Cowboys of course, an' missy 'ere can be your squaw," continued Josh, then he walked up close to Roger and poked him repeatedly and painfully in the chest.

"What about you, Bodger, are you up for bein' an Injun then?" he sneered daringly at him. "Fancy yer chances of rescuing yer squaw 'ere from us Cowboys an' goin' on the warpath, do yer, eh?"

Roger felt his heart thumping in his chest. His mouth felt as dry as sandpaper, and his usual trusty and logical 'scientific' brain was all fogged up with nowhere to go. The gang of brutish bullies were now openly and blatantly laughing at him.

"Look, he's goin' to cry," yelled out one of them, pointing derisively at him. "Brainiac Briggs is a blubbering bug, ha-ha-ha!"

"You leave him alone, he's not done anything to you, you morons!" Mary screamed out.

"Now, now," said Josh, using his very best 'smoothy' manner again, "we're not really gonna hurt him; well, not that much, me darlin'. But I'll tell you what I'll do, if you're really, really nice to us poor, lonely boys, then, I promise yers, we'll be quite nice to ol' Bugsy Boy 'ere; now 'ow does that sound?"

Mary glared at Josh in disbelief. If looks could kill, Josh was dead! Josh was a cinder!

But something now snapped in Roger's head. All logic was switched off, and all and any sense of self-preservation had gone with it. He could not let this happen. It was just too much, an innocent girl, a total stranger, put in danger by his blind, blundering panic and cowardly running away from danger.

He stepped in front of Mary and clutched his satchel tightly to his chest, and said to her as firmly and as boldly as he possibly could, "I'm so s-s-sorry, miss, I really didn't mean to g-g-get you involved in any of this. You r-r-run for it, I'll hold them off for as long as I can!"

At this, Josh wheeled swiftly around and angrily smacked Roger with the back of his black gloved hand, striking the side of his head. Roger reeled and was momentarily stunned and dazed and fell to his knees.

He then heard himself yelling at the top of his voice, "Go, Miss, run! Please, please run!"

Even while being scared out of his wits, Roger still somehow managed to maintain his natural politeness towards the fairer sex.

But the gang of vile yobs now gathered ever closer around him. Eager to give him a good bashing and pummel him to a bloody pulp. He was caught in a ring of hate and ignorance, and there seemed to be no escape.

He gripped his satchel and suddenly felt the weight of it. It held but a few slim books and some other science related bits and pieces. It wasn't the best of weapons by any stretch of the imagination, but it did have, sitting in its bottom, an ammonite fossil he'd collected while on holiday with his parents in South Devonia, in the West End Country.

This fossil gave the old school satchel a certain amount of much needed physical heft.

Roger sprang and, whirling the satchel, gave Josh a quick, single blow to the head.

The surprised thug clutched at his scalp, screaming and reeling in pain. "Why, you little, squirmin' worm! Get 'im, guys, get the bleedin', 'orrible worm now!" he raged.

The gang threw themselves at Roger as one, like a many-limbed, ravenous beast, hungry and hell bent on its blind revenge and bloody kill!

That's it, I've had it, Roger briefly thought as they charged, fists and cudgels raised.

He screwed his eyes up tight and then felt a moment of brief regret. He had never gotten the chance to complete his own museum collection, and who on Erf was going to look after his pet insects at home now; and what about his precious Fleas? What would happen to them? He stood silent and stoic, ready for the blows to rain down.

But none came. Instead, he heard a loud, bloodcurdling, battle cry.

He then, very bravely and very cautiously, opened one eye.

He then opened both eyes, and saw, standing in front of him, an extremely furious Mary. She was screaming and cussing and was effectively thrashing at the cowering thugs with two, long branches of bramble, that she deftly cracked about her like two, flashing, thorny whips!

"Aaaargh!" Josh cried out in pain, as one of Mary's makeshift whips caught him around the head, leaving a nasty looking welt, blazoned redly across his left cheek.

Mary knew her plants well; she had seen the clump of thorn-brambles growing beside her. She knew that if she firmly gripped such brambles below where their thorns began, just at ground level, and then quickly pulled at the roots, she could safely arm herself.

And now she was making battle with makeshift but very effective bramble-branch whips. Just like her hero, Indy-anna Jones did in the movie picture serial; so, she'd done exactly the same thing, but with brambles for whips.

Josh and his cronies desperately dived for cover while Mary darted and danced amongst them, like some crazed ballerina. Like a girlish-whirling-dervish. Like a tornado-tom-boy-top; now spinning and hissing and hitting out at anyone stupid enough to get in her way.

Roger could see she was very, very angry!

Mary, of course, had seen that despite Roger's unexpected bravado, he was in no way a fair match for a dozen or more brutish thugs, fully intent on making him pay for his ill-timed act of valour and defiance.

Her sudden attack had the needed benefit of the element of surprise; but not for very long. Josh was now rallying his troops.

Mary turned to Roger with an urgent look in her fiery eyes and yelled out at him.

"Run, you fool, run!"

Roger took off, with Mary following hard on his heels.

As they thrashed and crashed through the bracken and the undergrowth, the gang of bullies came charging after them, howling for blood. Indeed, they were even more like the howling, bloodthirsty pack of Higheenas Roger had first thought of them as.

But these Higheenas were Human and even more vile and vicious than wild animals.

"Head for the Quaggy," yelled Mary. "We've got to make it to the Quaggy!"

CHAPTER 3:
ACROSS THE QUAGGY.

Rocks and branches came whizzing by their heads, as the yobbos threw whatever they could get their hands on. Roger and Mary blindly ran on, sweat streaming down their faces.

"The Quaggy must be somewhere near us now," Mary called, as they blundered onwards.

Then, all at once, there it was, she could see it! The River Quaggy, bubbling its carefree way through the woods, dividing the so called 'Good' Wood from the 'Bad.'

The much wished for bright sliver of river lay before them, and soon they were sliding down a crumbling cliff, toward its green and gurgling waters. They made their way over several slimy, moss covered rocks, Roger very nearly tumbling over, face first, as he did so.

He didn't want to say anything to Mary, but he was now feeling scared witless. But not so much because of the bullies chasing them; Roger had become well used to such things from a very early age and throughout all of his lonely school years. No, the dread that filled him now was from the simple fact that he couldn't actually swim.

But the gang were nearly on them now. There was no time to explain, or for him to come up with any other solution. He just had to hope for the best and so brave the bubbling waters of the River Quaggy.

Together, they both plunged headlong into its chilling, frothy swirl. The river, although relatively small, was still wide enough to need a strong swimmer to get safely across to its infamous 'Bad Wood' side.

Mary was soon several yards ahead of him, and Roger was floundering about and bobbing up and down. He was trying desperately to keep his footing on the gravelly riverbed and then pushing himself upwards, to catch gasping gulps of air. Instead, he was now out of his depth and was gulping water and not air.

Mary grabbed him quickly by the arm and hauled him around, face up; then gripping him tightly around the waist and under the chin, she pulled him through the swirling rush of the river. She obviously knew what she was doing, Roger realized with some relief.

His panic subsided, but the water felt icy-cold, and Roger kept swallowing great mouthfuls of it as, with Mary's help, they made their way steadily across. Then, before he knew it, they were both paddling knee-deep in water and once again felt the pebbly riverbed.

Soon, they were making their way up onto the opposite bank. Roger heaving heavily, coughing and spluttering like the half-drowned, human Erfling he was!

"Why on Erf didn't you tell me you can't swim?" Mary demanded, glaring at him angrily, as soon as she'd gotten enough breath to give him the telling off, she felt he richly deserved.

"I d-d-don't know. I'm sorry, Miss. I didn't want to slow you down, I suppose is all," Roger answered her sheepishly.

They now quickly scrambled into the cover of the trees that crowded along the riverbank. Roger lay panting as Mary took a quick look behind her as they hid themselves amongst the leafy foliage to ensure they hadn't been followed.

But the hollering and chasing Cold Arbor Gang had gathered on the opposite bank and not one of them had dared to follow them across the river.

"Huh. Just as I expected, they're too spineless an' scared to come after us." Mary cried. And Roger saw she was right. Josh and his cronies just stood there jeering and hurling sticks and stones and insults at them but made no move to cross the river.

They were obviously far too wary of the rumours and evil reputation the Bad Wood had. Like all bullies, they were just puffed-up cowards, all desperately trying to hide their own terrible teenage fears and inadequacies.

Mary and Roger lay down on the bankside, breathless and out of sight, letting their hearts slowly settle as their mouths gulped in much needed lungsful of oxygen. Roger could hear the yelling youths slowly lose interest as the last stone was hurled, and after a while, the gang finally gave up and disappeared back into the greenery of the Good Wood.

Josh, the last to leave, hurled his final stinging insult at them.

"We'll get you two loony lovebirds later, don't yer worry none, yers 'ear me, we'll get yer," he yelled at them peevishly. "And a real bird in the hand is worth two Loonies in the bush like you any day!"

He cackled gleefully at his own cruel joke and then was gone, and nature's soothing sound of wind and water replaced him. It seemed, for the time being at least, they were safe.

But then... not everything is as it seems.

They lay there on their backs, with just the backdrop of the nearby gurgling waters and the rustling trees, easing their troubled minds. Then Roger suddenly realized, with some surprise, that Mary was quietly sobbing to herself. He'd thought she was the toughest, bravest girl he'd ever met, but hearing her distress tore at his heart. He wanted to help her, to tell her how brave and amazing he thought she was, but he didn't know where to start, so he just lay quietly next to her, and said nothing, waiting for her sobs to subside.

Without knowing it, that was exactly the right thing for him to do, as Mary didn't want to talk about it yet. She didn't want Roger to know that being called a 'Loony' had gotten to her and had hurt her far more than any of the other inane insults and physical threats had done.

Her mum had been called a 'Loony' back in the days when she'd been taken away from her. She had even heard the neighbours all whispering, as the ambulance came for her mum, "she's a loony, a loony, a loony, a loony." And ever since then, that one particular word had echoed menacingly in her mind, haunting her day and night, like a silent, evil curse.

The Psychonomists had been prescribing her mother with ever increasing dosages of their costly Psychotropic Thalamic Stimulants, (or PTS Pills, as they were called) supposedly to counteract the severe, repetitive episodes of her so-called delusory visions. Her visions had just persisted and got ever stronger, though.

The Psychonomists' pills had only seemed to make her more agitated and more unable to sleep and function at all. Mary now secretly believed that these so called 'Mentality Doctors' didn't really know what they were talking about. But there was nothing she could do about it, not now, nor back then either. It was just something that was always there, always painful to her, and something she had never really understood.

After a while, Mary's sobs subsided, and in their place once again were just the half-heard, distant sounds of the world of nature she loved, of the wind, the wild and the wood.

She felt better now but also somewhat self-conscious at blubbering in front of a boy. And one she'd at first taken as a bit of a weedling. But her mind was now changing on that score.

Now they were both in the so-called 'Bad Wood', and it somehow did feel different to her. Whether it was just her imagination being full of the old stories she'd heard, or whether it was an actual difference, she wouldn't have been able to say. What was true for her though, whether real or imagined, was that this wood, this so called 'Bad Wood,' had a very different sort of air and feel to it, almost like being in a dream or having gone off to that magical land of Woz she'd seen in the motion picture her Gran had taken her to at the local Eltingham Gaumont Picture House, barely a year ago now.

As she lay there, she could hear the wind in the trees above, sighing and whispering to her.

It feels just like someone is calling to me from far away, she thought dreamily.

Roger stirred himself from his own daydreams and thought it would now be okay to say something to her. But as usual when it came to actually 'talking' to someone, especially girls, his mind went blank and his tongue felt like an over-sized sausage, stuck inside his mouth.

"Th-th-thank you," he managed, at last, and then fell silent again.

Mary sniffed and turned towards him and gave him a smile and an acknowledging nod.

"You're welcome," she said quietly.

"My name's Roger, Roger Briggs," he said, politely offering his hand in introduction.

"Mary, Mary Maddam, very pleased to meet you," she replied, shaking his hand.

"Erm… Likewise," said Roger, hesitantly.

And then all at once… they both just started giggling.

Sometimes, when you've just been scared right out of your wits and then found somehow, against all the odds, you've survived, the only sane thing to do is to cry; but to cry with the joyful tears of relief and the cathartic laughter of disbelief too.

They lay on their backs, side by side, the deep blue of the heavens arched above them and framed between the leafy branches of beech trees, soaring into the distant mystery of the sky. There were just a few clouds dotted about, but nothing else to bother the summer sun from beaming down on them, radiating through the broad trellis of the tree's branches.

It was very pleasant and pleasing to just be able to lie there, drying themselves, without a worry in the world. Well, no 'worry' other than having just been chased across the forbidden borderline between the Good Wood and the Bad Wood of course.

Roger started to idly muse over all they'd been taught at their School and State Church, about the Great Forest of Lundun and the similar wild and untamed pockets of Forest yet to be cleared and brought under Mankind's management.

"We really shouldn't be here, you know," he murmured to Mary. "We'll be in big trouble if we get found out. There are only supposed to be criminals and mad people who come into the Bad Wood. Or so we are told. But you know, it doesn't seem that bad to me at all."

"No, it's exciting, isn't it?" Mary replied eagerly. "My Gran's always forbidden me to go across the Quaggy. But she ain't never explained properly as to why though."

"Well, if it's really because there's loads of dangerous animals and mad people and such, what I don't understand is, then why don't the Government Council just clear them all out? Surely, with all our modern, twentieth century technologies and great advances in Science, we Humans can handle a little problem like that?"

Mary, though, had drifted off again and was now peacefully dozing. Roger thought he'd do likewise. But as he lay there, he got a strange feeling that he was beginning to float away.

It was as if his conscious mind was slowly drifting off, away from his body and he was being summoned by someone calling to him from out there, out in the Bad Wood somewhere.

"Erm. Mary. Can you hear anything, anything at all?" he cautiously and drowsily asked.

"Yes, I can hear Mother Nature softly singing to me," she replied dreamily. "Now just rest yer body and mind a wee bit while we get dry, then we'll go and explore a while. I thinks it'll do you some real good to juss relax and be as one with Mother Nature for a change."

"Wh-wh-what do you mean one with Nature?" he asked, wondering if Mary really was a bit touched in the head, or whether maybe, in fact, they now both were. Anyway, whether they were both 'loony' or not, he thought, one thing was for sure, this day certainly was.

"Oh, it's nothing really," Mary dreamily answered him. "It's juss me… me being a bit over metaphorical, I s'pose."

Roger just smiled and relaxed as directed, still not sure what she was on about, and slowly let himself slip away into daydream again, floating off with the cotton-wool clouds up above.

But just as Roger was drifting off to sleep, Mary nudged him. Roger looked at her and saw she looked surprised at her audacity and then a little uncertain. Roger was about to ask her what was up when she suddenly blurted out exactly what was on her mind.

Roger found himself being told all about her life. He now realized she needed to confide in someone and for some reason it was to him she felt she could do that. And she was right, Mary instinctively knew he was different, his having a big heart and not just a big brain.

She now found herself telling him all about her mother and how she felt about what had happened to her. She quietly told him about her mum getting ill and finally being taken away by the Psychonomists and put in an Institution somewhere. And she told him how she'd lived with and been looked after by Grannie Maddam ever since, but also, how, a lot of the time, really, it felt like she was the one looking after her dear old Gran.

Roger, thinking himself as having a 'scientific' turn of mind, had some questions though. He'd never really understood this so-called 'New Science of Psychonomy' at all.

What he had read about it though, he'd found to be a load of over-complicated and near meaningless jargon and in fact all very unscientific indeed. They couldn't even make up their minds as to what a 'Mind' actually was!

When Mary had finished her story, he turned fully towards her and smiled. "Thanks for telling me all that, Mary. It's good that we know more about each other. I'll tell you about me but first, can I ask you… what was it that the Psychonomists found wrong with her? I mean, what was the diagnosis and treatment those pill-pushing Psychonomists prescribed for her?"

"Loads of gibberish, gobbledygook and argle-bargle, is all my Gran says they gave to her; that and loads of their useless pills, an' that made her even more ill," Mary answered sharply, with a shiver of disgust.

"Oh, I see. Right. Fair enough," Roger replied apologetically, not wanting to upset her and question her too hard. No point in causing her any further, unnecessary sadness, he thought.

"Well, what was really going on," Mary heaved with a sigh, "was me Mum was seeing things, an' hearin' voices, alright! An' they were scaring her, an' no one would listen; an' it was juss 'orrible is all, really, really 'orrible!" she finished, on the edge of tears again.

"It's alright, Mary. I understand; really, I do. I bet your mum felt like she was just trying to tell people actual things; trying to tell them what she was truly seeing and hearing, but they always insisted on telling her different and explaining it away for her; you know what I mean. Just like they do at school with us kids, especially certain subjects like the Arts and Religions. She probably didn't have anyone she could talk to about it," he finished morosely.

"Yes, exactly," Mary said, seeming a bit better now at being understood. "Me Mum always said that what she was seein' was the future – or *a* future anyway; one that really upset her." Mary became silent then.

But before Roger could say anything else, she quietly added, "She said she could see the end of the world, Roger. Everything was on fire, and everything was dead or dying. It was really terrible, and it really upset her a lot."

"What about your Gran, though? Wasn't your mum able to talk to her about it at all? Surely, she'd be the sort of person to at least listen and try and understand," Roger asked.

"Yes, she would have, 'cept me Gran wasn't around then, she was up North living in the Forest of the Mad Jester, an' when she did visit us it was too late; the Psychonomy already had their claws in 'er by then."

"Oh, I see," was all the Roger could say to that. It was becoming obvious that Mary's Family background was a strange and rather sad one.

Roger was intrigued though as to further details on what Mary's mum had actually seen, but he felt right now wasn't a good time to ask, so he said nothing further.

Roger had turned out to be a good listener. And he realized he was genuinely interested in hearing about someone else's life and experiences and what things were like for them, well, for someone like Mary Maddam, anyway. Even though a lot of the details were different; there was a lot he could empathize with. He too knew how it felt to feel lost and all alone, confused and not understood by anyone. So, when Mary had finished, he felt more able to tell her a bit about his own home life too.

He didn't want to say much about how he really felt about some things though, such as his feelings about his own Mother and Father especially; (he never called them Mum and Dad), as sharing anything about his private life was such a new and unnerving experience for him. But he told her enough that she understood the sort of life he'd had to put up with, despite all the apparent rich trappings, privileges and big house and everything.

Mary realized Roger was a lot shyer and more introverted than she was, but he was also a very kind-hearted and intelligent person, as well as being a naturally curious one. Though his curiosity took a more scientific bent than her own nature-loving and artistic one.

Where they lay was very warm and very peaceful; and, as yet, nothing at all had given them any reason to believe that here, in the so-called 'Bad Wood,' they had entered upon some wicked realm of dastardly evil and wicked ill-fortune, like the Psychonomists went on and on about in their weekly School lesson on Basic Psychonomy for the well-child.

The two new friends lay together, side by side in silence for a while, but then Mary awoke and began nervously chewing on a stalk of grass and growing increasingly restless. Then she sat upright, suddenly fully alert and grabbed Roger's arm. In a hushed voice she whispered urgently in his ear.

"Can you hear that noise, Roger? I think there's something moving about over there, along the riverbank, down by those reed beds?"

Roger listened intently but at first could hear nothing and started to say so, but then froze; he'd heard a definite rustling noise from the reeds Mary had indicated, down by the edge of the river, and not that far away from them.

Meanwhile Mary had regained her calm and composure and was once again alive and alert to all the background sounds of the surrounding wood and the nearby riverbank.

"Quickly, Roj, roll over under these bushes here; whoever it is won't see us in these."

Roger quickly did so, following Mary's urgent lead.

The rustling noises seemed to be getting closer and closer and moving alongside the reed-lined riverbank right in front of them.

Roger was now quite certain that there was indeed something, in fact some *things*, coming along the riverbank, he couldn't quite make out. Whatever they were or were doing there, they were being noisy about it and were getting steadily nearer.

Roger and Mary kept as low as they could, hugging themselves to the ground, furtively peering through the bush concealing them from the noisy intruders.

"Oh, my Doddering Diogenes!" whispered Roger to himself, "What on Erf can they be? Look what happens. We've been in this Bad Wood for less than an hour or so, and already we're under attack from some invisible monsters!"

"I think there's definitely more than one of 'em fer sure, whatever 'it' or 'they' is," Mary answered, peering along the riverbank, and into the reeds, as penetratingly as she could.

But she still couldn't see a thing; but could definitely hear them. And so could Roger.

"Yes, you're right!" whispered Roger. "I can hear them clearly now; it sounds like there's a lot of them too; sounds like they're eating up the reeds on the bankside or something!"

Roger could see that the reed banks were indeed being shaken and broken in the wake of whatever these creatures were.

"O.K. Let's keep our nerve, Roj. Whoever or whatever, let's pray they just pass us by, eh," Mary told him, trembling slightly, as she lay hidden beside him, fingers crossed.

"Look, look, that bush over there, it seems to be shaking," Roger cried out softly in alarm. "Oh, my P-p-potty Pythagoras, it couldn't be carnivorous crocodiles, c-c-could it, Mary? Or even w-w-wild wolves? They may have come down to the river for a drink?"

"Now, don't be silly, Roger, you don't get any ol' crocodiles here in Inglande, you knows that!" But then very quietly and half to herself, added, "Well, at least, I thinks you don't; but this *is* the Bad Wood after all, ain't it? Who on Erf knows what sorts of bloodthirsty creatures are lurking around here, just waiting to pounce on a person, unexpected an' out of the blue?"

"Yes, indeed, who knows?" whispered Roger, gulping again, in barely contained panic.

CHAPTER 4:
THE BAD WOOD BEGINS.

"Could it be Josh the Cosh and his gang again, do you think?" Roger whispered, staring intently at the area where the sounds were coming from. "Could they have crossed up-stream and then crept up on us, on this side of the river, while we've been lying here recovering?"

But then, before Mary could answer, there was a huge splash from the nearby riverbank.

The noisy intruder now showed itself at last. But it was not at all what Roger or Mary had expected. It was a large, brown, furry animal with big, dark eyes and long, white whiskers. And it definitely wasn't Josh the Cosh, it was in fact … a Giant Otter!

And it wasn't alone, there was a whole family of giant Otters; the large mother and father and then three smaller baby Otters, or 'pups', as they're properly called. They were noisily making their way along the side of the bank, within the reeds; keeping to the Bad Wood side and threading their sinewy bodies in and out of the tangles of tree roots and through the forest of reeds and mats of wet undergrowth. The two adults were busy, desperately trying to keep their three playful pups in some order.

"By Alexander Graham's Bells, Mary, they're huge! B-b-but why aren't they swimming?" croaked Roger in disbelief.

"I don't know," Mary whispered. "But don't shout, just lie flat and keep very still, O.K."

Roger did as he was told and then heard a deep but rather pleasant voice calling out.

"Come along, Lutie, my dear, do move them along please, we don't have all day, you know. We can't keep the Tree-King waiting," the big Daddy Otter pleaded to his wife, who was trying to shepherd her noisy family along the riverbank's edge.

"Oh, those horrible Humdrums!" came another, shriller voice, "Always butting in where they're not wanted, they are; with their smelly wood-mills an' all their wasteful nonsense. What do they want to go an' poison another bit of our lovely river for, eh? I ask you, Artie, what sense is there in that, eh?"

"Yes, I know, dearest, I know, there's just no understanding the Humdrums at all these sad days, but we've got to keep moving as best we can, we have to get to the meeting on time."

"Harrumph!" snorted the harassed Lutie, with a sardonic air and reluctant agreement, as she nosed a dawdling otter pup along in front of her, despite its own preferred intention being to explore a nearby water-rat's hole.

The big male Otter, Artie, now forged on ahead of them, closely followed by his family, his ever-complaining wife Lutie, and their three energetic offspring.

Roger held his breath as they went on by. After a short while, the Otter family had passed, disappearing among the roots and reeds further along the riverbank. Roger watched in silence and wide-eyed wonder, mouth agape and looking like a startled marmoset.

"By B-B-Bunsen's Bakelite Burners! Those animals were t-t-talking," spluttered Roger. "Wh-wh-what's going on here? Erf Animals d-d-don't talk!"

"Well, these ones obviously do," whispered Mary.

Mary had heard all the old stories about animals that talked; and of other creatures as well, belonging more properly to myth and legend, but this was her first time of really experiencing any in the flesh. (With the exception of Jemima, their pet South Amerigan Parrot of course!)

As for Roger, he was now sitting upright and furiously wiping his glasses. For him it was somehow, something even harder to come to terms with.

"After all, it isn't at all Scientific, is it?" he thought. "Maybe I'm just suffering from some sort of delayed nervous reaction or, or something!"

But before Roger had a chance to get his head fully around the strange procession he'd just witnessed, there came yet another loud noise; a cra-a-a-ash and cr-r-r-runching sound, but this time from the woods right behind them.

"By Aristotle's 'airy Armpits!" Roger exclaimed. "Now what?"

(Roger had taken to swearing in his own indomitable fashion a lot more than usual, which was a sure sign that things were indeed, most definitely **not** 'as usual,' at all.)

This time though, there was a much bigger commotion occurring in the wood, much more widespread than the Otters had made at the riverbank. And it was a lot stranger too.

Trees were swaying and shedding their leaves, and twigs and branches were bending and crackling noisily. And, whatever it was, was getting nearer and nearer to them every second.

"Oh, my fizzly-figs, this looks a lot bigger than Otters," Mary yelped, pulling at Roger to get up and run to some nearby rocks and take cover from the advancing monster.

Roger threw himself down behind the rock next to Mary, and just barely in time, to see the first 'monster' breakthrough into the open, just above the rocks where they both lay hidden.

Roger couldn't believe his own eyes. It wasn't a monster at all. In fact, it wasn't just one creature, but a whole galloping herd of them. More and more of the strange and furry beasts now came into view. What he was seeing was a large troop of wild Satyrs or 'Goat-men' as Humdrum's called them in their myths. They were half man and half goat. (They, of course, had their own name for their kind, which the Humdrums knew nothing about, and anyway, Roger, as with all Humdrums, had always considered them mere fantasies of Myth).

Roger heard various yells, yowls, and yips, coming from out of the woods, as more of the Goat-men came into view. Soon the full troop of Satyrs was clearly visible.

They gathered together down by the River Quaggy, just a stone's throw away from where Roger was watching, now barely daring to even breathe.

"By Einstein's Eyebrows!" he exclaimed. "First, it's talking Giant Otters, and now this... a troop of galloping Goat-men! I just don't believe it," he finished, still open-mouthed and staring, wide-eyed with utter disbelief.

"What on Erf's going on here, Mary?" he whispered to her anxiously, cowering behind the protective rocks, "talking animals and now these ... goat-men creatures. They just don't exist. Everybody knows that!"

Mary turned toward him. "I know! But I've heard about these creatures, Roj," she replied, earnestly whispering to him. "My Gran's told me lots about all the mythical things like these; they're called Goat-men now, but in Myths, they're usually called Fauns or Satyrs."

"Well, they're not supposed to exist, that's all I know," Roger answered her.

"Well, they do, and my Gran says her people up North calls 'em Goat-men an' they tells stories about 'em to scare their kids. 'Ow they come an' steal away babies to roast 'em on their fires an' eat 'em at their wild, all-night parties in the woods."

"Bu-bu-bu-bu-bu...." was all Roger could manage.

The Satyrs had now gathered into a group; there were about forty of them, Roger counted, (always the Mathematician), and they seemed to be taking a breather. Some went down to the water's edge for a drink, and others just idled about sitting on the nearby rocks and chatting.

After a short while, one of them trot-walked over towards the exact rock where Roger and Mary happened to be hiding, whistling nonchalantly as he approached them.

Roger and Mary both stifled a gasp.

"Just what would these creatures do if they were discovered?" Roger thought, anxiously. He really didn't want to end up as a Satyr's Sunday Roast!

The strange goat-like creature, the top half, man, and the bottom half, hairy goat, stood above them and started humming to himself. He then brought out a set of wooden pipes and started to play a jaunty tune. Its lilting little melody caught Roger's attention, and as he listened, he felt more and more caught up in its strange, hypnotic rhythm. It was having the same effect on Mary too. Roger could feel her tapping her fingers to its beat and humming along… and then he realized he was doing exactly the same thing.

Roger snapped himself awake and lay rigidly still, biting his lip, and quickly and quietly dug his elbow into Mary's side to jolt her awake from the trance-like effect he could see the Goat Man's music was having on her.

The problem now was to keep as still and as silent as they could and not be lured into any sleepy state of mind from the strange pipe music. But they also had to be ready to run for it if they were discovered.

Roger was the closest and carefully peeked up at the musical Goat-man; ready to give Mary warning if they were about to be discovered. As he looked, he heard a deep, wild sort of a voice, coming from another of the Satyrs, who now came trotting into view.

Roger could see that this one had shaggy, gingery hindquarters, whereas the nearer Satyr was more of a chestnut brown in colour. Both though, had long, pointed ears and two short, goat-like horns, sticking out from their crinkly, brown-weathered brows.

"Don't go wandering off now, will ye, Taog; We don't want to go annoying the Cap'n now, do we, me bothersome little brother?" said the newcomer gruffly.

"Oh, go shake yer old shanks elsewheres, Yllib!" replied Taog, pausing from his pipe playing and rudely sticking his tongue out in brotherly protest and defiance.

"Well, you can says what yer likes, yer knows Cap'n Caprinus will 'ave both our hides if ye causes any delay to the troop. We've got ter get to the meeting by sundown an' that's a fact that is. So, as I'm yer caring, big bruvver, yous keeps up with me, you hears me?"

"Alright, hold yer hooves, bruv, juss let me relieves meself, an' I'll be right with yers."

With that said, Roger soon heard a tiny tinkling sound that then became a much louder splashing, as the Goat-man, Taog, sent a long stream of steaming pee cascading down, over the rocks they were hiding behind. As the Goat-man duly relieved himself, Roger sat hunched tightly up against the rock face with Mary and looked on aghast.

Soon a pool of the frothing, yellow liquid gathered in a depression in the rocky floor right next to him. He then felt Mary shuddering, as she sat rigidly beside him, and so he turned towards her, feeling concerned that she might be terrified by these wild, uncouth creatures.

But he needn't have worried though.

Mary looked at him with a big grin on her face. Her blue eyes streaming with the gleaming tears of suppressed laughter. She spluttered and squealed and desperately tried to keep herself from guffawing out loud, quickly slapping a hand over her mouth. She'd obviously found the whole thing highly amusing.

"Well, I don't see what's so funny," hissed Roger through gritted teeth. "Getting peed on and then being eaten by wild cannibalistic goat-men isn't my idea of a fun time!"

Taog had now finished his call of nature and was re-joining the troop of Satyrs.

Roger prayed that their whereabouts wouldn't be given away. He reckoned that just as long as they remained quiet and still, they would be fine.

Mary had recovered herself too now and was leaning across Roger to get a better look at what was going on with the Goat-men. She was fascinated by this sudden evidence of such new (to her) wonders of nature. Actual Mythical creatures being real flesh and blood!

"I think they're about to leave now," she said very quietly, "they seem to be gathering around their Captain, that big tall chap over there, Captain Caprinus, I think they called him. Shhh, let's listen, he's talking now."

Roger didn't have any time to protest that he wasn't the one actually making any noise. The burly leader of the Satyr troop, these rough and rude Goat-men of the Bad Wood, spoke, calmly addressing his motley, caprine brothers, in a deep and commanding voice.

"Harken, my Hairy Hircumen, * gather and attend me! We arrive at the Tree-King's Court by turn of dark. But we must there present ourselves as best we can.

"Let us not arrive before our King, soiled and stinking. No, my brothers, no more battering, pell-mell through the trees and the bracken; from now on, we make our way downstream."

The Hircumen all nodded and grunted and stamped their agreement.

"And we must be alert for those filthy Humdrum poisons, for we'll head along the River Quaggy and go around Hooter's Hill and then on down to the grassy sward of the Green Lea. There we'll wash our flanks and cool our hocks and hooves. For down at the Green Lea, we can rest and groom ourselves as is fit an' proper for attending the Court of his Majesty, the Tree King." He paused, ensuring his audience were paying full attention, then continued.

"From there, my fine an' fearsome Hircumen, we will leave the River Quaggy and head on across the Kyd Brook, deep into the South-eastern woods and straight onto the meeting place at the Royal Green-Acre; are we all understood and agreed?"

A thunder of hooves erupted in reply, along with a loud and bleating chorus of "agreeeed," the Satyr troop answered as one.

"Very well Hircumen, forward trot!" Caprinus commanded.

(*Hircumen: The name the Goat-men or Satyrs have for themselves.)

Then, just as they were all setting off and charging down to the riverbank and weaving their boisterous way through the rocks and the reeds, in order to get to the River Quaggy as their new pathway onwards, a terrible thing happened.

Mary slipped!

She had been leaning too far over, and her hand had suddenly skidded from under her and she now fell heavily across Roger; banging her head on the edge of the rock as she did so.

Roger cried out "Ooof," as Mary gave out a short screech of alarm.

The Satyrs all froze in place. They were all suddenly as still as statues, standing among the scattered rocks, their eyes scanning along the edge of the river. Not one made a single sound.

Roger and Mary lay as stiff as two statues themselves, frozen with shock as they hid.

Then Caprinus called out, "Hircumen, there is somebody here, it could well be a spy! Watch out for any worm-Minions or spy-snakes; now fan out lads… and find 'em!"

Roger gulped, his skin crawled with fear; sweat was beading and trickling down his neck. He had absolutely no idea what a worm-minion or a spy-snake was, but he didn't think that they'd be all that friendly to two uninvited Humans either. He really didn't know what to do; there was nothing that he could do. These Hircumen were bound to find them.

Mary lay, huddled up beside him, holding her smarting and bleeding head; she was in despair at being so clumsy; she felt very guilty at putting them both in such terrible danger.

"They probably shoot spies, don't they?" she quietly groaned.

Then, just as one of the searching Hircumen got very close to where they were lying, Captain Caprinus, called out to his troop again.

"It's alright, men. Look over there, it's just that inky old Night Imp, up to his usual tricks. Let's get on again, an' leave him to get on with his, always up to something, that one is."

Roger looked right where Caprinus had indicated and just caught sight of a slim, shadowy shape, flitting up and away through the trees, just above the rocks where they'd been hiding.

"Whew, talk about a lucky escape," he sighed softly and with great relief.

"Oh, I'm so sorry, Roger, I should have been more careful!" Mary whispered, tearfully.

"Don't worry about it, it could've happened to anyone," he told her.

The troop of Satyrs now returned to the river and noisily made their way along its waters, following their noble Captain, who galloped on ahead, signalling for them all to keep up with him. The din of their passing slowly faded away into the distance as they cantered onwards.

The two human youngsters had somehow escaped, but luck had nothing to do with it!

Mary sighed thankfully, and asked, "What do you think we should we do now then, Roj?"

"Well we'd b-b-better wait a bit, I think, we don't want to run into those Cold Arbor yobs again, and we know roughly where those Goat-men have gone to at least," he replied, sitting up and stretching himself. "Anyway, it's well p-p-past lunch-time now. I'm getting hungry, let's find something to eat, O.K.?"

"Well, that's no problem," Mary told him. "We'll find some clean water from the Quaggy, just have to keep an eye out for any poisons an' pollutants though; Remember what that Otter said, somethin' about us Humans poisoning their rivers!"

"Yes, I do, and I wonder what that was all about? And they called us Humdrums too, us Humans I mean, and they seemed to think we'd been purposely poisoning it!"

"We don't do that, now do we, Roj? And according to the Psychonomy, all the territory of the Great Forest of Lundun is illegal and off bounds to Humans. Anyway, I'll find us a few juicy fruits and some tasty roots that are safe to eat. You can come an' help me find 'em too. The woods always have stuff you can eat. I'll show you where to look."

The two new friends rooted about in the bushes, Roger dutifully following Mary's detailed instructions. Soon, they were sitting comfortably on a soft lawn of grass under a chestnut tree full of lovely, white blossoms. Their recent trials and tribulations, with the Cold Arbor Gang and the odd surprise of Giant Otters, and the storm-troop of Satyrs, all temporarily forgotten.

Mary had gotten hold of some large, broad leaves that she'd fashioned into makeshift but very useable drinking bowls and plates. And these were piled high with assorted roots, bulbs, berries and nuts.

And there they sat side by side, cross-legged, like two happy little Buddhas in a garden. And munching away at their very own hand-picked, 'teddy-bears' picnic.

"How do you know all these are safe?" asked Roger, as he gnawed and crunched his way through a particularly crisp and tasty vegetable root. "I've always b-b-been told never to eat b-b-berries and roots, and stuff like that, not out in the wild at least, where they've not been properly processed. Wild things have germs and bacteria!"

"Oh, real food is wild, silly, and anyway, I've learnt lots an' lots from me Gran about it."

Roger nodded between eager mouthfuls of his home-made salad of crunchy asparagus stalks, wild watercress, spicy chic-weed, and hop-clover leaves.

And then all washed down with a leafy green cup full of fresh spring water they'd found. And despite his misgivings, their impromptu meal was surprisingly tasty and fully satisfying.

"It's just like," Mary continued, munching, "if you ask what food you can get from trees, most people will just say fruits an' nuts - like your cherries or chestnuts. But lots of trees and plants have other edible parts too - like the leaves and the roots, or even the bark sometimes. There's lots of cool stuff to know about the Vegetable Kingdom, you know."

Then she laughed mischievously. "And of course, I learnt a lot from Old Mother Nature herself. She's the best teacher of all, that's what me Gran always says, an' she should know."

She held his gaze and then looking very wise and serious said, "that's what I love most, learning all about the things that grow, how they start as tiny specks of almost nothing and then just grow and grow and grow and become something entirely different like a great big, mighty spruce tree or a lovely, scented, red rose bush!" She sighed wistfully and then said, "It's all such a miracle really, isn't it?"

"Well, you p-p-probably think I'm just weird, me being into scientific stuff, and all that," Roger told her, with a weary and self-deprecating sigh.

"No, I don't," Mary said softly. "I reckon you've got hidden depths, Roj! That's what my Gran tells me I've got, an' I think you've got 'em too, so there. That's what I think."

Roger listened intently and was slowly realizing just how comfortable he felt in Mary's company. Despite them being such different sorts of people, they actually liked each other.

At last, their late pic-nic lunch was finally over and done with, and there was thankfully, of course, no washing up to do. They just launched all their leafy 'crockery' into the River Quaggy and watched it float away, bobbing along in the swirling flow of the frothy waters. Cast off to an as-yet-unknown fate. Very much like themselves, in fact!

After a while watching them, Roger said, "That was quite a trick you pulled with those bramble roots, you know. I couldn't have done that. You're very c-c-clever, and b-b-brave."

Mary was feeling a lot better now and had had a chance to bathe and cleanse her wounds. "Well thank you, kind Sir," she answered him, "you were something of a bold knight of old there yourself too, you know."

"Well thank you, fair maiden," Roger replied, and then blushed and then quickly stuttered, "S-s-sorry, Mary, I didn't mean to be so p-p-presumptuous." His showing, yet again, what a really 'nerdy swot' he could be.

Mary just laughed though and gave him a thump on the shoulder and said, "Oh don't be silly, you can always give a girl a compliment if it's well meant you know," then continued, "but, there's something we still haven't decided on yet though, isn't there?"

"Decided on what, yet?" Roger asked, puzzled.

"What we do now, of course, silly, now that we're here, here in the Bad Wood, I mean," she explained, looking all about her and then smiling winningly at him, "I think we should explore a bit, Roger; we juss might as well take advantage of having been chased over here you know, an' we can have a real adventure together fer a bit, don't you think?"

"Are you m-m-m-mad?" exclaimed Roger, without thinking. "Oops, I'm s-s-sorry, Mary, but d-d-don't you think we've had adventures enough for now?" he stuttered apologetically. "And anyways, shouldn't we be getting ourselves back home?" he continued, ploughing on. "I reckon it's gone past mid-afternoon already; you know!" he finished rather embarrassed, not really believing in his own argument at all.

The truth was, that despite all his reasoning and reluctance, Roger was slowly changing. And he secretly felt he was now firmly caught between the proverbial rock and a hard place.

The choice before him was of deciding between the strict and stark discipline of life with his parents and the wild and airy temptations of being free to adventure whenever he wished and wherever he wanted to go. He was secretly feeling more fully alive and excited by all the possibilities of adventuring than he'd ever felt in his life before. He knew what he wanted in his heart of hearts, but he still had to come to terms with it all.

And it was actually much more like he was being caught between a rock and a *soft* place. The soft was his supposedly easy and pampered life at home and the rock, well that was the more compelling attraction of adventure and the call of the wild and the undiscovered country of the forbidden 'Bad Wood.'

Besides, he couldn't get rid of the silly idea that something or someone was calling to him, something silently but forcefully beckoning him onwards, on to some unknown fate.

It was a new idea to him, but it secretly felt like his ... Destiny Awaited!

CHAPTER 5:
HOOTER'S HILL.

"Oh, come on, Roj, please don't be a wet wuss! That's not really you, you know, is it? How about we just go up Hooter's Hill? We can get a good look from up there. Let's go an' see if there really is anything bad about this 'Bad Wood,' that everyone's warned us about."

"What about things like those Wild Goat-men though?" Roger gulped at her.

Mary just stared at him long and hard, with hands on her hips and tightly pursed lips and a scolding look on her face.

"Well, I don't believe the Bad Wood is really all that bad, Roger. So, we've seen some talking Giant Otters and some Wild Goat-men. Well, so what? What other wonders could lie within these woods, eh? Just think of that, we'd be true explorers!"

She didn't dare mention that she'd also been hearing some sort of distant, beckoning call, echoing in her head. Like someone urging her to go further into the woods. She didn't think Roger was ready for that sort of idea yet. He might even think that she was suffering from the same mental malady her poor mum had suffered from.

And Roger, of course, didn't want to lose 'face' with his new-found friend, and a girl too. He had the strangest notion he had some sort of a position to maintain; some manly status to uphold; as the gallant and chivalrous Knight Irritant, Sir Roger Briggs, or something like that.

He wasn't quite sure what a Knight Irritant was though, but he knew that it was a good fit for Mary calling him a 'bold knight' and his having 'hidden depths' and such.

He squared his drooping shoulders as best he could and looked Mary squarely in the face, then took a deep breath, and told her, "Okay then Mary, let's explore, just for a b-b-bit then; There can't be anything worse than those hairy g-g-goat chaps or Josh's gang of b-b-bullies, now can there?" he finished lamely, and somewhat unconvincingly.

Now Roger had only had any use for the 'out-doors' before for purely scientific research. The idea of exploring unknown, dangerous territory was something quite beyond his normal comfort zone. And besides, there was still that insistent, nagging idea he should somehow change his ways and go on an actual adventure. Which, in fact, was just what he was doing.

"Good, I think we should at least look things over fer ourselves. We can't believe all the stories we're told about it," Mary said, with her best 'brave and determined explorer' voice.

"What st-st-stories have you heard then?" Roger asked worriedly.

"Well, I've heard that the Bad Wood is full of Boggles and Hoblins," said Mary brightly.

"And poisonous creatures and deadly insects too?" Roger asked.

"And Ghostly Ghouls and Horrible Hags!" Mary answered.

"And Withering Worms and Man-eating Maggots," Roger retorted, now getting the idea.

"And Fiery Fantasms and Finickity Witches!" laughed Mary.

"What's a Finickity Witch?" asked Roger, looking puzzled.

"Oh, I just made that last one up," Mary teased. "You fell for it too; come on, race you to the top of Hooter's hill," she said, pointing to the hill behind them. "We'll get a great view of all of the Bad Wood from up there." And off she sprinted.

Now Hooter's Hill represented the very limits of Mary and Roger's paltry knowledge of the specific geography of the mysterious Bad Wood. This was largely due to it being such a large and prominent Hill.

It lay just across the Quaggy and so was easily viewed from Mottington and Eltingham. And it was also reputedly one of the highest hills in the whole of the Great Forest of Lundun.

"Hey w-w-wait for me!" Roger yelled, grabbing his battered satchel and chasing after her. The last thing he wanted was to be left all on his own at the edge of the infamous Bad Wood, but he wasn't going to let Mary know that now, was he?

"Y-y-you don't want to go off without your Knight Irritant, do you?" he called after her, muddled up in his meaning, but feeling much bolder and braver than he'd ever felt before. Something seemed to whisper to him that he really could be an explorer and adventurer too.

Mary was already well ahead of him though, so with a stiff upper lip and a cloud of wild butterflies fluttering nervously in his stomach, he stoically ran after her.

As Roger crashed his way through the undergrowth, following in Mary's wake, up the lower slopes of the hill, he noticed that the woods all around him now seemed to be somehow strangely shifting and changing in some way; so gradually though, that he couldn't quite put his finger on what exactly those changes were.

Then he realized their shadows and colours seemed to be getting darker and deeper as well; the bark of the trees here was getting shaggier, and the leaves were a darker green. The whole wood, in fact, seemed to be getting thicker and heavier;

and somehow distorted and different, and some of the trees were even becoming downright twisted and scary looking.

And then he noticed the eyes!

As they steadily made their way up the wooded Hill, more and more gleaming eyes, all of various sizes, flickered open and stared down from the dark, foreboding trees around them.

These luminous orbs were peering down from hundreds of increasingly raucous birds of all sizes and sorts, all sitting up in the trees, perched there, rank after rank amidst the thick, dark green foliage. And all starting to screech their heads off.

"I think we now know why it's called Hooter's Hill," whispered Mary. "My Gran's told me stories about all the birds of the forest being ruled by the owls here and how they're supposed to hold their Owl Parliament up here on Hooter's Hill. Maybe it's not just a kids story after all!"

They slowed their pace and walked even closer together, craning their necks as they kept a watch on the birds above them. Leaves and twigs had begun to fall from the agitated birds. Not to mention a few dollops of bird-poo as well, splattering on their heads and shoulders.

They finally came to a halt. The screeching and hooting and piping and chirping had risen to such a crescendo, that it was just too much. These birds of Hooter's Hill obviously weren't there to give them a warm and friendly welcome. They stood holding their hands over their ears, and both secretly wondered whether they should continue or not.

Roger and Mary were feeling increasingly afraid and un-comfortable at the reception they were receiving, but neither wanted to be the first to admit it. But both were thinking the same thing, "What if they really turned nasty and started at-tacking them! They'd be pecked to bits within minutes if they did that!"

"Just what the dizzy Diogenes do these birds want with us anyway?" Roger muttered.

Mary kept quiet; she really had no clue as to what was agitating this avian choir so much.

Also, as Roger surveyed the lower branches around him, where he could more clearly see the birds there, he noted that many of them seemed to be of very large size for their species. An even louder noise began, from even higher up in the trees. This was of a deep-throated thrumming, hooting nature. A grand chorus, of very large Owls, had now joined the choir.

Roger realised as this deep hooting thrummed in his ears, that these must be the fabled 'Owls of Hooter's Hill,' and according to the legends and stories he'd heard, they weren't known to be the friendliest of birds at all. But he'd thought that had all been just fairy tales.

And now they were showing their famed belligerence, giving a raucous demonstration, especially to these two trespassing Humdrums, it seemed.

As he stood by Mary's side, he silently battled the nagging feeling, urging him to go forward and to carry on. Surely, he thought, the sensible thing to do, was to just quickly and silently turn back? But, a deeper part of him said no, now was the time to show his mettle and not act like the weak wimp people thought he was; he should stand tall and be brave and bold. Just like a true knight of old would.

With this idea in mind, he firmly took hold of Mary's hand and set off once more, looking nervously upwards, from left to right, and getting a bad crick in his neck as he went.

"C-c-come on then, Mary. We said we'd get to the t-t-top of this blooming Hill, didn't we? So, we jolly well shouldn't be put off by a load of screeching old birds, now should we?"

Despite his bravado, Roger felt increasingly nervous and fearful, as they now cautiously continued onwards and climbed through the dark trees, slowly ascending the lower slope of Hooter's Hill. The woods of Hooter's Hill only encircled the lower slopes, as above them the increasingly bald head of the hill rose from the trees like a giant Friar's tonsure.

The Owls and the multitude of other birds were still becoming increasingly noisy though. They were not at all happy at the invasion of their ancestral home. The further onward Roger and Mary walked the noisier they got, hooting and screeching from the branches of the trees all around them and obviously protesting the two Humans' presence.

"What on Erf are they so upset about, do you think?" asked Mary, as they made their way ploddingly along, wending warily through the trembling, bird-laden trees.

"Surely, we can't be any threat to them, can we? But they're really getting angry now!" she added, getting increasingly alarmed.

Roger said nothing and kept on walking. He wasn't going to be scared off by a bunch of belligerent birds, not on his first real adventure and journey into the unknown!

"I don't know," he grunted moodily. "Let's get to the top, like we said we would, O.K.?"

He tended to get snappy like that whenever he got scared. And this was definitely one of those scary times, for sure.

"Well, I certainly get the feeling that we're not wanted here, don't you?" Mary persisted.

"Yes, I suppose so," Roger answered curtly. He was not at all used to trekking across such unknown country and climbing up steep, wooded hills either, let alone then being bothered and bush-whacked by a bunch of rude and raucous birds.

Wings were being flapped and feathers ruffled, and talons scraped bitingly against bark. But the incessant cawing, chirping, and hooting was the worst and was still getting louder. All the branches above them were raining down debris of twigs and leaves, some were even bouncing off their heads and shoulders.

They were both well and truly caught up in the middle of a 'mad maelstrom of arboreal ire and dire ornithological out-rage,' as Roger would have put it; or, at least, would have, if he'd had his usual wits to think clearly with; which of course he didn't have right then.

Mary, of course, would have just said that they were in an angry wood full of angry birds!

Then, without warning, everything went suddenly quiet. All the birds, as one, stopped their chirping, and the rain of leaves and twigs dwindled to nothing. Roger froze in his tracks, with Mary standing right behind him. A few late after-noon sunbeams came through the branches of the trees above, and the last drizzles of dirt and dust swirled eerily in the air around them.

Mary stepped toward Roger and was about to say some-thing, but then froze too, her eyes widening, and gazing poin-tedly at Roger, in a mix of horror and amazement.

"Wh-wh-what's up, Mary?" he asked, looking at her, and getting even more worried.

"Y-y-yes, exactly!" she cried, wide-eyed. "Up, up, UP!… Above you, Roger! Look up!"

Roger shrank into himself, suddenly gripped with the fear of what might be above him.

He stood, stone-statue still, frozen immobile, swallowing hard and trying to decide when he would actually dare to raise his head and look upwards and behind him. Then, after a heart-stopping second or sixty… he finally decided to look.

He lifted his head slowly upwards and raised his eyes to-wards the leafy branches of the tree above, that loomed so dark and menacingly behind him.

There, perched on a low, broad branch, sat three huge, ro-tund and dish-eyed birds.

Roger, in his confusion, didn't at first recognize what they were, but of course Mary did, right away.

"They're owls, Roger, three huge, enormous owls!"

"Oh, by Newton's Nobbly Noggin, it seems there are some unusually big creatures in this Bad Wood, aren't there, Mary?" he whispered to her incredulously, trying to control his steadily rising panic. "Wh-wh-what do you think they want?"

But Mary said nothing. She too was on tenterhooks as to just what they were in for now.

Keeping his eyes on the three giant owls, Roger cringed and felt his stomach shrinking, then he started to very slowly step backward, taking hold of Mary's hand and preparing to run for it. "Prudence is the better part of valour!" he thought.

Then one of the Owls spoke.

"Whooooo are yooooouuu?"

"I'm n-n-not anyone, s-s-sir," replied Roger meekly, after a short, tongue-tied hesitation.

"Hmmmmm, not anyone, eh? Oh dear, dear, dear. I'm sooo very sad to hear that, indeed," said the giant owl, speaking slowly and in deep and sonorous tones. "Well, young Humdrum, I am someone, and my name is Strix, and these are my Co-Primes, Tyton, and Athene; and we three represent all of the Birds of the Greater Lundun Owl Parliament."

Roger gulped and didn't know what to say. These were like no owls he'd ever seen or had heard of before; they had massive, razor-sharp talons that tightly gripped the branch on which they were perched. Each Owl had a short hawk-like beak on a flat, dish-like face and very large, forward-facing eyes, surrounded by conspicuous circles of feathers.

One had a mix of dark brown and tawny-coloured feathers with orange-gold eyes, another had black and white feathers with pale amber eyes, and Strix himself had mottled grey-silver plumage, with bright yellow eyes. However, the most striking feature for all three of them was the fact that they were each at least five-foot high.

These, indeed, were truly Giant Owls.

The three owls now patiently waited for Roger's reply, but Mary came forward and took the lead, quickly realizing Roger had temporarily lost his power of speech, and possibly his mind, as well.

"Please, Master Owl, please do excuse us, we didn't mean to disturb you, really we didn't. We're just sort of… well, we're sort of exploring, is all," she finished somewhat bashfully, feeling quite inadequate in her explanation, as well as in herself. After all, these large and noble creatures seemed so very regal and so, well … important.

"And whooooo are yooooouuu?" Strix now asked her.

"M-m-my name's Mary." She curtsied, feeling a bit ridiculous doing so, but still wanting to make as good an impression as she possibly could. "And this is my good friend Roger," she added, pointing at Roger. "We're really not used to talking to animals, you see, or such big b-b-birds like you."

"**Big Birds**?" cried out one of the owls; Athene, by the look of it, Mary judged correctly.

"Maybe it's rude to call a bird Big," she thought, "oh dear, I bet I've put my foot in it!"

"We are not Big Birds!" Athene huffed, ruffling her tawny feathers in indignation. "We are the Co-Primes of the G.L.O.P., The Greater Lundun Owl Parliament, and as such, are the elected leaders of all avian peoples. Also, my little Humdrum, we are not all 'Masters' either; I for one, am a 'Mistress' and you will kindly address me as such, if you please."

"Y-y-y-yes, Sir, Ma'am, M-m-mistress — sorry!" Mary answered, getting more and more flabbergasted by the second.

The third Giant Owl, Tyton, had remained silent throughout. He had sat and quietly maintained a lofty and unnerving gaze on Roger and Roger had begun to feel even more uncomfortable than he had been already. Tyton's gaze was unwavering and somehow very penetrating. Roger felt as if the

Owl was slowly stripping his exposed soul away, layer by exposed layer, like an onion; which, strangely, in a way, was just what he was doing.

"I wish to hear the boy speak," said Tyton in a commanding tone whilst still staring at Roger, his large amber eyes glowing as if lit with an inner fire.

"Wh-wh-what would you like to know, Sir?" Roger stuttered.

"Now, that's a very good question," replied Tyton, "that's a very good question indeed. What would I like to know? Hmmmm, well, let me see. I would like to know many, many things, young Humdrum, but right now I would like to know why you are here, in our wood, disturbing our Owl Parliament?"

Roger felt that it was about time he stopped being such a wet-blanket and a 'wet-wuss' (as Mary had put it). He was sick and tired of always being chased and threatened and scared.

"And, on top of it all, I'm now about to be bullied by a bunch of over-sized bird-brains, who really if they're so wise ought to know better," he thought, getting himself worked up.

"Well, if you really want to know," Roger replied, in his best dignified but defiant manner, "I'm here on a scientific expedition, w-w-with my friend here and we're just here to find out, well, what's here actually, and that's about the start and end of it. We are not here to disturb anybody really, and 'specially not the screeching, scratching and horrible-hooting creatures on this horrible hill!" he finished, in a rush and now very red-faced and breathless.

Mary looked on, appalled at his outburst, and Roger realized that he'd been a bit silly; losing his temper in such a place and at a time like this; he knew it wasn't exactly the wisest course of action he could have taken. He bit his lip and stood in silence, awaiting the worst.

"Oh, Roger," Mary gasped out, "don't be so rude! We're so s-s-sorry, Master Tyton. Roger really didn't mean…"

But then she was cut short by Tyton's sudden, loud Hoots. If Mary had known anything about owls at all, and especially the Giant Erf Owls, such as the three they were confronted with, she would have quickly recognized an Owl's distinctive whooping Hoots of Laughter!

"Well, well, well, not such a timid little mouse after all!" Tyton laughed.

Then before anything else could be said and done, there appeared before them another, much smaller owl, a messenger owl, that came fluttering down to them from the tree above.

To Roger, this particular owl looked even smaller than the normal sized Owls he knew of, this one being but a few inches tall.

"That there's what's known as an Elf Owl, I recognize it from me book of Inglishe birds," Mary whispered to him, looking rather smug in her superior knowledge of the natural world.

The Elf Owl now busily fluttered and flittered about in the air right before them and then daintily perched itself on Athene's shoulder and began to busily twitter and toot.

It quickly imparted its high pitched and unintelligible message to the Giant Lady Owl. Unintelligible that is, only to the children. Athene obviously understood it very well, every piped, shrill cheep and rapid, sharp chirp of it.

"Do please excuse us for a moment," Athene said politely, the tiny owl having finished its message. "My little friend Whitney here tells us we have an important messenger arrived for the Owl Parliament. Would you excuse us for just a little while? You will both be escorted to a parliamentary 'Guest-Nest' and you will be quite safe and comfortable there, I assure you."

And with that said, a flurry of beating wings descended and suddenly, Roger found he had two large talons tightly gripping his arms and shoulders. And Roger could see the same was happening to Mary.

Two Owls had appeared and were now hoisting them both up into the air.

They soared smoothly upwards through the branches of the trees and soon came to where a huge oak tree stood, imposingly wide and tall. Roger saw that this was a very ancient tree, with a tall, wide trunk and thick, crooked branches; All whorls and gnarls and knots and scars, but still full of life. Its broad branches cloaked in ragged oak leaves and clusters of glistening, green acorns.

"Ooh, what a lovely old tree!" Mary cried out.

Their Owl guards flew midway up the trunk of the tree, and Roger saw that they were heading for a dark, round knothole there. The hole loomed nearer, and Roger cringed, thinking they'd hit it and just smash into the trunk. "Surely, that hole is far too small for us," he thought. But it wasn't. As they flew toward it, the hole seemed to expand and just swallow them up whole!

Inside, Roger blinked, having to get accustomed to the gloom all around him. As his sight returned though, he gasped in astonishment. They were now in a huge round chamber lit with an eerie, green glow that seemed to stretch high above them and far below them.

As they flew upwards, within the oak tree, Roger saw tier after tier of circular galleries, with ornately carved balconies ranked all around the walls. This was the Prime Owl's Tower Chamber, (or the OTC, as the Owls called it: their very own Houses of Parliament).

The inside of the massive, old oak was a lot bigger than what it seemed from the outside, Roger noted with amazement, his eyes goggling like an Owl's at the strange architecture.

"By Billy Bunsen's Burners, what is going on?" he yelled to Mary. "This must be some kind of magic trick or an illusion… or something… it just doesn't make any logical sense!"

"Yes. I think it is a kind of magic, Roj, and not a trick!" Mary answered, gasping in awe.

High up within the tower, the big Owl Guards deposited them onto the assigned 'Guest-Nest' and flew off. This Guest-Nest was a large, hollowed-out area between two balconies. And in the wall at the back of the nest was another knothole that served as a small window.

Roger sat down beside it and peered through, but thankfully could only see more branches and oak leaves, obscuring the dizzying view downwards.

But he felt sick in his stomach, anyway; he really wasn't very good at heights at all.

"And what if we're now just helpless prisoners to these Giant Owls, what do we do then?" he thought glumly to himself.

CHAPTER 6:
A PARLIAMENT OF OWLS.

The Guest-Nest had been lined with moss and twigs and was in fact, dry and comfortable. Roger sat crouched by the oak-wall as low and far away from the edge of the nest as he could. While Mary excitedly scrambled about on her knees, exploring their surroundings.

"Don't worry, Roger," Mary beamed, peering over the edge and down into the deep gloomy depths of the hollow tree. "I don't think these Owls are bad creatures at all. In fact, these 'ere 'Bad Wood' Owls seem quite good and wise to me." She smiled at him. "But they're a little bit pompous too," she added brightly.

Mary, in fact, quite enjoyed being up in big trees, so this one didn't really bother her at all.

"We're not that high you know, Roj, though if you did fall that'd be the end of you," she said matter-of-factly, peering over the edge of the large nest. "I could easily climb down from here if I wanted, but it'd be a bit strange climbing down the insides of a tree instead of up the outsides of one, wouldn't it?" she mused, half to herself.

"I wish you wouldn't move about so much," Roger complained, "we really don't know how safe and stable these Guest-Nests are, after all."

Roger just sat glumly where he was, not daring to move; Mary's blithe indifference to their precarious height had totally failed to instil any confidence in him at all.

"Wh-wh-what do you think they want with us then?" he asked her.

"I don't know, but I don't think they want to eat us. Owls only eat mice and insects an' stuff like that, so come on, Roj, be brave; we're having our adventure after all, aren't we?"

But Roger was rapidly losing any glimmer of enthusiasm he'd had for this so-called exploring and adventuring business.

"Don't see what being dragged up into a Tree-Tardis, by Giant Owls, has to do with us exploring anyway," he grumbled knowing full well he was contradicting himself as he said it.

Because, even as he said it, he knew it wasn't true; they really were on an actual, real live exploration and amazing adventure; but he just fervently hoped that this one didn't abandon all bounds of human dignity, comfort, and reason.

"Well, just don't expect me to sit down to an Owl dinner and munch on a morsel of mouse or scrunch on a crunchy insect or something," he grumbled, mumbling disdainfully at her.

Then, as if right on cue, there was a fluttering of wings and two medium-sized serving-owls flew up from the shadowy depths of the tree's inner trunk. They were wearing what looked like small white bibs or pinafores and were bearing little baskets, full of delicious tidbits and delicacies for their guests to eat. Unfortunately, the Owls, just as Roger had feared, weren't at all familiar with the usual and more accepted eating habits of humans.

"Oh yuk!" cried Roger, "what on Erf is this stuff?"

The basket lying in front of him was indeed full of such diverse, tasty morsels as live, wriggling, pink worms, writhing, green centipedes and scuttling, black beetles, all mixed with a nice salad of yellow, pond-weed strands, brittle, brown twigs and the finest, home-grown mosses of emerald green!

Mary dug him in the ribs with an elbow. "Shhh, Roger, don't be so rude; we're their guests, after all, you know. They don't know what we like, so be polite. We don't want to make any enemies here, now do we?"

"Thank you very much," she said to the two birds, taking the two baskets in her hands.

The serving-owls bowed, hooted and blinked their saucer-like eyes and seemed happy they had done their duty; then fluttered out through the knot-hole window and disappeared into the canopy of trees. When she was sure they had gone, she quickly threw the basket's contents out of the window as well, then innocently put the two empty baskets down onto the floor of the Guest-Nest.

"What a lovely meal that was. Hope you enjoyed it too, Roj!" she said, rubbing her belly.

Mary's teasing wasn't of the malicious kind though, and her natural exuberance and sense of humour were very infectious. Roger's sullen mood melted somewhat, and he grinned back at her, joining in and contentedly rubbing his own stomach.

"Yes, indeed! Those were some of the finest worms I've eaten in a while," he laughed.

Mary explored the Guest-Nest some more, but it was just a very clean and tidy nest, and there wasn't anything of further interest in it at all. Then she looked up and around her at the tiers of balconies that stretched high above them, and she saw very high up, a balcony much bigger than the others. There she could just about make out the bulky figures of the three Owl Co-Primes. And she could also just about hear that all three of them were engaged in some sort of urgent conference.

"Look up there, Roj," Mary whispered. "I can see them; the Owl Co-Primes are up there; they seem to be huddled up on that larger balcony, talking to someone. Can you make out who it is they're talking to? I can't see who it is."

Roger dutifully bent his head and peered intently up in the direction Mary was pointing. He quickly spotted the three Giant Owls and saw there were a lot of other birds up there with them as well; all of them of different sorts and sizes, and all listening intently to some other dark and shadowy shape, but he really couldn't see who it was that was doing the talking.

Roger resumed peering out of the knot-hole window and could tell the sun was getting quite low in the sky now, as a green-tinged gloom spread through the oak tree's branches. Whatever it was that was happening up there, high inside the ancient oak tree, was something quite important though, as the three Co-Primes were all listening very, very attentively.

Then, just a few minutes later, Roger saw the mysterious inky shape separate itself away from the three Owls and other birds there, and rapidly flicker like a shadow, off and away, through another, but much higher, knot-hole window.

"Well, whatever the Humpty-Dumpty, Humphry Davy, was that? Did you see it, Mary?"

"Yes, yes, I think so, Roj," she replied. "I sort of saw it, I think, but it moved so quickly. But it definitely wasn't an Owl though, whatever it was."

"I thought I saw s-s-s-something like that before, you know, back when we were hiding from the Goat-men, I'm not sure," Roger muttered, "it looked a bit creepy to me though."

But then, all at once, their waiting in the Guest-Nest was over. Whoever the visitor had been, and whatever his urgent business had been, it was now all done and dusted.

The three Co-Primes, Strix, Tyton and Athene, left the lofty meeting-place balcony, and flew, gliding down to the Guest-Nest below them. For such big birds, they were incredibly versatile and aerobatic flyers, Roger admiringly observed.

The three Owls swooped silently onto the Guest-Nest and gently perched themselves around its wooden rim, folding in their magnificent and beautiful wings as they did so.

Then Athene took the lead and stepped towards them. It had obviously been decided that, of the three Co-Primes, she should be the Owl Parliament's official spokesbird.

"Well, dear children," she began, "we sincerely apologize for causing you any delay, but we now understand the extreme importance of your mission; although, as I understand it, you yourselves do not, as yet. But no matter, we, of course, will allow you to go forwards, and we will do what we can to assist you in fulfilling your mission... ahem, well, I mean continuing your journey, at least taking you to the top of Hooter's Hill from our Parliament at Castle Oak here, in this our ancient and avian domain of Castle Woods."

"Hmmmm, now that's a bit of a change in attitude!" Roger thought.

"Th-th-thank you, Mistress Athene," Mary stammered; unusually for her, she was almost totally lost for words. But she quickly recovered and pressed on with her explanations. "But, you see, we really are just exploring a bit, an' we really didn't mean to annoy or upset anyone. Isn't that right, Roj?"

"Yes, that's right." Roger agreed. "But, what does she mean, our 'Mission'?" he thought.

"And we're not actually on a mission as such, either," Mary continued, "well, not other than fer me, keeping an eye out fer some White-Willow Bark fer me ol' Gran, fer her poor bone-aches. But you really don't have to, well, you don't have to, you know, put yerselves out, or anything... erm."

She stumbled to a stop, as the giant Lady Owl just looked at her very intently and looked very much like she was somehow, well, just smiling at her.

"How on Erf does an Owl smile anyway," Mary thought to herself, incredulously, but realizing that, after all, here she was in fact, having a conversation with a live, giant one… and up in a magical tree to boot!

Roger thought he had better say something as well, just to back Mary up. He felt that he had to somehow show her he really could be like a bold and brave knight of old, if needs be.

"Yes, er, M-m-mistress Athene, that's quite right, what Mary says, an' as it's getting on, we best be going, you know; got to get home for tea and all that. Our p-p-parents will worry. So, you really don't have to bother yourselves. We'll come back another day, though, if that's alright; so th-tha-thank you very much, anyway."

But Athene said nothing in reply to that. The three Giant Owls just stood completely still and silent, perched at the rim of the Guest-Nest and looking intently at the children with their big, unblinking eyes boring down on them, and their sharp, hooked beaks agape, as if each was about to say something, but just couldn't quite decide what.

What the Owls were thinking though was, "Hopeless Humdrums; what can yooou dooo?"

The Owls were far too well-mannered however, to say anything like that out loud.

What Athene had decided was to take a good, firm wing and claw with these two young humans. They may not be too 'well-nourished in the head' department, which was really her way of saying 'stupid,' but she now knew they were here on Hooter's Hill for a very good reason; and one that demanded the Parliament of Owls' utmost respect and attention.

She and her Co-Primes had been told enough by their mysterious and shady visitor, but she was also wise enough to know that the Co-Prime Owls had not, as yet, been told all.

The Tree-King would soon set that right though, she thought. At the up and coming Court meeting. Also, it seemed, these two skinny and poorly prepared Humdrum children had not yet actually been told anything about what was really happening in the world at large, at all. Seems they were to be nudged and guided – but not coerced and enforced.

"Now, Mary – it is Mary isn't it?" asked Athene. "All I can say is that you are quite right; yes, you are on an adventure, and you are exploring too, Roger," she added, looking at Roger. "We know that your kind isn't used to our kind at all, and you may even have some strange ideas about us, but we do wish you well, and we are definitely not your enemies. I hope you do appreciate and understand that?"

Both Roger and Mary realized by Athene's tone that they were being spoken to in an adult way and about very important matters, though they weren't at all sure why.

"Yes, Mistress Athene, we understand," Mary answered for them both.

"Now despite you Humdrums, excuse me, you young humans," she continued demurely, "encroaching as you have upon our avian territories, we do know it is but a relatively few of your own kind who are dedicated to a belligerent and bellicose course of action, and who are truly responsible for the chopping down of so many of our ancestral trees and the polluting of so many of the Great Forest's pristine streams. But we do not blame the child for the hate and greed of the parent! Do you understand?"

"Y-y-yes, Ma'am, I m-m-mean, Mistress Athene, I understand … I think," said Roger, now looking like he'd just been told off, but quite politely, by some Headteacher at school.

"Yes, me too," said Mary, "but, we can always come back and visit you here another day, you know. And we'd only come if we were invited, honest we would. We don't want to harm anyone at all, as I said, really, we promise, we don't!"

"My Dear, **You,** are not the problem, I can assure you, but alas there won't be another day, I do fear, not unless you and your friend take the true path and the adventure that awaits you! Please believe me when I tell you … your destiny lies ahead of you, and not behind."

Athene now paused; her tawny chest feathers ruffled as if a shiver had run through her.

"Children, I can tell you this much; you both have a much higher calling, and I advise you very strongly to listen to that calling. The age-old realms of Mother Nature and of Mankind and Machines are at odds and have been increasingly divided. The rift between our realms grows ever wider. I urge you to listen to your true natures. If you do so, then you can help heal that rift. Now, no more chatter and chirp; for now, we must fly!"

And with that, the Giant Owl, Strix, spread his wings and arched over Mary and took her firmly in his talons and beating his mighty wings took off, gliding out through the magically expanding knot-hole of the oak-tree, and up and away, heading to the top of Hooter's Hill.

Then Tyton did the same with Roger, and the two Owls soared skilfully upwards, Roger dangling a little behind Mary, through the soft blue haze of the late afternoon sky.

Athene took off and swiftly followed. The three Giant Owls flapped and flew upwards, curling higher into the sky, catching the thermals there in order to ascend the ever-steepening gradient of the top half of Hooter's Hill.

As they flew onward and upward, Roger and Mary could see the lush, wooded landscape spread out below them like they'd never seen it before, a patchwork of meadows and woods that stretched into the distance all around. Behind them the little silver trail of their own river, the River Quaggy, pencil-scrawled its winding way, marking the forbidden border between the so-called 'Bad' and the 'Good' Woods. But right ahead of them loomed the ever-rising, tree-covered slopes, of Hooter's Hill.

As they paralleled the slant of the wooded hillside, the trees grew more and more stunted, becoming increasingly scattered and scarce, until the very last of the trees and owls, or any other birds, lay far beneath and behind them. Then, at last, they were nearing the very top of the highest hill in South Lundun.

The curved top of Hooter's Hill jutted like a monk's shiny, bald head, above the higher, wind-blown scrubland and the lower-lying, dense, green tresses of the Bad Wood.

The never-before-seen inner-reaches of the Bad Wood, beyond Hooter's Hill, now spread out before them, in a grand and sweeping panorama of undulating treetops, swaying in the breeze. A sea of wild, green trees of all sorts and sizes, that flourished as far as the eye could see. It was to their eyes, a vast verdant ocean of unknown and unexplored Treedom!

The Owls gently dropped them onto the crown of the hill, which was a broad and grassless area of sand and rock, sitting high above the treeline from which they'd flown.

Athene, Strix, and Tyton stood together, like three solemn, giant Owl-Statues, looking out over the green expanse of the Great Forest of Lundun. To them, this was home. There was nothing 'Bad' about it at all.

Athene finally ruffled her feathers and spoke her parting words of wisdom to them.

"We have brought you this far and no further as it is believed best that hereon you decide yourselves on what your next course of action should be. Remember, Children, the wise bird knows he yet has much to learn. Do not assume all you have been taught is either true – or even all there is to know. I would advise you both endeavour to learn to unlearn – and having unlearned – then learn anew – and then what you do know … is what is truuue for yooou!"

Roger was bewildered by all this and just stood, saying nothing and looking down at the ground, nervously shuffling his feet. He'd found the whole flying experience very unsettling. What on Erf was this Owl telling him? That all his hard work at school and being top of his class each year, was a waste of time and something to unlearn? He really didn't get that at all!

Mary though, did understand what the wise, old bird was getting at. Or she thought she did. Her dear Gran had said something very similar to her, many times, over the last couple of years or so.

"You do what you can do at yer School Mary, and you does yer best, but the best lessons there are, are the ones you learns yerself, especially from ol' Mother Nature."

Athene now lifted one of her stately wings and plucked a large tawny feather from it with her pointed beak and lifted it towards Mary. "Take this, young one. I believe it will help you both on your ways, whatever way that happens to be!" she told her, with a bright twinkle in her large, round eyes. Mary graciously took the offered feather, twirling it around between her fingers and thanking the Giant Tawny Owl for her gift.

"What on Erf are we going to do with a feather?" Roger gasped at her, but Mary gave him a sharp, hot glare, and he quickly apologized.

"Oops, s-s-s-sorry, Ma'am. Thank you, very kind, I'm sure," he said meekly.

The three Giant Owls now took flight again, swooping and hooting and circling together, right over them. As they dived and flew away, Athene called out in her regal, Queenly tones.

"Farewell and Fare Well, yooou Adventurers Twooo, we will meet again soon, but before we dooo, you must see the Sign; you will know it when you see it. Too truuue, too truuue!"

And with that, she flew away, with her fellow Co-Primes in tow, swooping and gliding back down the hill to the bird-filled trees of Castle Woods and their Castle Oak-Tree and the pressing business of the awaiting Owl Parliament.

Roger though, was a bit peeved about it all. "Well, what's that s'posed to mean, anyway?" he griped. "Oh, we're in for it now aren't we? We've got even further to go now haven't we, just to walk back home?" he moaned rather grumpily, standing glumly with his arms crossed while surveying the forest scenery stretched before him; all with a very serious, 'grown-up' frown on his petulant, boyish face.

"Oh, I reckon we'll find out somehow," Mary replied kindly. "I think those Owls know a lot more than even our so-called Teachers do, let alone all your Scientists and such like!"

"Well, whatever those Owls are on about, if we don't watch out, our 'higher calling's' going to be at least a month's worth of detentions!" he continued, with a shrug and a sigh.

Mary just smiled at him and then did a joyful pirouette, twirling about with her arms flung out wide, and yelling out at the top of her voice, "Oh, but isn't it all simply wonderful, Roger, eh? A whole New Wood for us to explore. It's just like we really are explorers now, isn't it? And all of this is ours – a totally new and unknown woodland-world, just for us!"

"Yes," muttered Roger, unenthusiastically, "but just why is it called the 'Bad Wood' then, Mary, eh? That's what I'd like to know, you know. Things aren't just called a bad name for no good reason, now are they?"

Mary abruptly stopped her dance, and with hands on hips, gave him her most penetrating and serious look yet; she gazed deeply into his eyes; almost directly into his soul, he felt.

"Aren't they?" was all she said.

CHAPTER: 7:
THE SMOKING TREE.

The sun was sitting redly above the wide canopy of trees and was steadily sinking lower.

Roger guessed that they had no more than a couple of hours or so of daylight left.

More and more clouds had gathered as well, and the scene, unfolding to Roger and Mary, across the 'unknown' Bad Wood, had a far sadder and sombre aspect than the Good Wood they'd left behind had done.

Roger observed that here, the Bad Wood seemed to be full of much older, shaggier trees. He could see between the trees the ground was blanketed with wild thickets of bramble and bush, spilling and sprawling, wherever they could manage to survive.

There were also many fang-like, rocky outcrops, haphazardly scattered throughout the woods and rising-up like broken teeth from the riotous greenery.

As he keenly gazed, scanning from left to right, over the distant tree-tops, like some lofty, ancient Lighthouse set high above the Sea of Trees, he could feel how very ancient the Bad Wood really was. But despite his lack of overt enthusiasm for knightly deeds of derring-do, he did feel a strange compulsion to explore this new and mysterious woodland and especially to be the first to discover its many secret entomological wonders.

To Mary, the Wood had the silent and slumbering air of having a lot of well-kept secrets. Most of them long forgotten. But some secrets were light ones, but some very dark ones too!

Although Roger didn't seem to show much interest in the pastoral and floral wonders of the arboreal panorama set out before him, Mary on the other hand was totally enthralled and was eagerly champing at the bit to get down the hillside and discover all the wonderful plants and flowers she felt sure must be hidden within its dense flanks.

"Look, Roger, the North face of Hooter's Hill is a lot steeper on this side than on the south side we flew up with the Owls. I think we'll have some trouble getting down it, don't you?"

But Roger was still recovering from his head-dizzying flight with the owls. He reluctantly looked down the hillside to where she was pointing but was still torn between coming up with a good excuse for persuading Mary to return to the River Quaggy with him or instead, just to throw caution to the wind and actually try and go onwards and explore some more.

Then Mary suddenly cried out, "Look, look over there, there's the top of a big tree, Roger. It looks like a bit like a Wych Elm to me, and look... it's smoking, it seems to be on fire!"

"What, where?" asked Roger, his interest piqued and so now keenly peering out towards where Mary was excitedly pointing.

"There, there!" she said, jumping up and down and pointing directly North. "See, there's a sort of a clearing, way over in the middle of the Wood there, you can just about make it out from up here, it's sitting there all by itself, and it's got some grey smoke billowing out of it. Can you see it, Roger?"

"Yes, I see it! How very strange. Wonder what's causing that then?" Roger answered her, getting more enthused, his natural scientific curiosity finally being aroused.

"And remember what Athene said to us, Roj? 'Look for the sign, and you'll know it when you see it!' Remember? Well, we've seen it! That must be the sign, I just know it is!"

"Hmmm," mused Roger, rubbing at his chin and squinting his eyes, looking every inch the intrepid, young scientist. "It's very curious indeed, for sure. It must be a very big tree, though. Bigger than the trees around it anyway. How far away do you think it is, Mary?"

"Oh, that's really hard to say, Roj. Distances with Old Mother Nature can be quite tricky at times, 'specially like this, when you're looking from high up, like we are."

"Yes, I see what you mean," he replied in a ponderous tone, "it must be something to do with the perspective and the parallax, I expect."

"Oh no, not really," said Mary brightly, "I think it's just Mother Nature being playful, more like."

"Harrumph!" Roger grunted, barely containing his disdain for her lack of scientific rigor.

"Anyway, it's not too far off, is it, so let's go an' look see, shall we? Let's go an' find out. We're explorers after all, aren't we? And, well, I think this could be our destiny, Roj!"

"What! You must be joking!" Roger gasped. "We can't just go traipsing off miles through the Bad Wood now can we, for Furry Freud's sake? N-n-not with there being no one knowing we're even here! And besides, what if there really are 'b-b-bad things' out there, what do we do then, eh, what sort of a destiny is that?"

Now it was Mary's turn to conceal her disdain, but she didn't grunt, gripe or even groan, she was much cleverer than that. She just put her hand on his shoulder and with her steady, blue-eyed gaze, told him, "Oh no, don't worry, Roger, I'm not at all scared. I'll be quite safe. I have you as my bold Knight to protect me, after all, now don't I?"

"By Newton's Nose, this girl is tricksy!" Roger thought. "I can't back down now!"

Roger studied the terrain below them more closely, looking for a way down. He could see that the hillside here definitely was steeper on this side, just as Mary had observed. "Maybe, there was no real way down anyway," he thought, "maybe, they would just have to turn back, and it wouldn't be his or anyone's decision or fault then." Roger quickly and guiltily tried to suppress such thoughts and turned towards Mary with a shrug.

"Well, I'm game if you are…" he said nonchalantly, "if we can actually find a way down there that is. We may well be forced to come back and try it another day, you know."

"Oh, there must be a way, surely?" Mary pouted. "I'm sure that Smoking Tree is there for a reason, we can't just give up, Roj! We should at least investigate that, I think. Don't you?"

Roger could see that Mary was determined for them to go on, but he couldn't see how they possibly could, not safely at least. Then he saw that below them, beneath a large line of rocky outcrops and just above the treeline, the woods there were of a different sort of tree entirely. The bottom of Hooter's Hill on its Northern flanks was covered in a steep sweep of fir trees. Some sort of dark, evergreen pine forest, and then beyond those, the deciduous forest proper, stretched away towards the Smoking Tree and beyond.

"And we'd have to get through that Pine Forest down there first too," he told her dutifully, pointing down at it, "and get over those rocks above the trees as well."

Mary stood silently beside him and then sighed. "Maybe your right, Roger. But it just feels like we should be going on, you know. I know it don't make much sense … but, well … it just feels like we should, that's all," she finished lamely, feeling disappointed and subdued.

Roger had no answer to that. Despite his arguments otherwise, he still felt it very hard to actually turn away, turn back, and so end their adventure together.

Mary didn't move either and just carried on gazing across the wild woods to the distant Smoking Tree and twiddling away with the large Owl Feather as she did so.

After a moment Roger dug his elbow in her side and quietly told her what he'd just seen, despite his hardly being able to believe his own eyes.

"Ahem, Mary. Look at that Feather you're holding. I do believe it's growing!"

She took a step back in sudden shock, as she looked down at the Owl Feather in her hand and saw that it was already three times the size it had been. She quickly dropped it to the ground and stepped away in amazement.

"What on Erf's going on 'ere?" she squealed.

Roger watched in fascinated silence as the Owl Feather steadily grew. After only a couple of minutes, it had become the size of a small rowing boat. It lay there quivering, its curved, mottled plume sitting on its spine and now beginning to slow in its rate of growth.

"It really does look like a small boat, or canoe, doesn't it, Mary?" Roger piped up. "I think those Prime Owls were one step ahead of us, at least. We can use this magic Feather to get ourselves down the hill!"

"I reckon yer right, Roj!" Mary beamed. "I told you there had to be a way, didn't I?"

"Yes. Well, we'd better have some sort of steering device and a brake too. We don't want to go plummeting to our deaths with no way of controlling our descent, do we?" he told her.

Mary nodded her agreement and immediately walked off over the brow of the hill to a nearby scrubby old tree she'd seen barely clinging on to life there. Before Roger could say Newton's Nobbly Kneecaps, she was back and carrying a piece of gnarled branch.

"This should do the trick, Roj," she told him with a big grin.

"Right," Roger agreed. There was nothing left but to just get on with it now, he realized. "Give me that and let's get going then," he told her. "I'll drive!"

They pointed the Feather-boat straight towards a shallow dip just above where the rocky outcrop began. Then they pushed it over the hill-brow, and both jumped in, one on each side. The Feather-boat sliding easily over the scrubby, barren surface on the hill's top.

Mary went into the front and Roger sat at the back with his trusty tree branch at the ready, as they began their bumpy and exciting slide down the steep hillside.

Roger tightly gripped hold of the chunk of branch and then wedged it into the ground at the rear of the Feather-boat, creating a long, winding wake of turned-over dirt and stones trailing behind them. But it worked. He soon found he could control their descent; that was, just as long as he could keep his balance and his concentration.

That wasn't easy, though. The Feather-boat was a light craft and very skittish.

"You'll have to look ahead and guide us, Mary, I can't do both!"

"Okay, get us more over to your left, Roj. We don't want to crash into those rocks, or even worse, miss them altogether. I'll try and get us into that hollow there in front of the rocks."

They careered on down the hill, Roger soon feeling very hot and sweaty from keeping the Feather-boat moving in the right direction as well as from stopping it suddenly shooting off at an uncontrollable rate of speed by use of his makeshift rudder-cum-brake.

Soon they were zig-zagging their way closer to the rocks and to their target, the particular hollow in the ground that lay right in front of that part of the rocky ridge.

"We're nearly there, Roger. Miss those scrubby trees, though. Just a bit more to the right and we'll have done it!"

she yelled above and despite the whipping wind whistling past her ears and her long hair lashing wildly at her face.

Roger was straining away with all his mustered might, beads of sweat spilling from him, and wearing a face that was screwed up with a fierce determination. Whatever happened now, he didn't want to let Mary down; it was very important to him to show her that he could be like a heroic Knight Irritant. It was also important to him that he didn't kill himself!

Roger put his full weight into thrusting the branch to the left so they would turn right.

"Well done, Roj, we've missed the trees and here comes the hollow. Brace yourself!"

The Feather-Boat skidded into the hollow and Roger soon realized that it was filled with soft grey sand, as they shuddered to a juddering halt just several feet from the line of rocks. The sand helped give them a soft landing and Roger breathed a sigh of relief as he pulled his sturdy branch into the boat and turned forward to congratulate Mary.

But the words choked in his throat. Mary was gone!

For a bare moment, he sat stunned and speechless in dumb-struck panic. Then he saw her. She had been flung from the Feather-boat and had been shot like a human cannonball into the crumbling sand of the hollow. He could see her legs sticking out and frantically wriggling back and forth. He smiled just momentarily, observing the undignified and embarrassing position she was in but then realized with a gasp that she was in deadly trouble.

"Oh, by Heavenly Hoyle! She can't breathe!" he exclaimed in horror.

Mary was trapped, and unless Roger or somebody acted quickly, she'd suffocate and be a goner. Roger looked frantically around him, but there was no one else to call for help; the Giant Owls were long gone, and it looked like it was up to him alone to rescue her.

Roger hurled himself to the front of the broken Feather-boat and leaned out as far as he possibly could. But it was no good. She was just out of reach.

He still had his school satchel on his back and the length of tree branch with him too, but he soon realized that he didn't have anything useful in the satchel, and even if he could reach Mary with the branch, there was no way she could grab hold of it.

Roger was on the verge of sheer, blind panic. He felt so helpless and useless. Just how was he going to save his one and only friend; a friend he'd only just met and was getting to know? He knew that he only had minutes to come up with something. But his mind was a blank.

As he stared out towards the rocky outcrop that lay just beyond Mary's still thrashing legs, he thought he caught a sudden glimpse of some dark presence, flashing between the rocks. He peered up at the cracks and crevices along the rocky wall but couldn't see anything else.

"Maybe I'm just seeing things!" he thought.

He lunged once again, trying to catch hold of Mary's ankles, but again, it was just a matter of being mere inches too far from her.

"What if I use my satchel straps?" he thought. "What if I can hook them around her feet and pull her up that way? I've got to try something!"

But before he could even begin such a desperate attempt at an unlikely rescue, a muffled explosion shook the whole sand-filled hollow. Spurts of grey dust and pebbles skittered down from the rocks, and strange jets of inky, black smoke came shooting and billowing from out of several fissures in the rock face. Then, the sands in the hollow suddenly heaved upwards and shivered and shook and then another muffled explosion occurred. And then another.

This time, the sands started sinking and swirling about in a steady clockwise motion.

Mary was being relentlessly sucked down into a whirlpool of sand.

Seeing this, Roger flung himself, without even a second thought, off from the prow of their Feather-Boat and grabbed hold of Mary's leg with one hand, the other still clutching his trusty bit of branch. Together, they were swallowed up and relentlessly sucked down into the maw of the swirling morass of sand, both as helpless as two bugs flushed down a plughole.

He found himself quickly choking as his eyes, throat and ears were filled with the shifting, stinging particles of sand, whirling all about him. But no matter what, he wasn't going to let go of Mary. No matter what. If this was the end of them, then so be it!

But it wasn't the end. Roger found himself sliding down a short slope, bumping along, with Mary tumbling beside him and himself, still steadfastly and resolutely refusing to let go of her, no matter how much they were being thrown and twisted about.

The sand was hurting his eyes so he could barely dare to squint to try and see where they were heading. But when he did manage a peek, he found they were now tumbling into what at first looked like a cave full of black smoke. But then he realized it wasn't an actual cave they were tumbling down, but more like a narrow, underground tunnel. And the inky smoke was somehow already beginning to clear away.

But then he saw that they were heading into even greater danger. The cascading sand was gushing like a roaring river down towards a large pothole at the bottom of the tunnel, and they would soon be following and plummeting into its inky depths.

Roger again acted without thinking. He tightened his grip on Mary's ankle, causing her to yelp in pain, but also as he did so, he fiercely jammed the branch into the side of the tunnel, and the packed sand piled up around the boulders at its edge.

This slammed them into the rocky tunnel wall, just short of the deadly pothole.

They were battered and bruised, but they were alive. Roger sat against the rock and peered through the dust, grit and gloom. Together they waited several minutes as the rest of the sand from the hollow flowed relentlessly by them and disappeared down the gaping hole.

Roger quickly rummaged in his satchel and brought out his old and trusty torch. He shined the torch around them to see what he could see. The short answer to that, at first, was nothing. But with the help of his torch and his eyes slowly getting accustomed to the gloom, he saw high above them there was a narrow ribbon of open, if dull sky. They were in fact not in a tunnel at all but were in a long gully or gorge, running like a deep gash between the rocks.

Mary sat next to Roger, gasping and getting her breath back. Most of the inky smoke had cleared now, and the last silvery tendrils of sand had trickled on by, down into the inky well.

"Th-th-thanks for saving me, Roger. You were incredibly brave!" she spluttered to him.

Roger felt rather bashful at being praised like that and really didn't feel he deserved it.

"Well, I think there was something… or someone else… at work, you know, giving us both a helping hand there. If that sand hadn't been shifted so it fell into this gully down here, then we'd both have been drowned in it, up there in that hollow," he told her.

"Well, I don't know about that. But I do know you threw yourself after me and if it wasn't for you, we'd be down that pothole right now… and most probably be as dead as Doo-doos."

"Um, erm! OK then. If you say so. But what do we do now then, Mary? Aren't you a bit worried that things are getting a bit weird, not to mention downright dangerous?"

"Well, that's what happens on exploring an' adventures, isn't it? At least, it is on ours!" she lightly replied, as she dusted herself down and stood up, stretching her limbs and so checking all her bones were still working and intact.

"Come on then, Sir Roger of the Royal Tree Branch, let's get around that nasty old 'ole and see what's at the end of this gully 'ere, shall we?"

Roger sighed and stood and followed Mary along the edge of the gully wall, cautiously skirting around the edge of the eerily smoking emptiness of the pitch-dark pothole.

"I reckon this hill we're on, Hooter's Hill, must be well riddled with caverns and caves," he mumbled to her. "I don't like dark underground places, and I don't like high ones either!"

"We're nearly there, Roj!" she called back to him. "Look, there's the end of the crevice. We'll be able to see where we stand soon."

The steep walls of the crevice-gully ended and opened out onto the lower, northern slopes of the hillside and then they were stepping onto the flat ledge of a protruding rocky shelf.

There in front of them stretched the hazy panorama of the Bad Wood and directly beneath, the dark, brooding trees of the Pine Forest began. Thick and foreboding and very close now. Beyond the Pine Forest, the Bad Wood proper unfolded in all its green glory.

"Look, there's the Smoking Tree!" Mary yelled excitedly. "We can still see it. Well, some of the top of it anyway, and it's still smoking!"

"Well, there's no turning back now, is there?" Roger huffed. "Let's get on with it, eh? Let's finally find out what this mysterious Smoking Tree is all about, shall we?"

CHAPTER 8:
SHADOWS IN THE DARK!

They made their way, step by step, down through the last yards of the rocky outcrop and across a short stretch of wild scrubland full of prickly gorse up to the edge of the Pine Forest.

They paused before entering. Roger was not feeling too brave and adventurous now as he looked in at the gloomy, dark interior of the awaiting Fir trees. They seemed so un-friendly and unwelcoming. He rubbed his bruised posterior as he stood and contemplated the thick wall of trees that loomed before them.

There was much less undergrowth here; the Pine Forest floor was a carpet of pine needles and old brown pinecones scattered haphazardly about. As they stepped into the dry, gloomy confines of the trees themselves, the very air seemed to still and deaden. And Roger noted that it all seemed very quiet and lifeless, as if it was a place always shunned and avoided by any normal forms of natural life.

I wonder if there are any new insects to discover here though? he thought to himself. He couldn't stop the inner Scientist showing through, no matter what the circumstances.

The Pine Forest stood on the lower slopes of Hooter's Hill, and as they trudged onward, they soon found themselves falling into a rhythmic pattern of walking and wending their way down through the tall fir trees, passing tree after tree, with the same view surrounding them. Everywhere they looked, they saw the same sight. All the trees looked exactly the same.

Also, they were both starting to feel quite weary and drowsy. The quiet and the gloom had a monotony to it that induced somnambulance, as Roger would have put it. Or making them both very sleepy, as Mary would simply say. Whatever it was called, they were both plodding along now, almost as if sleepwalking.

After a while, Mary came to a stop and turned to Roger with a puzzled look on her face.

"Do you know which way we're going, Roger?"

"Haven't a clue," he answered her morosely. "I thought you knew!"

"Yes… well, I thought I did … but I'm not so sure now!" she replied worriedly.

"It's very gloomy and eerie here, isn't it?" she asked him, yawning. "I'm not sure we're still heading for the Smoking Tree, is all," she muttered, wearily and half to herself.

"Well, let's just press on and get through this depressing place, O.K? We can't have gone that far off course, and we know from the view we got from the top of the hill that the Pine Forest doesn't go on for too long. I bet we'll be through it in another ten minutes at most," Roger told her as confidently as he could.

But ten minutes went by, and then another ten minutes. And after nearly half an hour of trudging through the dark and dismal trees, they came to a halt again.

"It's no good, Roj, there's something wrong!" Mary exclaimed. "It's just getting gloomier and gloomier, and I'm usually very good with my sense of direction, but here I feel like I'm just walking around in figures of eight and going nowhere!"

It was very late in the afternoon now, and Roger was getting secretly worried about being caught here in the dark. "What if there's Wild Wolves or things even worse … now we know there actually are weird and magical creatures living in the Forest of Lundun!" he thought.

"S'pose we better just press on, Roger, or we'll get caught in this creepy place in the dark," Mary told him, just as if she'd read his mind.

But after another ten minutes, nothing had changed.

"I think this place is enchanted somehow, Roj!" Mary whispered to him. "I don't think it wants to let us go at all! Oh, what are we going to do?"

Roger was beginning to feel very scared now. He looked around and realized that he had no sense of direction whatsoever. His heart began to thump in his chest and a lump of fear sat in his throat. Everywhere he looked, there were just the same trees and the same brown bed of needles and cones.

The air had grown even heavier and was full of an earthy, musky scent.

"We've got to make a run for it, Mary! That's all we can do. Don't think about directions, just run as fast and as straight as you can, O.K?"

"O.K., Roj, but we'd better hold hands, so we don't get separated!"

Roger grabbed her hand, and they set off, pounding across the flat, springy needle-carpet, the thudding of their feet dampened by the thick layer of mulch and pine needles. But they ran on into nothing but the same surroundings of Fir Trees flashing by but with no sign of the end of the forest in sight.

Then right ahead of them a loud 'Crrrrump!' noise erupted, along with a black cloud of billowing darkness suddenly welling up between the trees. Roger immediately swerved away to avoid the billowing tendrils of black smoke.

"Strange, that's just like the smoke we ran into in the gully, up in the rocks!" he thought.

Then another explosion of the inky darkness erupted in front of them. Roger pulled away to the right, and they carried on running. But then another erupted, and he went to turn left, but another explosion of dark cut him off, so he veered right, running onwards with Mary's hand clutched tightly in his own.

But again, and again, billowing clouds of the dark smoke erupted, time after time; just coming seemingly out of nowhere, as if born from the very shadows between the trees.

Roger quickly got the idea that something or somebody was doing this on purpose.

But who and why? And were they trying to lead them into even worse peril, into the heart of the Pine Forest for their final destruction, some gruesome arboreal sacrifice to the Pines? Or, were they being helped in some way? There was no way to know.

Mary was gasping, and Roger was getting a painful stitch in his side. He knew that they couldn't keep running and dodging about for very much longer.

"Come on then, just show yourself, you coward!" he screamed out in pain and frustration. "If you want to kill us at least do it honestly and openly!"

"It's alright, Roger, Look!" Mary yelled, just as they veered away from another explosion. "There, ahead of us. I think we're coming out of the Pines now!"

And it was true. There were no more eruptions of dark smoke, and they found themselves stumbling out of the stand of Pine Trees and into a glade full of bushes and, a little further on, were leafy green, deciduous trees they both knew so well; Beech, Elm, Alder and Ash.

Mary pulled Roger down onto the grassy meadow, tears welling up in her eyes. Both lay panting and sweating like two bolted colts just returned from a wild stampede.

After a while, they had both got their breath back. Roger realized that somehow, they had both been guided and saved from the evil enchantment of the Pine Forest. But by who, he had absolutely no idea.

"That was very, very strange... and very scary!" Mary muttered to him.

"Yes, and just how are we going to get back through that place again when we go home?" he replied, rubbing his ribs.

"Look, Roj, we've made it this far… and well, I think there's something here that wants us to make it, you know, all the way to the Smoking Tree."

"Yes, you're right, Mary. I sort of have that idea too. O.K, let's get on then," he told her. "But which way is it now? I've got no idea."

They, of course, couldn't see the Smoking Tree at all now, it being well hidden beyond the dense canopy of the trees. And the race through the dark Pine Forest had been most confusing and disorientating, to say the least. But even though they currently had nothing visible to aim for Mary was, in fact, not worried. She had some of Mother Nature's 'Uncommon Sense' in her young but wise head, and so she confidently pointed.

"It's that way, Roger!"

"And just how do you know that?" asked Roger, feeling slightly annoyed by Mary's rather nonchalant, but as it happened, quite correct guidance on the matter. And this was because he had been ready to pull out his pocket compass from his satchel, and so show himself to be the resourceful and intrepid Forest Tracker and Scout that he thought he was.

"Moss!" Mary chirped, simply and pointing. "You see over there on that old Beech tree. Moss only grows on the North side of trees, and we're heading North, so that's the way."

"Oh," said Roger, feeling even more peeved now, and also a little bit jealous of Mary's far superior knowledge of 'Nature in the wild.'

Mary walked onward, taking the lead this time and feeling full of ebullience and bravado; She felt very much in her element now. This was more like it. This was a proper Wood.

"Well, we can't see the Wood for the Trees, but we can sure see the Smoking Tree from the Wood!" she cheerfully called back to him.

Roger just grunted, plodding along behind her and now deciding to just concentrate on discovering any new insects he could.

Mary though loped excitedly along, crying out with gasps of surprise and little yelps of delight whenever she spotted a new plant or a flower she hadn't known of before.

Of these, there were many. There were strange, perfumed flowers of vivid blues, curious, green, coiling vines and big bursts of spikey red bushes. There were large-leafed, umbrella-like plants too, as well as many smaller, multi-coloured orchids.

Then she came across some very large and garish velvety violets, all the size of tubas, growing out of huge tangles of thick and thorny green, bramble-like stalks. The brambles though, all quivered and shook at them as they passed by.

"I wouldn't want to get caught up in that lot!" she remarked spryly, hurrying past.

They were now walking through a Botanist's dream-world, continually coming across brand new and exotic species of flora, completely unknown to Mary. Her old Book 'The Flowers of Merrie Inglande', which she'd lost way back in the Good Wood, now indeed seemed totally redundant.

Soon they came to a grove of trees that looked very similar to weeping Willows, but these had hundreds of thin, trailing green branches, full of eerily, glowing, coral-like blossoms of red, orange and yellow. And these flowers were shaped like large, fleshy lips and seemed to mutter and moan at them as they made their way onwards.

The Willows were whining and were getting louder, the nearer the children came as they went through them, the 'Whining Willows,' (as Mary now named them), were obviously very unhappy at having the children there. Or maybe, Mary thought, they were just hungry!

As they passed by, Roger gave out a sudden cry of alarm, with a strangulated "erkkk, erkkk!" he gargled and gasped, his arms and legs flailing wildly in the air.

He had been grabbed tightly around the neck and the waist and the Whining Willow Tree was hauling him upwards into its hidden maw; Roger was to be eaten as plant-food.

Mary quickly spun around and rushed to his rescue. She found he'd already been pulled several feet up into the green, leafy mass of the writhing Willow Tree. A particularly hungry 'Whining Willow' had suddenly lashed out, with several of its long, whip-like branches, and had caught him as an unexpected but most welcome and tasty morsel.

Very soon, Roger would be swallowed and gobbled up and gone!

"Oh, Grizzly Gremlins! A Carnivorous Tree! We don't want those, do we?" Mary cried.

Roger couldn't properly answer her, though. He was too busy swinging high above her and being slowly strangled to death.

Mary ran to where Roger was dangling and trying to loosen the tree's woody grip from around his neck. She could see he was growing somewhat purple in the face.

"D-d-do something, erkk," Roger managed to choke, "its ch-ch-choking, erkkk, meeeee!"

"Hold on, Roj, I'll get you," she cried, jumping up and trying to stop him going up higher.

She started pulling at his legs, but that just made things worse, she soon realized, as Roger yelped in protest. She somehow had to loosen those thin, rope-like branches that were coiling in an ever-tightening stranglehold around his neck. Every second counted, as Roger began to shake and splutter, no longer able to talk.

Then, before she could do anything else, the Whining Willow Tree itself suddenly began to violently tremble and shake. Leaves and fronds scattered on the ground all around her.

Mary then saw there was something up in the tree that she couldn't quite make out.

The atmosphere around the Whining Willow had suddenly become shadowy and ominous. Even the spaces in between the trees had darkened even more.

The whole copse of Willows, in fact, seemed to have sunk into a somber, twilight gloom, where the very idea of something like day or sunlight seemed completely strange and alien.

The Willow tree's whining now grew louder and shriller. Mary knew there was definitely something up in that tree; and the tree didn't like it one bit, or at least, didn't like whatever the mysterious something was doing up there.

Then without warning, the tree shivered and trembled, and then stopped its shaking and suddenly let Roger go. It just uncoiled, pulling its branches away; and as it did so, all the dim shadows lightened, and the natural greenness of the Wood returned to normal. Whatever it was that had been up in that tree, it had very effectively come to Roger's rescue.

Roger tumbled from the fronds down onto the ground, still choking and falling heavily into Mary's arms. He clung to her for a short while, spluttering, red-faced and breathless.

Eventually, he got his breath back and rubbing his sore neck, he looked urgently upwards and all around him, in order to see who, he could thank for saving his life; as did Mary too, but they couldn't see anybody there at all.

"B-b-by Galileo's Galloping Grasshoppers!" Roger exclaimed. "What on Elrond's Erf was all that about? I think that Willow tree th-th-thingy really wanted to eat me, you know!"

There was simply no sign of anybody or anything else there at all. The grove of Whining Willows was as docile and as well behaved as you'd expect any 'ordinary' willow trees to be; even their incessant whining had reduced to but a barely audible background wuthering.

"It's almost like we've got a guardian Angel or something," Mary mused quietly to herself. Then she turned her attention back to Roger. "Are you all right, Roj; no broken bones or anything I hope?"

"I'm f-f-fine thanks," he groaned with a pained look. "Huh, and some Knight I turned out to be!" he said wryly. "Must have looked a right twerp dangling there like that!"

Roger quickly retrieved his fallen satchel and brushed himself down, then put on the bravest face he could. He was sure there had been someone up there with him who had done something to the Willow. But he hadn't been able to get a good look at anything, not while swinging around and being hanged.

He turned toward Mary and said, "Really strange that was, Mary; not the sort of behaviour I'd expect from a normal tree at all, and I think there was someone up there as well who somehow persuaded it to let me go, you know?"

Mary nodded her agreement. Then they turned North and set off once more. After a short while she told him, "There's obviously things in this wood that we just don't know anything about, Roj, so we should probably be prepared for anything."

"Right," Roger agreed ruefully. "Let's get on and get to this Smoking Tree then, eh?"

They were now well on their way to the much sought for Smoking Tree. And Roger was feeling in a better heroic mood now, having survived a death-tangle with a Man-eating Tree!

He followed in Mary's wake. And in fact, both were feeling hypnotically drawn onwards, but by something more than just simple, idle curiosity. They both secretly felt like they had some important purpose for being there, in the 'Bad Wood' that was, but without the faintest idea as to what that purpose could possibly be.

Mary though was also feeling puzzled. "Hmmm, there's definitely more to this Bad Wood an' the things in it than meets the bloomin' eye," she quietly mused, as she loped onwards.

But she too, was soon in her stride and her element once again, peering all about her with a keen eye for any as yet undiscovered wonders of Mother Nature that might be on display in this wonderful, brand-new world of spectacular, botanical splendours.

One thing that soon took her fancy was the strange, luminescent and large mistletoe-like plants, with their round clusters of milky, moon-like orbs. She saw these sprouting more and more frequently up amongst the branches of the bigger trees. These were all nestled in green, waxy leaves surrounding a cluster of several large, creamy berries, that glowed pale and cool, like tiny, full moons.

"Just a mo', Roj, I gotta get some of these Moon-berries, they're wonderful," she called.

She picked a few sprigs she could barely reach, hanging from the branch of a nearby tree. The tree seemed to shudder slightly as she did so. Seemingly, it did not like giving up any of its 'Moon-berries.' Mary duly noticed this and so only took a small handful of the berries and then quietly and politely apologized to the tree for not asking its permission first.

"This place is very strange, but it's really wonderful too," she sighed. "Juss think of all the new plants an' herbs I could name an' discover, Roj! I bet there're all sorts of new medicines and tasty foods too; all sorts of fantastic stuff I could find here."

"Harrumph!" Roger grunted at her. "I think you need to actually 'discover' them first, Mary, and then you can name them after that. You're not just making up names for some new mental illnesses like those Psychonomy Doctors do all the time, now are you?"

Mary's face immediately dropped at the mention of such mental illnesses. Roger quickly realized his thoughtless mistake and immediately apologised, "Oh, I'm so sorry, Mary, please d-d-don't listen to me; what do I know, you're the B-b-botanist, after all."

"Oh, that's alright, Roj," Mary answered quietly, "It just made me think of me mum when you said that, that's all. I do wish she was with me now, you know, more than anything, I do. She loved flowers and plants, even more than me, I think."

Roger felt rather sheepish about having upset Mary and reminding her about her poor mother locked away somewhere in an Institution. But he was also now getting increasingly concerned, the further they went on through the Bad Wood. The plain fact of it was, it was very late in the day now, and he just couldn't see them getting back home before dark.

"I'm going to be grounded for a gazillion weeks for this!" he thought to himself, ruefully.

He decided he should at least say something and get Mary's agreement that they'd just go on as far as the Smoking Tree and then go no further. After all, as they'd told the three Giant Owls, they could always come back here, another day, when they would be better prepared, couldn't they?

"H-h-hold on a bit, Mary!" he called to her. "Can we agree we go as far as the Smoking Tree this trip and no further? I really am in an awful lot of trouble for doing this, you know."

Mary could tell by the tone of Roger's voice, that this wasn't the right time to tease him.

"That's O.K. Roger. Sure. If you insist. I think we'll both be grounded for weeks, but let's get to the Smoking Tree at least, and then we can go home and maybe return another day."

Roger nodded, and with that agreed and done and dusted, he set to, a wee bit happier now. He trundled along, satchel bumping on his back and his magnifying glass now in his hand.

And every now and again there was an enthusiastic cry of "ooh!" or "aha!", or an "oh my!" And on one such encounter, Roger got very excited when finding a very peculiar green caterpillar, nearly a foot long, splattered with red dots, and which seemed to be wearing a big and bright, yellow moustache!

"Oh, Mary, come here, you must look at this!" he called out to her.

"Now, now," laughed Mary, "just look who's dawdling around now! Come on; let's get there before dark so we can at least see about this mystery of the smoking tree. There must be some reason it's billowing smoke like that. There's no flames or anything. Weird, huh?"

"Yes. O.K. Mary, Northward-Ho then!" Roger replied.

Roger carefully returned the bright, green caterpillar to its branch, and trotted on after her.

Just a little while later, with less than an hour of daylight still left, they found themselves standing at the edge of a round, grassy clearing. Here the woods came to a sudden halt, and so did they, now both gazing at a most grand and curious sight.

At last, they had found the long sought for, 'Smoking Tree!'

Ahead of them spread a large, bowl-like clearing, like a raised, round swelling of green, right in the middle of the so called 'Bad Wood,' between Hooter's Hill and the River Tymes. It was as if this grassy and flower-speckled meadow was some sort of grand stage or a raised royal dais, put there on purpose, like a natural open-air throne room or a royal audience chamber, for some great Wood-land King.

The mighty Smoking Tree stood there alone, tall and proud and still billowing out smoke; Towering up from the middle of the greensward. And soon to be the centre of attention for all of the creatures of that particular area of the Great Forest of Lundun!

CHAPTER 9:
OF UPS AND DOWNS.

The gentle, up-sloping mound was a broad area full of beautiful, lush green grasses, speckled with little white and yellow flowers. "Oh, what a lovely meadow!" exclaimed Mary excitedly, as they moved eagerly onward toward the majestic tree.

At the meadow's center, the smoking tree stood like a mighty hand spreading upwards and outwards, as if trying to grab the very sky itself! Its thick shaggy, grey trunk and its mossy, leaf-filled branches were gnarled and ancient looking. It was like some lonely monument, signifying the relentless struggle of all life on Erf.

And from its branches, gouts of grey smoke coiled up into the early evening dusk.

Mary saw that it still had an abundance of leaves, and these were large and a grey-green color, but in some areas all the leaves had died away, leaving brown patches. She assumed this was due to the smoke that belched in repeated billows from its trunk, roots and branches. It was almost like it was puffing on a pipe.

"This Smoking Tree's a worse smoker than even my Gran!" she thought.

"Well, what do you think's causing this smoke then, Mary, any ideas?" Roger asked her.

"Not really," she answered, "but, if it was the tree itself on fire then we would see some flames somewhere, wouldn't we?"

"Yes, I'm sure we would," Roger agreed.

He looked over the tree, studying it closely, looking for any sign of flames; but there was none to be seen at all. "This is very mysterious," he thought, "after all, you can't have smoke without fire, can you? That would defy the laws of Physics!"

Above him, a hazy stratum of cloud was being swept away into the slowly darkening skies of the eastern horizon by the warm, westerly wind. Roger felt torn between staying longer and solving an intriguing scientific puzzle or leaving for home immediately.

But he didn't want to seem too eager to tear Mary away from her treasured reward of reaching the Smoking Tree, as he'd agreed and promised. He knew though, it would take them a good two hours of hard walking to get back to the Quaggy, even with them taking the easier route and going around Hooter's Hill.

"Well, well," said Mary, in her most teacherly voice, and inadvertently disturbing his reverie. "It's definite; this **is** an 'Ulmus Glabras,' no doubt about it; but a really big one!"

"A what?" exclaimed Roger. "What are you on about?"

"Oh, that's just the fancy Lateen name for a Wych Elm tree," she replied. "An' I bet you don't know a Wych Elm tree is also the symbol for the spiritual connection of all Humans to the Erf itself? My Gran taught me that, you know."

"No, I didn't know that," muttered Roger, once again grudgingly impressed by Mary's vast knowledge of the natural world.

"Anyway, I'd say there's a proper an' real ol' mystery here," Mary continued, musing half to herself. "Either this 'ere tree's got a very bad smoking habit, juss like my ol' Grannie does, or there's something else goin' on! What do you think, Roj?"

"Well. Yes, indeed," muttered Roger, as together they walked warily around the tree's large trunk. "Can you see any f-f-fire anywhere; or anything like that?" he asked her.

"Not a flicker or a flame," she answered, in a bewildered tone. "But I know what me dear ol' Grannie always says; she says there ain't never no smoke without no fire!"

"Yes, I know. But then where is it, where is the fire making the smoke?" murmured Roger, increasingly intrigued despite the lateness of the day. He was definitely getting the idea that there was indeed some real scientific exploration to be done here.

"Well, we've not got very long to find out, now, have we? We'll have to come back and explore another day, I s'pose," Mary replied in a disappointed tone.

"Yes, we did agree we'd only go as far as the Smoking Tree, didn't we?" Roger replied.

The sun was now hovering very low in the sky and Mary glumly nodded her agreement.

"Well, least we got to where we said we would, didn't we?" she said, with a forced smile.

They both knew they would have to make a very hasty return indeed now, before the full darkness of night-time descended on them. This would require them running a lot of the way back just to get to the River Quaggy, and thereby to the safety of their familiar Good Wood.

But they weren't that keen to return to the hot water they knew they were both in, either. Roger was still feeling torn between staying and going. And unbeknownst to him, Mary was feeling the same.

Mary, however, felt she should have at least one quick climb up into the tree's branches, just to see what she could see before they left for home.

"Listen 'ere, Roj, will you let me 'ave one look up the tree before we go?" she asked, imploringly, looking at him with her pleading blue eyes. "I promise it'll be a quick climb, cross me heart and hope to die and all that!"

"Oh, Mary, do you really have to?" he answered, pretending reluctance in allowing her request. He well knew though, before he'd said anything to her, he was going to agree.

"We'll be able to come back another day, you know, Mary, and it's getting near dark now. We should really be heading back."

Mary did her feminine magic trick again, saying nothing, but gazing intently at him and biting her bottom lip and just allowing him time to realize he was still going to say O.K.

"Oh, O.K., then Mary," he ruefully agreed, "but you b-b-better be careful. I'll stay down here and keep a l-l-lookout for you, but you promise not to get into any trouble, all right?"

"Oh, all right, Sir Roger," Mary laughed, "I'll be very careful," and with that, she quickly pulled herself onto the first branch and began her exploratory climb, up into the green depths of the 'Ulmus Glabras', as she called it. Otherwise known as the mysterious, 'Smoking Tree.'

Mary was a very accomplished climber and this tree was a very climbable one indeed, being full of large and broad branches. "I won't be long," she called down to him, as she disappeared into the green, trembling world of the leafy canopy above.

"Make sure you avoid the smoke," Roger called up to her, "and please don't do anything silly!" he added, gazing upwards and anxiously watching for clues of her progress, shown by the occasional shaking of branches and fluttering of disturbed leaves.

Mary speedily and easily climbed upwards and indeed made sure she kept well clear of the dead areas where smoke had billowed through more often and sometimes was still doing so. She was well used to finding the right footholds and handholds for tree climbing, and this tree was one of those trees that seemed to have been specially grown for children to climb in.

She found it very exciting being up, right in the heart of a tree. She always felt she had been miraculously transported to another world; simply by climbing up into the shimmering, green world within a tree. There you could really think and breathe and be like the tree.

And soon she had got to as near to the top as she could go. Whenever Mary climbed a tree, her objective was always to get as near to the top as she possibly could.

Up there, the branches were a lot thinner and she could feel the bounce and sway of them as she climbed up higher and higher. She felt like a tree-sprite, flitting amongst the trembling leaves and the crackling twigs. She was, once again, an intrepid explorer, discovering a new tree-world; Just like Amerigo Vespucci did, discovering Ameriga, in the Fifteenth Century.

But this was the world of the Tree, and at the top of it, the wonderful world of the sky. That was where clouds and birds soared, through the vast, limitless freedom of the sky.

It was then, as Mary poked her head up out from the top of the tree, that she suddenly realized she had seen no birds, none whatsoever. Which she knew was very unusual for any sort of a tree and especially a whole Wood.

"It must be all this smoke," she mused, "but what on Erf could be causing it?"

Then, she suddenly realized something even more astounding. Something that had been so blindingly obvious and had been staring both her and Roger in the face, ever since they'd left Hooter's Hill. She wondered how they could possibly have ever missed it?

THEY HAD SEEN NO ANIMALS IN THE BAD WOOD AT ALL!

Ever since they'd left the Giant Owls at Hooter's Hill, they had only seen various sorts of plants and insects and nothing else at all. They must have all left; there didn't seem to be any sorts of woodland animals in this part of the Bad Wood anymore. She had seen no dogs or deer, no wildcats or wolves, no ferrets or foxes, no badgers or bears; no rats or mice, no squirrels or snakes; just no animals whatsoever!

They had been so busy with their own individual excitements and interests in plants and insects, that the obvious fact of not seeing or hearing even one lone bird or one single animal, had just completely escaped their notice. *Juss where can all the bloomin' birds and beasts of the Bad Wood be?* she wondered to herself.

Sitting up in the top of the tree, she looked all around her, far across the broad, speckled meadow that the Smoking Tree was in the middle of. She could see right down to the edges of the surrounding woods. And the odd, lifeless silence of it now struck her for the first time.

The light was now definitely dimming. But up here at the Smoking Tree's top, she could feel the last, lingering fingers of the sun's rays, stroking and warming her face. It was almost a shame to have to climb back down into the gloom again. But she knew she had to report back to Roger; he'd be worrying, and she had to let him know that there was an even bigger mystery here than that of the Smoking Tree. Just where had all the animals gone, and why?

Then, as she gazed outwards, pondering on this thorny question, she felt a small tremor pass through the tree, like a rippling wave, and she and all the leaves around her trembled together in its aftershock.

"That's strange!" she thought. "We don't usually have Erfquakes in Inglande!"

Then she noticed something else or thought she did. Some sort of a motion by the trees. But it wasn't a quick movement, like an animal, nervously darting behind a bush that just suddenly caught your eye. No, this was like the whole surrounding edge of the wood out there was moving. Or at least, the wood's trees containing things you couldn't quite see.

Some things out there were moving and filling up the shadows at the edge of the woods. Like a host of grey ghosts, or dark unerfly creatures, flickering between the tree-trunks.

"That's spooky!" Mary thought to herself, worriedly. "That's not just trees swaying in the wind, more like a host of haunting shadows; all twitching and scratching, like some restless, fidgeting crowd; all gathered together and impatiently waiting for something."

She peered out into the edges of the darkening woods that encircled the Smoking Tree's broad meadow, and suddenly got goosebumps.

"I can't actually sees 'em but I can feels 'em!" she told herself. "Maybe it's the trick of the fading light. What does Gran call the feeling now? That's right, the 'Crepuscular Creeps!' But I'd swear there's something out there, just silently watching and waiting!"

Mary felt her skin crawl as another chill shudder of fear passed through her. "Must be getting cold," she told herself. She didn't want to think that out there, at the edge of the meadow, there might be nasty things surrounding them, things far too scary and horrible for Mary or Roger to deal with.

She hadn't got any closer to discovering why the Smoking Tree was smoking but she decided she'd best hurry back down to Roger anyway and tell him what she had discovered about the missing animals and the shady creatures in the distant trees, before he started to get too impatient; but it was too late, Roger was already on her case.

"What are you d-d-doing up there?" he yelled. "Come on, Mary, we've really g-g-got to get going; it's definitely getting a lot d-d-darker now!"

"O.K., Roj, I'm on my way," she called down to him. "I won't be long."

She could tell that Roger was becoming very anxious and started making her way down, nimbly retracing the route she'd taken to get to the top. "We're definitely coming back and getting to the bottom of this strange Smoking Tree and 'Disappearing Animals' business," she resolutely muttered to herself.

Inside the lower part of the tree, it had already become a dark and dismal world of inky, glaucous gloom. She had to slowly feel her way from branch to branch. She lowered her feet, one after the other, like two tentative, searching tentacles; feeling out for a firm foothold and getting the instep of each foot stably onto a branch below her. While at the same time, tightly holding onto the branch she was lowering herself down from. In the deepening gloom of the tree it was very easy to make a mistake and slip and fall; and after all, she'd promised Roger she wouldn't get into any trouble.

But as she made her way cautiously downwards, she suddenly caught sight of something lurking within the tree, hidden within the multitude of dark leaves. There had been a flicker of – something. She couldn't tell what it was exactly. It had been so fast and so, well, blurry! She got the definite impression there was something else alive in that tree, and she was right.

But this, so secret and hidden something or someone, wasn't yet ready to show itself.

Roger could hear that Mary had finally gotten to the lower branches. He stood there nervously, hands on hips and impatiently craning his neck up and waiting for her to appear. He heard every rustle of leaf and crack of twig, as she made her descent. Then, all at once, there she was, smiling and cheerily waving down at him. She nimbly swung herself down from the bottom-most branch, landing near to him, between two, large tree-roots.

As she did so, Roger heard a sudden, very loud crack, and then a great gout of thick grey smoke billowed up from where she had landed.

Without a single moment's warning, Mary had been swallowed up and completely disappeared. She had totally vanished under the ground.

And Roger was left, with jaws dropped wide, utterly and terribly alone!

*

Seconds slowly ticked away to minutes in the stunned silence that followed Mary's sudden and dramatic disappearance. Roger's heart was beating madly, and he was feeling sick, dizzy and lightheaded. He felt caught in the blood-draining grip of a relentless terror and panic.

He rushed over and dropped to his knees, right next to where Mary had last been standing, and saw a gaping crack; a gash in the ground, in between the roots where Mary had landed when she'd jumped from the tree. He peered down into it, staring into its dim, damp-smelling depths. But there was nothing to be seen. She had really gone; just vanished without a word, and without leaving a single shred of evidence that she had ever existed at all.

Roger's mind had seized up with the sudden shock of it. "What d-d-do I do, what do I do?" he kept babbling, over and over, looking wildly about, unable to focus on anything.

All he could see below him was impenetrable blackness. Then he realized he should at least call out to her and see if Mary could hear him. After all, maybe she hadn't fallen far; maybe she'd soon be scrabbling to the surface, any minute now, and they'd both be laughing about her little fall down a rabbit hole. Desperately he yelled down into the dark, murky pit.

"He-e-e-ello! Mary, are you all right? C-c-can you hear me?"

He called several more times; then waited, listening for a moment, but there was only a still and eerie silence. He had never ever felt so alone in his life.

After a while he spent several painful seconds having a difficult argument with himself, just trying to decide as to what he should exactly do next.

"Now, let's be scientific here! Let's just keep calm and be logical about this, shall we?" He umm'd and err'd, frantically talking to himself, not knowing whether to stand up or crawl, whether to come or to go. "Surely, the best thing I can do now is to go and get help, isn't it? I can't possibly do anything all by myself, now can I?"

He was having to face up to his own fear and uncertainty. He was having to look himself very squarely in the heart … and ask himself a very simple but very hard question:

"To Flea or not to Flee?"

After calling for Mary several more times and still not getting any answer, he finally got a grip on himself and began to realize that in actual fact, he didn't have any real choice at all. He just had to thoroughly convince himself of that first though.

"Well, R-R-Roger, me lad, it's just up to you now and n-n-no one else, let's face it!"

Roger was rapidly realizing, that whatever happened now, whatever the future may hold, for both himself and for Mary, it was all down to the decision he made, right there and then.

He cautiously approached the edge of the smoky hole that had swallowed up Mary and got down onto his stomach and peered into its murky depths.

"Maybe I can be like a real Knight and rescue a damsel in distress, after all!" he thought. "I can't just leave her down there, in the dark, all alone and defenseless; and prey to any wild animal that might come along, can I?" he argued, desperately trying to convince himself.

"Anyway, let's not be silly, eh? Let's be realistic. I'd get lost in these woods all by myself, but I'd get lost going off down into the dark too, now wouldn't I?"

He rolled onto his back and looked up into the depths of the great Smoking Tree above. He saw that its leaves and branches were hazily blending together, darkly coalescing into the gathering gloom of the oncoming twilight.

"You definitely wouldn't be able to tell the smoke from the wood now, Mary," he thought, gazing up at the gathering gloom of the night sky, now being slowly filled with the distant bright dots of the Heaven's host of flickering stars.

"O.K., Roger m'boy, no time to dither, it's time for action!" he said to himself out loud.

Roger knew all along, in his very heart of hearts, that he always only had the one choice; there was after all only one thing he really could do, and this time, it definitely wasn't to run!

He emptied out the contents from his satchel and found his school journal. He tore out a blank page and hurriedly wrote a note. Just in case, he thought, meaning … just in case he never came back!

The short note read: "To whom it may concern: My name is Roger Briggs and I have gone down under this tree to rescue my friend, Mary Maddam." He then very carefully wrote out his full address: The Manor, Mottington, Under-Lundun, South East - Sector 9, Inglande, Erf; and dated and signed it.

He returned what he was going to take with him into his satchel, his torch, his compass, his old school scarf as well as assorted hankies and a packet of biscuits and a flask of water. He folded and wrapped the note up in a hanky and placed his ammonite fossil firmly on top, to keep it from getting wet or blown away.

As for his precious tobacco tin of highly trained Fleas, he just couldn't decide what to do. "Just who'll look after them, eh, if I don't make it back?" he grimly thought to himself.

Eventually, Roger made the very painful decision to let his Fleas go.

"If only they were b-b-bigger, they'd just hop down that horrid hole and bring Mary up in a jiffy, no p-p-problem!" he ruefully muttered,

He knelt on the ground and carefully opened the lid of the tobacco tin, and then gently tipped it onto its side. He then ensured that all twelve of his precious fleas hopped safely away, off on their new and unknown roads to freedom.

"Goodbye, fellas, take care of yourselves," he sighed, wiping away the tears in his eyes.

He then realized he'd been talking to himself for some while, and so started feeling a bit embarrassed, as well as scared. Which he knew, in the circumstances, was a bit daft really. He should just be scared!

He then had the idea, and he didn't really know why, but he just felt that somehow, here in the so-called Bad Wood, even tiny unimportant creatures, like his Fleas were supposed to be, would indeed be safe and be able to flourish.

Roger was now fully prepared. There was only one thing left for him to do, and that was ... to just do it!

CHAPTER 10:
DOWN THE SLIPPERY SLOPE.

Roger got to his feet and again approached the edge of the yawning pit. The sky up above was streaked with the bloody colors of the darkening sunset, and all around him was a strange air of silent expectation.

As he prepared to lower himself down into the depths of the pit, in between the Smoking Tree's roots, he felt a sudden shudder, as of icy fingers running up and down his spine, or of a thousand piercing eyes boring into his back. His skin crawled with a clammy, cold fear as he gave a final look to the darkening world around him.

Directly above him, within the grey gloom of the Smoking Tree's foliage, he thought he'd fleetingly glimpsed a pair of pale luminous eyes. They flickered then vanished into a patch of shadow that seemed to rapidly melt away.

"There's something very w-w-weird going on here, that I just d-d-don't understand," he whispered to himself, feeling the hairs rise on the nape of his neck. He again had the definite idea that he was being watched.

He got to his hands and knees and prepared to lower himself down into the waiting crack between the tree's roots. As he was doing so, he thought he saw, or at least, half saw, several flickering shapes, flitting between the trunks of the trees, at the edge of the distant clearing. He also thought he saw strange, dark, spidery things, falling from the branches there, as well as bat-like shapes flapping about between the trees.

He couldn't really be sure, but right now, it didn't really matter.

Whatever was out there would just have to wait. The only important thing now was to rescue Mary!

One thing he briefly noted though was that as the deepening gloom of night descended, there were scattered clumps of eerie, pale light glowing and lighting up, all around the wood. He dimly registered that more and more of the Moon-berry orbs, glowing with their unerfly, pearly-light, were appearing, giving the Bad Wood an even spookier look than it had before.

But Roger was fully committed, there was no turning back now, and anyway, he thought, what was there to stay for? Whatever was happening above-ground, would just have to wait. His one and only quest now was to descend into the dark and unknown depths of the Erf, down beneath the Smoking Tree; to seek and hopefully find his new-found, dearest and only, human friend, Miss Mary Maddam.

As Roger cautiously lowered himself over the edge, grabbing hold of any roots he could find and with his torch weakly beaming from between his clenched jaws, he heard the faint, restless murmur of the shady thing or things, above him. He tried to ignore whatever uncanny goings-on were taking place up there. He had decided and was now absolutely determined. He had some very important rescuing to do!

"I do hope Mary's all right, she must be all right, she really must be!" he prayed fervently, as he lowered himself into the fuming pit.

He lowered himself just a few yards down into the crevice, clinging on to a nearby root. The light from his torch was weak, only illuminating a small patch of darkness around him. But already, the world had changed. The dank smell of the erf and decaying vegetation filled his nostrils and the cloying combined sensations of dread and claustrophobia filled his mind.

"By the Fearsome Fur of Faraday's Face! This could be a bottomless pit; or just an endless void of Nothingness down here, for all I know!" he exclaimed to himself, aghast. "This torch is next to useless. Just how am I going to do this?"

Despite the chill of the air, he was sweating already, and his heart was beating like a Big Band's Drum Solo. He at last found some hopefully safe foot and hand holds, and as he went lower, the inky darkness relentlessly drew in, smothering and blanketing him with blindness. He tried his best to just concentrate on making his descent and to just ignore the distant and mysterious whines, whistles, croaks and cackles coming from the mysterious creatures above.

Then, to his great horror, his concentration slipped, and so did he!

He had lost his footing and his torch at the same time and found himself swinging in the dark now desperately hanging on by one hand, to just a single, frayed tree root.

It was only that one hairy root that had saved him though. That miraculous old root had somehow managed to get itself snagged under his belt buckle as he fell; and that one stroke, of so-called 'luck', was all that now separated him from plummeting to his certain death.

"Oh, Ruddy Rutherford's Rabbits, help!" he cried feebly, swinging in the inky darkness, and feeling totally helpless and utterly alone.

As he swung there, back and forth in the inky dark, desperately trying to keep a tight grip of the root, he just managed to keep his courage intact, as well as the contents of his belly.

He really wasn't built to be any sort of a Tarzan, at all. The real problem now though, was to get back to the wall of rock and erf he'd been climbing down. He had to get a good, firm grip there again. But how? His eyes were slowly getting used to the dark but weren't yet good enough to see any clear route by which he could rescue himself.

Also, he now realized, his hand was starting to hurt, he must have strained his wrist when he grabbed onto the snagged root and he knew he couldn't hold on for much longer.

"Right! About now is the time for a bit of clever scientific thinking," he thought.

But without his torch, there was nothing to show him how deep the drop below him was. He then had a brilliant, 'Roger the Swot,' idea:

"So, I need to know what the depth below me is, don't I? So, let's get a measure of that first, eh? That's what I need to do," he muttered earnestly.

With that, he looked around for something he could drop down into the chasm below him. All he could find though, were three penny coins, one of which he managed to scrabble from out of his trouser pocket.

He took a deep breath and dropped the coin beneath his feet and waited anxiously to hear it strike the bottom of the pit.

He had been tensed and ready to count out the passing seconds and calculate the distance before the coin hit some solid surface below. But before he'd managed to even draw a single breath, the tinny clink of the coin rang up from below him, in fact, just a couple of feet below where he was hanging.

He in fact, wasn't swinging over a bottomless chasm, after all.

Roger steeled himself and just jumped, trusting to science and its physical laws. But also adding a silent prayer to whatever God might have any interest in him, just as extra insurance.

It was actually less than a yard down, and his feet thumped firmly onto a solid ledge with a satisfying crunch. He took a step backwards and accidentally stood on his battered, old torch, 'luckily' it had been caught in a root sticking out just where he'd landed. He picked it up and found it wasn't working but he gave it a shake and it flickered back to life.

"Must be a loose wire or something," he thought, "only hope it doesn't die on me now."

He quickly pointed his torch down onto his feet and found he had indeed landed on a rocky shelf. A ledge that lay at the bottom of the cliff of the pit he had been climbing down. He cautiously sidled up to its edge to see what he could see. But with only the weak light of his torch, no matter how much he strained and stared, he couldn't see much at all.

In the dim light there were thick tangles of tree roots all about him; some half buried and some exposed and trailing off down into the gloomy depths. And above him he could see the walls of the crack he's jumped down, narrowed like a scar against the distant night-sky.

At his feet lay the hidden depths of the pitch-black chasm that Mary must have fallen into. And who knew how wide or deep that was? Once again, Roger would have to use his brains. But what he was really using was his courage. He shone the weak light of his torch along the rocky ledge, but other than the ledge and the tree's roots, there was nothing more to be seen.

"Can you hear me Mary, are you down there?" he shouted, but still no answer came.

He sat on the ledge to get his breath back and to ponder his predicament. Then without any warning, the wall of erf and the rock, and roots behind him started to madly shiver and shake. The rock wall seemed to be having convulsions, and he felt very near to having them too.

But, by some uncanny power of premonition, he threw himself off to one side, just as the tip of a Giant Erf-worm came boring through, erupting from the rock-face behind him.

It looked just like an ordinary Erf-worm except it was at least a hundred times as big and was glowing a faint blue. It was obviously much tougher than the ones he was familiar with. This worm could bore through solid rock, not just soil. He realized this was obviously a Giant Rock-Worm of the Under-Erf!

"Hmm, well, whatever else, it's still definitely a Megadrile, a variety of Erfworm of the family of Megascolecidae," he thought, being his old clever-clogs self again.

Roger lay as still and as quiet as he could, while it slithered on by him and disappeared down into a crack in the rock ledge several feet from where he lay. It hadn't tried to hurt him and in fact, hadn't paid him any attention whatsoever. But it had served one purpose though. Roger now knew there were very strange and unknown creatures down here in the realm of the 'Under-Erf'; and in the future some of them might not be so negligent of his existence!

After that horrible thought, and once his heart had stopped racing, he again yelled out as loud as he could for Mary, still hoping to hear her; but again, no answer came. He was now getting very worried about her indeed and had to stifle another wave of fear and panic.

He shone his flickering torch into the murky depths below, but as expected, it revealed nothing new; just a smoky void of impenetrable blackness. He then very cautiously peered over the edge and once more did the traditional and time-honored thing all heroes do when they're confronted by an unfathomable drop beneath them. He took a second penny from his pocket, and peering intently over the ledge, dropped it into the inky, black chasm below.

Once again, he was amazed to find that by doing so, he was not in fact on the edge of an endless chasm at all; but was instead at the top of a fairly, smooth slope of rock, that slanted away into the dark, seemingly at a steady angle. He could clearly hear the coin and disturbed pebbles skittering down the slope below him; He grabbed another handful of pebbles and threw these as well, just to make sure, and they also skittered down the hidden slope.

He then made some quick mathematical calculations in his head and taking time, velocity, mass and distance into account, he determined that there was indeed a slope at his feet, and it was at about a Thirty Degree angle, at the most. He sighed with relief. This meant that, if he was very careful, he could slowly and surely slide his way down into its dark dismal depths, and without tumbling to his untimely death.

"Sometimes Practical Mathematics is a real pain in the abacus!" he told himself ironically out loud, finding his own voice strangely reassuring down here in the darkness. But it made him think of Mary again. The only voice he'd heard so far had been his own. And it was Mary's voice that he most desperately wanted to hear more than anything.

"Still not a single peep from her yet," he thought, "but at least it's not a bottomless pit she's been swallowed up by; she must have rolled down the slope and then, gulp! Survived somehow!" He frowned, again now talking aloud to himself, trying to work out what to do. "O.K. first things first, let's get down this slope and then we'll deal with whatever we need to deal with then, right, Roger? Right!"

Roger was very, very scared; and yes, some of it was the smoky darkness and his horror of heights and the ever-threatening danger, but what he was secretly most scared about was:

"Wh-wha-what if she's dead?"

He could hardly bear to even think such a thing.

There were several wisps of grey smoke still rising up from the gloom. This was making breathing more difficult but other than that, there was nothing else to see or hear down there.

Then, suddenly, there was another shuddering Erf tremor. And parts of the ledge he was on began to crack and crumble and chunks of rock came clattering down from above.

Then a large cloud of grey, billowing smoke came up the slope from below, causing him to cough and his eyes to stream, momentarily blinding him; even though he was all but blind already, in the close claustrophobic gloom of the pit.

He quickly fumbled for one of his hankies from his pocket and tied it around his mouth.

Then, as his spluttering and wheezing subsided, he heard it; just very, very faintly, and sounding a long, long way off below him. He could hear a distant cry for help followed by several weak coughs. Then all was silent again. He listened intently; but once again, there was nothing to be heard.

All was just silence, smoke and darkness, as before.

But Roger knew what he had heard, even so faintly. It had been Mary, he was sure of it.

"That's her!" he thought, with great relief. "Oh, thank Galileo for that, she's alive!"

Then another gust of smoke billowed up into his face, causing him once again to choke and so give his own rendition of a coughing smoker rendering him temporarily unable to call back down to her and let her know he was on the way. But he wiped at the soot from his face, with yet another of his hankies, and then lay flat on his stomach, and leaned over the ledge. He held his breath, and listened for any sound, just to be absolutely sure that it was her.

"Roger. He-e-e-elp meeeee! Can you hear meee?" he heard he call once again.

"Yep, that is definitely her!" he thought, then smiling grimly to himself, ruefully added, "But that's a bit silly really; after all, who else is it likely to be down here?"

Roger leaned out from the ledge and yelled as loud as he could, down into the darkness.

"I can hear you, Mary. I'm coming, hold on, I'm coming!" Then gathering the very last shreds of his courage, told himself, "Well, Roger, this is it I s'pose; although it's not exactly scientifically exploring the depths of the unknown that I'd expected, but, well, needs must!"

With that, he hoisted himself over the side of the rock-shelf and sat knees under his chin, at the very top of the powdery grey slope that disappeared scarily below his feet, down into the billowing blackness of the unknown beyond.

Mary's Knight Irritant and rescuer was at last on his way!

Roger gingerly began his slow, ungainly bum-shuffle downwards. But once again, after a short while, the slope suddenly and violently lurched and buckled beneath him. It was just as if some long, dirty carpet had been caught tightly in the hands of an invisible Giantess doing her housework and given it a thoroughly good bashing and beating.

Huge clouds of dust billowed all about him, and once again he could hear the rumbling of nearby rock-falls. All around him came the noises of cracking stones and tumbling rocks, as he was suddenly enveloped in an even thicker mass of boiling smoke and dust.

"Oh, by Newton's Nappies! Hanky or no hanky, I've had it now!" he thought desperately. "There's no way I can breathe in all this smoke!"

The Erf-quake at last subsided, and Roger was left gasping; his chest felt like it was on fire and his mouth and nose seemed to have been convenient places to fill up with dust and soot. Any idea of using them for the actual function they were supposed to do seemed totally futile.

Roger realized, if he didn't get a breath of proper air very soon, he was going to die!

He fell onto his back, against the slope, writhing and choking, desperately trying to get one good lung-full of air; but it was impossible. He was drowning in a surging sea of smoke.

"So, this is it, is it?" he wondered. "Me dying of asphyxiation; who would have thought? Mary would just call it 'suffocating' though. Asphyxiation is just me trying to be a clever clogs. Anyway, it just means 'no pulse' in Latin, and you still have a pulse for ages after you've suffocated." Even as he choked, he felt amazed at himself, that even while he was dying of the aforesaid 'asphyxiation,' he could still babble away in his head and think of such seemingly silly and mundane matters as the meanings of words.

"Who cares about the blinkin' definition now?" he thought, realizing that he sometimes was a bit over-pompous and pedantic about such things. He felt that, even while his body was struggling and choking slowly to death, there was yet another part of himself, the real him as it were, looking on and surveying the whole scene, in a cool and detached manner.

"Just like being, sort of, well, disembodied, I s'pose. If there is such a thing!" he thought.

Roger realized that he only had mere moments left now; then he would black out and go unconscious and then he'd be just a lost and unknown corpse buried somewhere underground and un-mourned by anyone.

"B-b-but what about Mary?" he wondered. "I c-c-can't let M-M-Mary down, now can I?"

Then once more there was a sudden rumbling roar of sound from all around him.

"Oh, no, not another Erfquake!" he dimly thought, as he began to slip into dark oblivion. But it wasn't an Erfquake at all. Roger found that he was beginning to breathe again. He saw that several of the Smoking Tree's roots, just above him, had become very active and alive; now boring up through the ceiling of the rocky slope, and miraculously creating air vents.

But they weren't acting alone. Roger saw there were several Giant Erf-Worms that had burrowed their way down through the slope's roof as well. These were also creating tunnels to the surface above. The Smoking Tree's roots and the Erf Worms were working together, creating air vents so that the smoke could clear, and Roger could breathe!

He became fully conscious of all this as his lungs automatically filled themselves with air. Roger gasped painfully as he gulped down the reviving oxygen, while the boiling clouds of bitter smoke were sucked up and away through the newly created vents. And soon the blue, eerily glowing Erf-Worms were rapidly disappearing back into the hidden depths of their rocky world, just as the smoking tree's roots also retreated and became dormant once more.

Roger lay there for many minutes, panting and hardly daring to believe he was still alive.

"Oh, praise the mighty Megadriles and their Class of Oligochaetes!" he thought, as he slowly recovered.

For a while, all he could hear was his rapidly beating heart. All else was sunk into a dim, muffled silence as the rocks and dust settled; with just a few wisps of acrid smoke, coiling in the inky air before him. Then he heard, only very faintly at first, but more clearly the more he concentrated, Mary's voice, once again, very weakly calling up to him from below.

"Hellooooo! Are you O.K., Roger, can you hear me?"

"I'm fine, Mary. Hold on. I'm c-c-coming!" he called back.

Judging from the sound of Mary's voice, he was at last getting much closer now.

He just hoped to high heaven that there wouldn't be any further unexpected dangers to interrupt and distract him from the brave and daring rescue of his damsel in distress.

"Surely there can't be anything worse ahead of me now, can there?" he wondered.

CHAPTER 11:
THE RISE AND FALL OF
RATTUS MAGNUS.

Roger made his way down, once again sitting on his haunches, and again doing what could best be described as an undignified 'bum-shuffle.' But as there was no one there to see him, his slow and ungainly progress into the cavernous underground realms went by unremarked.

Every now and again there would be another cry of help from Mary, as well as further acrid billows of pungent smoke, blowing up from the depths below. Roger was by now extremely dirty, being black with soot from head to toe. And as he shuffled on further down the slope, he gave occasional cries of encouragement for Mary's imminent rescue, shouting out, **"I'm coming, Mary, hold on. It'll be O.K. I'm coming!"** as he shuffled, inch by cautious inch, down the slanting floor of rock, moving ever deeper beneath the tangled roots of the Smoking Tree.

"I just pray to Potty Pythagoras, this slope goes all the way to where Mary actually is," he muttered wryly to himself.

As he continued though, the smoke was again getting thicker and billowing all about him. It came on in gusts and was getting in his clothes and seeping into his skin. But what was worse, even with the hanky over his face, it was getting into his eyes too and making them sting and stream constantly. This made it very difficult for him to see anything clearly at all. His throat felt like a soot-caked chimney-flue in need of a good sweep. He started coughing and spluttering once again as another belch of smoke hit him full in the face.

"Just where was all this smoke coming from?" he wondered.

He rested awhile and let the coughing subside. Then he pulled out another spotted hankie, discarding the old one, and tied it around his mouth and nose again. He wiped the mix of soot and sweat from his eyes with another hanky and carried on his bum-shuffling way down the rocky slope, praying to all the great Brains of Science that he would make it to Mary.

He now noticed there was an area just to his left that had several old roots poking up through the sloping floor there. And some of those roots contained several strange, ball-shaped objects. They clustered together amongst the root-ends, like leathery, black footballs.

Now what on Erf can they be? he thought.

He sidled his way over to them and played the flickering beam of his torch over the roots. He saw how each ball was segmented, like a rolled-up Armadillo, and they were in fact at least three times the size of ordinary footballs. But also, they weren't really balls at all. As he looked, one started to uncurl itself, unrolling and showing what its true nature was.

Seemingly the light had disturbed it and Roger now saw a huge Woodlouse-like creature. Its small, stubby legs were wriggling madly and its two curving antennae were twitching and turning towards him. It now fully unrolled itself, found its footing and started scuttling away.

"Well, Bless my Bacon, it's a giant Isopod!" he cried out in amazement.

Roger, being a budding Biologist and specializing in Entomology, (the study, as you now know, of Insects), of course knew quite a lot about Isopods. These were the usually very tiny armored insects that people more commonly knew of as 'pill-bugs' or 'wood-lice.' And they would more normally find them underneath damp bricks or moldy logs in their back gardens. Roger's natural bug-hunting instincts and curiosity now fully came to the fore.

"Hmmm, I wonder what it's doing down here way under this tree?" he pondered, out loud, as he now watched the flat, armadillo-like creature scuttle away into the darkness. "Oh, yes," he exclaimed, answering his own question. "I suppose it's just like with the ordinary Isopods; They prefer moist areas, living under damp rocks or tree roots too. But how come these are so huge? We've seen Giant talking Owls, Giant glowing Erf-Worms and now whopping Giant Isopods! Just what on Erf's going on here?"

But the torchlight and the skittering noise from the departing Isopod had disturbed all the other large, curled up balls. One by one, those still buried among the old tree roots started to uncurl themselves. Roger could see their shiny, black, chitinous scales, gleaming in his torchlight, as they slowly uncurled their round, segmented bodies. Their long, quivering antennae and seven pairs of wriggling legs soon fully exposed to the air.

There were about a dozen of them over there, lumbering among the roots, like mini tanks. Despite their large size they were nimble creatures and were adept at moving about in the pitch dark and at some speed, when they wanted to.

"Well, I just hope these Giant 'Pill-bugs' are as shy as the tiny ones I know on the surface. I don't want trouble with any savage, man-eating woodlice, do I?" He chuckled to himself.

There wasn't any real worry though, as they seemed harmless. They had now all settled down again once he'd directed his torchlight away from them. One by one, they curled themselves up and nestled back into their root-tangle nests, and just melted away into the inky-gloom of their damp and dark abodes.

"It looks like they're more interested in having their snooze than they are in me! Ah well, I better press on, no matter what; I can't keep Mary waiting, can I?" Roger thought to himself.

Roger had descended but a few yards further down the slope when he saw a little way below him, some large and shadowy shape appearing from out of the smoky darkness. He couldn't make out what it was; He'd noticed fleeting, shadow-like things before up in the Bad Wood, and also up on Hooter's Hill, but this darkness was somehow different. There was something about its shape, and just the looming presence of it, that made the hairs on his neck stand on end and sent a shiver down his spine.

As he cautiously slid his way down the dusty incline of the slope, he observed there was even more smoke billowing up the lower he went. He would have begun to seriously worry again about how he would breathe as he descended further. But now, his worry turned toward something far more threatening and alarming. The huge, shadowy shape was climbing steadily towards him, ever closer, slowly emerging from the clouds of smoke below.

He rubbed his eyes clear of soot and smoke yet again; And he saw it now, looming out of the inky black and lumbering towards him on all-fours, out of the fog bank and up the slope. It had slanted, evil-looking eyes that glowed in the dark, burning with fiery-red gleams that smoldered and flickered. Its head swaying from side to side under hunched shoulders.

Roger stopped petrified. He'd not seen anything like it before and it definitely wasn't friendly!

It came nearer and nearer, pacing its way up the smoky slope. Roger could now see it for what it was; This creature was huge; It was gigantic. It was in fact, a Giant Black Rat!

"It's of the same species as Rattus Rattus, the Black Rat!" he thought, his academic self once more getting the better of him. But this thing was like no rat he'd ever seen or heard of, on or under the Erf, ever before.

"Oh, my Bothersome Boyles!" he exclaimed, plumbing the depths of his store of curses. "What on Euclid's Erf is that horrible monster doing down here? That's more like a 'Rattus Magnus' than the ordinary Black Rat, the Rattus Rattus!"

He well knew what an Erf animal of the usual size for this species was called; And that was simply, a rat, but this was a monstrosity. It was the size of a large horse; But it wasn't a horse, it was a Giant Rat... and it was coming for him, jaws wide and with razor fangs at the ready, and dripping a foam of poisonous, yellow saliva.

This creature was yet another of the oversized denizens of the Forest of Lundun and the Under-Erf. But this one was obviously extremely evil. It radiated hatred and malice and it was out hunting for its intended kill - and Roger was its definite and intended prey!

The Giant Rat padded onwards up the slope, now only a dozen feet from where Roger watched, hunched and transfixed. He couldn't run; He couldn't fight; He couldn't argue with it either; This was obviously a mindless killing machine, fully intent on rending him limb from limb.

It had matted, black fur and a twitching black nose and long, wiry whiskers sprouting from its furry cheeks. Its feet had large pads, encasing very nasty-looking claws, and it had a long, sweeping rat tail. This swished along behind it, ever ready to lash out as a deadly whip.

As it approached, Roger could see it crouch down lower, its head almost down to the ground. It was coiling its muscles, getting ready to spring in attack. But Roger still couldn't move, he felt paralyzed, just staring into those deadly, flickering, red eyes.

He could hear its growling now, and he could smell its rancid, ratty stench; it smelt of old, dead things and foul garbage; rotted vegetation and putrid flesh. Roger wrinkled his nose in disgust and waited helplessly for its sudden, murderous leap and its vile fangs slashing down upon him.

And then the Rat attacked. It sprang high into the air, its two front legs outstretched with their razor-sharp claws eager to rip into fresh meat. For Roger, there was no escape. The Rat knew it and Roger knew it.

Roger scrunched up his eyes tight and just prayed that it would all be over quickly.

He heard the roar of the Rat, and then… a thudding sound, and then another. A second passed. Nothing had happened! He cautiously opened one eye and then the other.

"This is impossible, that Rat couldn't have missed me… could it?" he thought.

But then he saw it. The Rat was tumbling back down the slope, back from where it had just come. It was rolling over and over and it was being repeatedly battered, in the sides, in the face, and in its rear too, as it rolled and twisted and skidded downwards and out of control.

Roger gasped as he realized it was being hit by Giant Isopod, after Giant Isopod. They'd come tumbling at great speed, rolling relentlessly down the slope from behind Roger and so knocking the Giant Rat for six! For the Rat, it was just like facing a continual fusillade of cannon, firing broadside after broadside from some mighty fleet of War Galleons.

Scores of the seemingly sleepy and shy Pill-bugs had come to his rescue!

"Whew! Well at least somebody likes me down here!" he wryly thought, "I'm definitely getting the idea that there may be something down here that doesn't actually want me to die."

"But, then again," he added as an afterthought, "there's definitely something down here that does!"

The Giant Rat had now fallen a fair way and disappeared down into the bubbling smoke below, along with all the valiant Isopods that had so soundly defeated the verminous ratty brute.

Roger heard a distant thud and then a screeching howl; Then all was once again silent.

The attack of Rattus Magnus was over!

Roger turned his attention back to his mission. He cautiously continued on his way down; Pointing his torch ahead and getting ever closer to the swirling lake of grey smoke below.

He needed to make sure Mary knew he was still on the way, and that she could hear him, so he called out to her again.

"I'm all right! I'm still coming, Mary, if you can hear me try and answer me, O.K.? Try shouting up to me, so I can better hear where you are, O.K.?"

"Help, help, I'm here, I'm here!" she called back. Followed though by a series of hacking coughs. Her fits of coughing were happening more often and more loudly now, Roger observed.

But Roger took hope that he, at long last, was now getting close to finding her.

Then all I have to do is get us both up to the surface and then get us home again, and back through the Bad Wood, and in the dead of night too! he thought. Will wonders never cease! he grimly joked. But knew in his heart of hearts, that the joke was on him.

Then... with a cry of alarm, he came to a shuddering stop. There was no more slope!

Roger found he was suddenly sitting in the dark and deep underground, and with his legs dangling into empty space. His stomach lurched, his heart went into overdrive and he froze again, sitting on his backside and sticking hard to the rock, like some petrified victim of Vesuvius.

"Oh, Jumping James Joules! Wh-wh-where's the slope gone?" he cried out, in great alarm.

Below him, the slope had abruptly cut off and had become a vertical cliff; All he could see down beneath him was a large cloud of smoke; just as if he was looking down onto the top of a big, grey thundercloud. It roiled and boiled in continuous agitation and flickered and flashed angrily with occasional bursts of glaring oranges and garish reds, from deep within its churning and heaving mass.

By Holy Hawking, thought Roger in alarm. Mary is somewhere under all of that smoke and flame! Just what the Devil-in-Darwin am I supposed to do now?

Roger's only course of action was for him to quickly do some hard thinking and turn to his trusted 'scientific method', and so follow the fine examples of his many scientific heroes, such as Einstein, Newton or Faraday. So, instead of simply panicking, Roger calmed himself and forced himself to think - clearly and logically.

And at least I don't have any rabid, giant rats leaping in my face now! he thought.

Hmmm, let's see, he continued to himself, now logically, if Mary has been down here all of this time, which she has, and she's been able to survive and therefore still breathe, well there must be a way down that I can survive too, and ... what's more, he continued, in a flash of realization, that means I can breathe under all of that smoke as well!

For a short while, Roger felt pleased with himself. This, however, didn't last very long.

For, as many people know just by doing their best to live life, let alone from also being Scientists, coming up with new ideas and explanations as a theory, is just something that has yet to be proven. This was the bit of Roger's logic that gave him the most cause for concern; for as with any theory, there was the continual, nagging doubt, the unquestionable and most worrying problem of all, but what if I'm wrong? nagging away in his head.

But this is what indeed made Roger special.

He had, as Mary had put it so very well, 'hidden depths!' Roger wasn't at all stupid, but in lots of areas, he knew that he was very ignorant, for he knew there were lots and lots of things he didn't yet know. This, however, made him quite a lot cleverer than most people.

Thinking you know all about something when you don't is really more stupid than thinking you don't know something when you do, after all.

And what Roger was finding out now that he hadn't known before was just how brave he really was!

But despite being brave, Roger was still actually and factually terrified.

But once again, he used his brains, and now for the third time, used the time-honored hero's trick, to determine just how deep the boiling cloud of smoke below him was.

He dropped a third penny and a clink and clatter came to his ears after only two or three seconds. He now knew that the floor of the cavern couldn't lie that far below him, but he'd still have to climb down, as it was too far to jump, he was now pretty sure of that fact.

With a dry mouth, a thumping heart and a fluttering stomach, he started to lower himself over the edge, but then he stopped in his tracks. For there, not far below him, was the grisly sight of the Giant Rat. Rattus Magnus. But it was all right, for Roger at least, anyway. The Rat was stone dead; It hung there, impaled and motionless and still bleeding copiously, it having been pierced by a large stalagmite, rising pointedly up from the cavern below right through its chest.

"Oh, by Holy Heinlein!" he gasped feeling somewhat sick at the sight of the giant rat's blood, still oozing and dripping, with continual soft plop-plop-plopping sounds, down onto the surface of the rock. The rat's blank, lifeless eyes bulged, staring up at him as if challenging him with accusing guilt and responsibility for its untimely demise.

Roger looked all about him to see how he would ever get down past that horrid dead creature. He could see by the occasional flashes in the red glowing mass of cloud below him, that there were, in fact, several more, spiraling towers of rock, rising like jagged spears from the depths of the cavern's floor. They jutted through the coiling smoke like deadly stone swords, raised in salute to some long-lost king.

"The bottom of the slope I've been sliding down must feed into this large cavern," he mused out loud, getting his bearings. "I must be entering the cavern now… at the top of this cliff and that's where Mary is, down there somewhere."

"Mary, Mary, I'm here at the bottom of the slope; Where are you?" he called down again, as loudly as he could, directly into the foggy bank of smoke, lapping under his feet like an eerie lake.

"I'm here, Roger, I'm down here. An' I've hurt my ankle an' stuff, but I think I'll be all right," came her muffled reply.

Roger took heart from hearing her reply. But he secretly wondered how on Erf she wasn't already dead.

That's a heck of a long way to fall! he thought, puzzled. But then shrugged that idea away. **"Well, I'm coming now,"** he called back down to her. **"I won't be too long now, Mary, I hope. Just hold on!"** Then muttered to himself, "Yeah! Just, as soon as I can figure out how to get down onto that cavern floor, and without choking to death, or plunging to it, just like that dead rat did!"

He could see that above him hung several spikes of rock, hanging down from the roof of rock over the slope and up from the yawning cavern too. These columns and spires, he knew, were scientifically termed, Stalactites and Stalagmites. They had an eerie beauty to them all of their own; Having been created by the Erf itself, over many thousands of centuries. And Roger could also very easily identify which of the columns of rock were the Stalactites and which were the Stalagmites, because of a neat trick he'd learned from his Geology studies.

"StalaCtites hang from the Ceiling and have C in the middle of the word, and StalaGmites have a G in the middle of the word and grow up from the Ground!" he casually reminded himself. "C for Ceiling, G for Ground."

But as he searched for a workable solution to the problem of how to get down to Mary it was these very thoughts, along with the grisly plight of the Giant Rat itself, that finally gave him one. A solution that is - not a grisly plight!

He saw that the tapering, cone-like spire of rock, the stalagmite in this case, that the giant rat was impaled on, could be directly reached from the cliff-edge he was sat upon. It would mean having to clamber onto and over the dead rat's body though and avoiding its' still sticky, trickling blood, and then he'd have to carefully climb down the spiraling formation of the stalagmite, right through the smoke and on to the hidden floor of the cavern below.

"Easy-peasy; I think not!" he snorted out loud to himself, with some sarcasm.

He slowly lowered himself, handhold by cautious foothold, over the slope's cliff edge and then carefully reached out, when he was level with the dead rat on top of the pinnacle of rock.

He took a deep breath and then made the small but scary jump across the short distance, onto the rat's back, not daring to think about the height or all of the possible "what-ifs" he had built up in his mind: What if I slip and fall, what if another quake comes, what if the Rat isn't dead after all, what if, what if…?

Just as planned though, he pulled himself onto the furry back of the Giant Rat and then sitting there like a noble Knight, astride his mighty battle charger, looked for the best route down the twisting, column of rock to the Cavern floor below.

Well, if anyone from school could see me now, he thought, they wouldn't believe it!

He tried his best to avoid looking at the thin spike of rock sticking up in front of him, through the rat's back, its blood, still slowly oozing from its horrible wound and looking like a dark crimson stain under his torch's weakly flickering beam. The rat blood though, became just another gruesome black puddle when he turned the torch away, attempting to peer down into the hidden depths of the smoky cavern.

"Oh, I really don't like heights… but at least I can't see down through all of this smoke." he muttered grimly to himself.

He lowered himself down the rat's furry flank and quickly found its bony rat-ribs very useful indeed, although distasteful, as handholds and footholds. He was now, at long last, standing on and descending the large, upside-down and corkscrew-like stalagmite itself.

"Now all I have to do is get through all this filthy smoke without suffocating while blindly landing on the floor of a cavern full of spikes!" he wheezed with grim sarcasm.

He tightened his spotted hanky-facemask and coughed and spluttered as he descended the spiral of rock, into the swirling fog billowing all about him, but he instinctively kept going, stepping lower and lower, around the stalagmite. Hugging tightly to its rough rocky surface and not daring to look down.

Almost like having your own spiral staircase, this is, he thought smugly to himself.

It was then, of course, that the ancient curse of 'Hubris'* struck!

(*Hubris - I suggest you look it up in a dictionary!)

CHAPTER 12:
SIR ROGER TO THE RESCUE!

The Giant Rat suddenly shifted position. It was still dead, but it hadn't been as firmly and as stably balanced on the pinnacle of rock as Roger had thought. The top of the stalagmite was slowly cracking and breaking off under the Rat's weight and in doing so, the body of the vile beast, had swung around and one of its legs gave Roger a sudden hard shove in the back.

He fell, toppling from the rocky staircase, into the boiling grey mass of smoke below.

But as he fell, the rat's long and sinewy tail came whipping through the air towards him. Roger grabbed it without thinking, in an automatic and mindless response to the dire peril he was in. It was either 'make like an ape' or fall to a dark and deadly fate, far below.

He fell, swinging and cutting through the smoke in a wide arc, desperately clinging on to the end of the rat's tail for dear life. It flashed through his mind that at one time he'd looked like a masked Cowboy, and now here he was, swinging through the boiling, cavernous smog, looking like some prehistoric Tarzan!

He hardly had time to scream. The rat and of course its tail were both still precariously perched atop of the stalagmite, but for how long? Who knew? He really didn't have time to worry about such things. The rat's tail was now drooping downwards and slowly coming to a stand-still from its sweeping, pendulum-like motion, and with Roger, of course, still clinging to it as tightly as he possibly could.

One very lucky thing had occurred, however. The rat's tail had swept downwards and had passed quickly and through the cloud of smoke. It now hung limply downwards, penetrating the cloud's underside, with Roger hanging over the cavern floor from its tip.

Roger could see that the rock-strewn floor of the cavern was just a few feet below him and all he had to do was slide the last few feet down the rest of the tail. And then jump.

But he felt momentarily paralyzed. "Oh, Muddled up Maxwell!" he cried out. But then he quickly swallowed his panic. All he had to do was… let go. And then he'd be home free. Well, at least Cavern free, if not quite Home yet! he wryly thought to himself, as he slid down the rat's tail and did just that.

And not a second too soon.

As his feet landed firmly on the cavern's floor, the pinnacle of the stalagmite holding the Giant Rat at last cracked and sheared fully away from the rest of the rocky column of rock. The Giant Rat along with a noisy cascade of crumbling rock and debris, hurtled downward, all ready to bludgeon and squash any non-rocky life-form that might be below, to a pulp! This, unfortunately, included Roger.

He dived away just in the nick of time, hiding behind some large, sheltering rocks nearby. There, he watched in horror, as the giant dead rat hit the floor with an almighty thud and a horrible squelch; blood spluttering against the nearby rocks. Roger waited, hardly daring to breathe as it lay there sprawled amidst the rain of rocky debris and dust.

A great cloud of powdery dust momentarily filled the air around where the rat had landed, and once more Roger was coughing and spluttering, his eyes again temporarily blinded, now stinging and streaming with tears. He felt like he really could cry anyway, so in a weird way, he felt guiltily thankful for the smoke.

His throat felt rubbed red-raw with all the gasping and coughing that racked his bruised and weary soot-stained frame. He was feeling extremely on edge and battle-weary now.

He took a moment to get himself together, wiping his face and clearing his eyes free of soot. He could now see that nearly all the smoke swirling about and above him meant there was several feet of relatively clear and breathable space down here at ground level after all.

He had been right! "Oh, of course," he muttered to himself, now realizing what physical properties were at work in this smoky cavern. "I see now! Hot air, or even smoke, as it is in this case, always rises!"

He then peered and gave a puzzled look, gazing up at the whirling cloud. "But where's it all coming from? Just where's the fire making all this smoke?" he wondered out loud.

Then his thoughts turned to the vital need at hand.

"I'm here Mary! Where are you? I can't see very well in this smoke," he called out.

"I'm over here, Roger. I'm in the middle of the cavern, just follow my voice," she replied. "But be careful, it's a bit of a maze and the ground's very rocky and dangerous, O.K.?"

Roger got a bead on the direction her voice had come from and started out towards her.

"Huh! Dangerous, she says!" he snorted derisively to himself. "Well, I don't think there's much else that beats 'dangerous' than being attacked by a Giant Rat!"

He could see the floor was strewn with many other stalagmites growing up from the floor, all of various sizes. But all much like the one he'd climbed down, that had so effectively skewered the Giant Rat, Rattus Magnus. And above him lay the bubbling sheet of dirty grey smoke, hanging like a permanent low-lying canopy of cloud.

He realized that his next task, after finding where Mary was in this gloomy old cavern, would be the seemingly impossible one of somehow... getting out of the place.

That's going to take some really tricky thinking, that is! he thought to himself.

But the immediate task now was to locate Mary, give her whatever immediate aid he could and then, with that done, they could take stock and figure out things from there.

He swallowed all of his worries and doubts and pressed on. Miraculously, he still had his trusty torch, but its weakly flickering beam did little to add any illumination of his environs. The glowing grey cloud above him cast but a very dull light and although there were several other fires flickering here and there around the cavern, the somber light from these was more like the last dying embers from near-burnt-out coals.

I do hope there isn't a tribe of savage, man-eating Cavemen, or Troglodytes down here! he thought grimly to himself.

There were several stalagmite columns he had to navigate past and avoid as he weaved his way towards where he'd last heard Mary call from, so he thought he'd best call out again and ensure he was heading in the right direction still.

"I'm not far off now, Mary," he yelled. **"Can you shout out to me again, it's very gloomy down here and difficult to see anything at all. Are you still all right?"**

"Yes, I'm all right, Roj; Well, at least... sort of. I'll explain when you get here."

Roger sighed with relief, he was heading roughly in the right direction and so trudged on.

But it was in fact lucky he had paused and not just rushed on, regardless. As he took a few further cautious paces and turned slightly to his left, to head more directly toward Mary's voice, his foot suddenly trod onto... thin air.

He barely kept his balance and played the beams of his torch over the ground, right where he'd been about to step.

He gasped in horror. There, just to his right, was a large gash in the ground; a deep, dark split in the cavern floor. How deep he had no idea. And he didn't want to know. If he hadn't stopped when he had and then turned slightly, as he had done, then right now he'd be at the bottom of that narrow chasm to nowhere. He'd be lost and dead for sure!

"Oh, my Leaping Leonardo da Vinci!" he swore, appalled, sweat breaking out on his brow and his heart hammering loudly in his chest.

He traced the edge of the long crack with his torch and saw that several yards further on to his left; the crack narrowed. He carefully picked his way across the rubble-strewn floor, following the line of the chasm's ragged edge, until after only a few yards, the crack had narrowed down to a split only a foot across. He then just stepped across, half expecting it to suddenly expand and gulp him down into the bowels of the Under-Erf.

But instead, he was safely across.

Whew! Well that was a lucky break! he thought, and continued cautiously on his way, intent on his chivalrous mission to rescue his friend, Mary Maddam; And this time taking extra care to ensure there were no more hidden cracks waiting for him to fall into.

Away on the far side of the narrowed crack, he could see that he was very nearly there. Just a hundred feet away, he could just dimly make out a large mound of rocks, with an area right by them that glowed, as if from burning red coals. These helped guide him on his way, as it was from that very mound, next to those glowing coals, that Mary had been calling from. He made his way towards them as fast as he dared.

"Hello there, Roger, so nice of you to drop in!"

He looked around startled and gave a great gasp. There, by the middle of the rock-mound, lay Mary. She was lying on her back, propped up against what looked like a huge jumble of boulders on the floor, and despite her cheery greeting, she seemed in pain. Roger could see she was torn and tattered and was tightly holding onto her ankle with both hands.

She was obviously putting as brave a face on things as she could. He could see she'd been crying, from the tell-tale tracks of her tears, running down her soot-stained cheeks.

Her eyes though still blazed bright defiance in the redly glowing gloom of the smoky, cathedral-like chamber of the cavern. Her pretty round face now lit up with a wide and welcoming grin of recognition, as Roger joyously ran towards her.

"Wh-wh-what on Erf...?" he said, hardly being able to speak. But then he calmed himself and gathered his wits. And his relief gushed out in a barely controlled torrent of questions.

"By Thomas Edison's Ten Toes, Mary, I'm happy to see you. I really am. But, are you hurt? What has happened to you? How did you end up down here? And how did you survive that fall?"

He saw she was lying propped up against a particularly large boulder and sitting pretty much right in the middle of the cloud-covered cavern. He still didn't understand how she'd made it... and survived. It seemed nothing short of a miracle.

"I'm all right, Roger, really. I've just twisted my ankle and stuff is all," she told him.

"Mavis here saved my life!" she continued. "But, oh, goodness, I'm pleased to see you, Roj. Seems like I've been down here for hours and hours. But I knew you'd come for me!"

Roger thought she was just babbling now. "What **is** she on about? A 'Mavis' saving her!" he thought, "But she's probably still recovering from the shock," he quickly decided.

Then, without warning, the large rock behind Mary suddenly moved and a quick flash of orangey-red flame, along with a great gout of grey smoke, erupted from out of it.

Roger jumped back and screamed, **"Mary, quick, we've got to run for it. There's something here in these rocks! And it… c-c-could be a giant… well, anything, in this dangerous sort of a place!"**

But then the rock suddenly moved again, and this time, two very large and heavily lidded, reptilian eyes blinked open, and shone out with a yellow, sulfurous light, and looked piercingly and directly, right at Roger.

"Oh, my Dizzy Diogenes!" Roger yelled. **"Quick, Mary! For Science's Sake, move!"**

Mary just laughed. "It's all right, Roger, this is Mavis, and she's a good Dragon," she said calmly, casually introducing the Dragon to him as if she were an old and dear family friend. "She caught me and broke my fall with one of her huge wings. If she hadn't, I don't think I would have survived, Roj. I really owe her my life, you know!"

Mary looked up at Mavis, the Dragon, with much heartfelt and teary-eyed gratitude.

Roger looked at Mavis too. He was stunned into a disbelieving silence. He rubbed his eyes with grimy fists and blinked and gawked in confusion, then blinked again, but still, he saw what he saw.

Right there, right in front of him, loomed the unbelievable, inconceivable, unimaginable, but the indisputable presence of… a real live and actual, fire-breathing Dragon!

She was huge though, at least the size of three double-decker buses. And Roger could see that she was also a very lovely creature indeed; a beautiful, shimmering, red and gold dragon; occasionally belching out ruby-red flames; briefly erupting into the smoky clouds above their heads; And thereby giving the clouds and the cavern its eerie, red glow.

And she also seemed to be in some pain, as her breathing was very ragged and irregular; he could sense the deep anguish and pitiful pain in her heavy-lidded, amber eyes.

Those large, reptilian eyes stared steadily down at him as if stripping his very soul bare.

"B-b-but, d-d-dragons d-d-don't exist!" was all he finally managed to stutter.

Mary laughed, although somewhat painfully, at the sight of poor Roger, standing there totally dumbstruck, with his smoke-stained face and his posh clothes all tattered and torn from his perilous journey to the underworld.

He stood there miraculously before her, with his dirty spotted handkerchief still over his mouth and nose and his bent, round glasses, glinting in the red flickering gloom of the smoke-filled cavern.

"Roger, you really do look like a proper wild-west cowboy now," she giggled, but then cried out again, wincing with pain from her bruised ribs and throbbing, sprained ankle.

"Owww! Stop! It hurts when you make me laugh, Roger!" she exclaimed, rather unfairly. "Oh, please don't make me laugh!"

"But I haven't said anything funny," Roger protested, with a puzzled look on his face.

Now Mary had thought she would die, all alone and deep down and lost in the dark. Just buried and forgotten forever beneath the unforgiving Erf. She had never felt so relieved and so happy to see anyone as much as she did right there and then. Even if she was still underground in a dark and dismal smoke-filled cavern; Trapped and injured as she was, and with a fiery and fearsome Dragon, at that!

Despite the evidence of his eyes, Roger stood rooted to the ground like a petrified statue and pointed up at the fabulous Dragon with an expression of complete disbelief on his face.

"M-M-Mary… is that really a D-D-Dragon?" he asked.

"Of course not, silly," teased Mary, smiling at him. "It's obviously a lost sheep taking a summer holiday underground, can't you tell Roger?"

Roger just stared dumbly at her, his lower lip aquiver, far too taken aback to say anything else. All coherent thought had completely vanished from his being suddenly brought face to face with an actual and for real, live Dragon.

Mary could see that a proper introduction and an explanation were now definitely in order.

"Let me introduce you properly," she said to Roger gently and waving her hand airily toward the huge Dragon. "This here is Mavis Davis, the Dragon Queen."

The Dragon lowered her head towards Mary's and gave a small growl.

"Well, it's actually Sivam Sivad, she says," continued Mary, "but we can call her Mavis, as she says that's much easier for us. She's a very nice Dragon too… and she's been in this 'orrible cave quite a long time, and, and…"

Here Mary faltered, her voice cracking and straining to keep herself from crying again. Roger thought it must be her ankle, but it wasn't. Some pains are even worse than physical ones like her twisted ankle or scraped knees and her bruised ribs; Some pains were pains of the heart; raw emotional pains, one might call them, and it was this kind of pain that Mary was feeling right then.

"She's dying!" Mary cried. "Oh, it's so unfair, Roger," she finished, sniffing and sobbing.

Roger could see she was extremely upset, and he felt his heart melting with compassion, now suddenly in sympathy with the Lady Dragon's very sad condition.

"I'm so s-s-sorry to hear that," he answered quietly, looking at Mary and then the Dragon. "Is there anything I can do?"

Mary held her arms out to him and Roger just let all logic and questions go for another time and flung himself toward her and held her gently as she wept, her head buried in his arms, all the pain and suffering now bubbling up out of her.

"Oooh, now mind my ribs, Roj" she sniffed at him after a little while, with a pained smile.

"Are you all right then, Mary? Are you able to walk at all?" he asked her anxiously. "We've still got to get ourselves back to the surface somehow, you know?"

"I'll be O.K. in a little while, Roj. Mavis says that I'll mend, and she's given me some of 'er Dragon Medicine to help too; Blue Dragon Flame' she calls it. She says I should rest up a bit before I starts rushing off and clambering up any smoky tunnels and such things though."

Roger looked at his new friend and smiled at her compassionately. He fully realized she was doing more than putting a brave face on things. He could tell she was in fact, in a lot of pain. Physical and emotional. Her tear-stained face was pale, and she wrinkled her nose and screwed up her eyes whenever another jolt of pain stabbed through her body.

"O.K., Mary, you rest up and get your strength back; we can just talk and catch up a bit."

"Well, come an' sit down then an' I'll tell you all about what I've gathered, so far anyway, or even better, if she wants to, then maybe Mavis will herself," she answered with a sigh.

Roger sat himself down next to Mary, not even being bothered now by the fact that they were both leaning against Mavis's scaly dragon flank and that one of her sharp looking claws was lying close to them. He had now realized they weren't in any danger from Mavis. Logically, if they had been, they would have both already been toasted to a crisp!

The Dragon was curled up behind them, her golden wings furled away. Her arching neck curled over her shoulder and her head facing towards them. Her breathing was still ragged. Now and again she'd raise her head up and give a growl and then blast a few gouts of smoke and flame into the air; But when she did, Roger noted, she always, very considerately, faced away from them. She's got very good manners for a Dragon! Roger thought.

Mary had only been alone with the Dragon for barely an hour before Roger had appeared; But in that time, they had had a lot to say to each other. Roger was told how Mavis had heard Mary fall, as she'd slid down the slope to her cavern. And she had immediately realized that unless she caught Mary, the little human girl would smash onto the rocky cavern floor and be broken beyond repair.

Mavis had pulled herself upright and had unfurled a great golden, bat-like wing, just in time, just as Mary had flown off the ledge, and flew in a great arc through the smoky cavern; Just like some sort of a human cannonball. And then the miraculous Mavis had caught hold of this strange 'ball' as skillfully and as deftly as any professional cricket or baseball fielder could have ever done.

"Most Dragons just like to go about their own business and not be bothering anybody else and not being bothered by them either," Mary told him, "just like us humans, really, but then there are always some exceptions, of course, as you already well know, Roj."

"Yes, there are always exceptions," muttered Roger, thinking of their recent encounter with Josh the Cosh and his gang of Cold Arbor thugs, whom they'd so narrowly escaped from earlier that day.

"Isn't it strange that just one or two rotten apples can spoil a whole barrel?" Mary mused. "Anyway, Mavis saved me," she continued, "and then, well ... then ... well... she talked to me... err, in my mind actually, I mean!" Mary meekly finished, feeling foolish and embarrassed.

"What? Wh-wh-what did you say?" exclaimed Roger, looking at her totally astonished. Had Mary completely lost her wits?

"Now, just let me explain," Mary said plaintively.

"No, please, allow me!" came a deep, throbbing voice, suddenly booming clearly inside Roger's head.

Queen Mavis had spoken. But not with a normal voice. Not as we humans would call a voice as such, anyway. There was no actual sound involved at all. Mavis was speaking to him telepathically!

"And hello to you, Master Roger," she said. *"I am very pleased to meet you, indeed!"*

CHAPTER: 13:
TRAVELS THROUGH THE
UNDER-ERF.

"V-v-very n-n-nice to meet you t-t-too, I'm sure," Roger squeaked back, totally astonished, not sure whether speaking out loud was considered correct etiquette or not for Dragon-talk.

Mary had been knocked unconscious when she'd been caught, just in time as it happened, by the Dragon's miraculous, bat-like wing. When she'd come around, the first thing she had heard was the gentle booming in her aching head, feeling just like a soft, nagging headache, but one that talked. But now it was Roger's turn to experience the strange and far-reaching mental abilities of a True Dragon.

"Wh-wh-what's happening here? Have I been hypnotized?" Roger asked, half to himself.

But, instead of a reply from Mavis, it was Mary this time, calmly answering his question, but not by speaking in his head like the Dragon had. Mary was in fact very excited and very relieved to talk to Roger again at all. For a while there, she'd thought she'd never see or be able to speak to anyone else ever again, so she now gushed out her news to him.

"Well, I heard Mavis saying, 'Little human, little human, come on, wake up, wake up,' over and over, and when I'd opened my eyes, there she was; Mavis, gazing intently at me. But somehow, I didn't feel at all scared; she's got lovely, gentle, amber eyes, you know, so I could see she was a very kind and… well, a concerned sort of person too, I s'pose."

Mary quickly told Roger how she'd felt herself being slipped onto the hard cavern floor. Then Mavis had blown a cool, blue flame into her face and had cleared away the last tendrils of grey smoke that had hung about her. She'd coughed and spluttered and then Mavis told Mary her own story, telepathically of course. And now, she reckoned, it was Roger's turn.

"Yes. child There are things you must be made aware of in the short time we have left together. Now, look into my eyes, young human," Mavis gently and telepathically told him.

"This isn't hyp-hyp-hypnosis, is it?" squeaked Roger again, very nervously.

Mary took his hand and assured him, "Don't worry, Roj, it's not hypnosis, I promise."

"Do not worry yourself, Master Roger," thrummed Mavis, softly in his mind, *"this form of communication is much more like waking up from a deep sleep and then being able to clearly see and understand things for the first time."*

Roger screwed up his face and his courage too and looked fearfully up at the great Dragon.

Her huge, amber eyes shone down upon his boyish, soot-stained face and he seemed to feel himself being pulled right into them as if he was being sucked down into a whirling, round, golden vortex of warmth and light.

He now fell head-long and heart-full deep into her steady, wide-eyed gaze and soon found himself feeling very peaceful and calm. As if floating in a lake of thick, warm cream or on a soft, woolen cloud full of blue-white light and gentle warmth.

Roger realized this was indeed a far superior intelligence; Not just some wild and savage beast, only interested in feasting on the flesh and blood of its cornered prey. And he could 'see' her thoughts too now, just like picture-stories in his head. They were so vivid and clear; It was even better than the Movies; Better for Roger even than the Xmas Royal

Academy Science Lectures that he loved listening to so much every year on the Wireless.

"This is like, well, like actually and for real, fully being here, right where I am!" he thought. But the 'here' where he was, was the him now looking out at the world from Mavis's eyes. From inside her head as it were. He could see all around the great cavern, very clearly. He could even see through the smoke-cloud above him right up to its rocky, high-arching roof, festooned with its many sharp, pointed stalactites, hanging like hundreds of dangling daggers.

"Now, dear children, I have been expecting you and this will be explained in due course. Firstly though, I must show you some of my own world and my own long and ill-fated past; And all the better for you to understand your present and your unfolding future, yet to be," Mavis thought-cast to them enigmatically.

And so, Roger now began a mind-traveling journey beyond his imagining together in the company of Mavis and Mary. But this wasn't their traveling as physical bodies; Now they were moving through the Under Erf as disembodied spirits. They were freely roaming phantoms; just ghostly entities, being guided along by the Dragon Queen and traveling down through the vast network of underground Cavern-Worlds. The hidden worlds within the World, ruled by the True Dragons of the Under-Erf; worlds never before seen by humdrum eyes.

They were witnessing a magical world of worlds within the World itself; being a vast and secret domain the Dragons had maintained peace and prosperity in for thousands of years, and all these many worlds together were called the 'Under-Erf. The only world that Roger and Mary knew, was just the single surface world of their Planet Erf, and the Dragons knew this as simply the 'Over-Erf.'

Roger could see the Under-Erf was a far more interesting and more varied place than even the Humdrum's surface world of the Over-Erf. To really and fully know a whole World, you needed to get under its skin and plumb its deepest, darkest depths. Then you could really understand it much, much better. Just like you did when getting to know new people and friends, or even alien races and unerfly creatures, for that matter.

Roger at first felt giddy and sick, but after a while got used to the strange, flying sensation.

"This is just what being a bird, or even better, an angel, must feel like," he thought.

"Or a Dragon!" came Mary's thought, giggling gleefully into his head.

"Hey! I can hear you, Mary! Can you hear me?"

"Yes, of course I can silly," she replied telepathically, *"we can telepath to each other now that we're with Mavis."*

"Oh, my Jumping James Joule!" Roger cried out in alarm. *"But t-t-telepathy doesn't…"* But he couldn't finish his thought. He was a scientist after all, and the fact was, he was now actually and for real, telepathing his thoughts, as well as, more wondrously, 'spirit-walking.'

The Under-Erf was a network of an untold number of worlds, many miles beneath the surface of the Erf and so was a gigantic place and much, much bigger than the Erf's surface was. The Under Erf had thousands of worlds, all within the one world of the Over Erf.

Roger, being clever, at once understood how this could be. Just how the inside could be much bigger than the outside. Just like it is with Dr. What's Tardis! he thought.

And the answer was very simple. On the outside of the Erf, all the Humans along with most of the animals and plants lived on just the one single surface. And as large as that one surface was, it was always only the one. But this was not the case for the Under-Erf.

"You now see below you many worlds within the rocky mantle and the magma of the Erf," Mavis said, *"you are passing by hundreds and hundreds of miles, and layer after layer of mantle rock, but within this rock and magma there are hundreds of these vast Cavern-worlds. The*

Under-Erf has many surfaces within; as with the rings of an onion, or as a better description, the many chambers in a beehive."

"Wow! It's just fantastic," Mary murmured, getting a vivid idea of the true structure of the whole Erf, as the many layers and unfolding terraces of the regions of the vast 'Under-Erf' went by, ever deeper and deeper. And as they flashed by, becoming increasingly stranger and ever more 'Un-Erfly.'

Mavis informed them that there were several regions of the Under-Erf that no Human Being could ever hope to visit, let alone survive, as they were completely alien and therefore deadly to normal Humdrum life. But the very worst and weirdest of these were all a very long way down, being inside or very close to the Erf's Core itself.

Mavis then explained to them that the Erf's Core was a region of unimaginable Hellish qualities, where you would think it would be completely impossible for any form of life to live at all.

"But... unfortunately, there are some who do!" she added, enigmatically.

Roger and Mary only got a very hazy idea of that region though, their attentions were being taken up with the stunning sights right before them, as they hurtled onward through the layers of rock mantle. They caught brief views of Cavern-world after Cavern-world, flashing by. There were huge underground caverns so vast that they even held their own deep oceans and long, winding rivers; As well as their own scorched deserts, snowy mountain ranges and hot tropical jungles.

Roger was stunned silent at seeing this seemingly endless network of vast Cavern-worlds and the many interconnecting corridors that joined these wildly different areas of the Under-Erf. Indeed, these underground realms were like nothing any man, woman or child on the surface of the Erf had had any slightest inkling of before.

"We are now approaching my own Home-world, the True Dragon's Home Cavern World," Mavis calmly announced.

As she thought-cast this, Roger saw that they had now burst through a ceiling of blurry, grey rock, down into the vast Dragon Cavern World; This stretched out below him, in a great mind-boggling panorama, causing him to gasp in awe at its sheer beauty and magnificence.

"Oh My!" Mary exclaimed, also awestruck by its grandeur, *"it's so beautiful, Mavis."*

"Why, thank you, young Erf-child," Mavis answered her, very pleased.

"How m-m-many of these Cavern-worlds are there down here altogether, do you think?" Roger asked incredulously.

"There are more than even we True Dragons know," Mavis answered. *"There are those of the Macrosphere and those of the Microsphere; But I have never, ever understood how you poor Humans can be so content with just having the one surface as your one and only world, when there are so many different environments; So many different worlds within the worlds, within the Erf to explore. And you've never explored any of them, but have just stuck to scratching around on your one-surface Erf. And most of that is water too! That really is a most peculiar puzzle to me."*

"I've never thought about it like that before," Roger replied, thoughtfully.

"I think Bees, Ants, and Termites would understand though," Mary thought cast to him.

"And you'd never ever get a colony of bees, for example, to live all together on just the surface of their hive, now would you? I think it makes a lot of sense." she added.

Unknown to Roger and Mary, a lot of the Under-Erf's creatures did, in fact, feel that the Humdrums were rather stupid. Fancy having a wonderful, beautiful home-world like the Erf and then just living on its surface and not even looking after that and not sharing in all its wonders! After all, it was like having the gift of a juicy apple and then just eating the skin!

"Come, dears, I will now show you some of my home Cavern-World," Mavis announced.

The phantom Mavis swooped down through the pink and gold streaked skies of her home, the Dragon Cavern-World, with the two phantom Erf children closely in tow.

Roger keenly observed everything he could take in, totally enthralled, as he mind-traveled over the many mercurial lakes and the liquid-gold lava-falls and the winding rivers of red-hot magma, ribboning through a colorful land peppered with mountains and smoking volcanoes.

The Volcano cones were continually erupting, engulfing their surroundings with bubbling, molten lava fields, flowing down from their flanks.

The vast and mountainous landscape below was streaked and puddled with many colored plains and beautiful lakes. Roger saw hundreds of brightly colored Dragons too, many flying and swooping about in the cavernous pink and gold of the high-domed sky and others travelling across the landscape, going about their daily business.

This underground world was so big the sky itself went up for many miles before it hit the undersurface of the rocky dome of the cavern ceiling, held high above them. This truly was the legendary and unbelievably wonderful Cavern-World of the noble and ancient True Dragons of the Under-Erf and Roger was very, very impressed.

In fact, Roger was ecstatic. He didn't know where to look first. There were so many other creatures there too; All sorts of curious beasts and birds and some that were unknown to Roger and Mary or any Human; As well as the many different species of insects and plants that he recognized or half recognized.

By Jumping Jim Joules! I wonder what the Fleas or Froghoppers are like in this place? Roger thought in amazement.

Roger suddenly gasped at seeing some helicopter-sized Ladybirds and hundreds of Dragonfly-like creatures flying right besides many colorful Dragons that flew close by to him, skimming their way over the colored lava plain below.

He could also see a pack of pink Giant Erf-worms, busily boring their way in and out of a multi-colored range of rocky hills; and then, a herd of shiny, black Stag-beetles hove into view, each as big as an elephant, thundering their way across the pale-red, rusty plain and disappearing into the distance behind them as Mavis and the two children swooped on by.

Roger found that everywhere he looked there was yet another fantastical wonder living on the land or flying in the sky. And as he watched in amazement he could see, that Mavis was heading steadily towards an area dotted with the ever-smoking volcanic cones, which were the True Dragon's natural homes.

He could see that each Dragon family, in fact, had their very own family volcano cone. Mavis dutifully explained how each cone was a Dragon family's ancient, ancestral home. The steep sides of each Home-Cone were all full of openings, balconies, and vents used for chimneys, doors and windows, some belching copious curls and some mere wisps of smoke.

He saw each Home-cone was artfully carved with many whorls and spiraling designs all over their multi-colored flanks, and in many complex and curious patterns that the Dragons obviously enjoyed and excelled in. These intricate designs were indeed famed throughout the Under-Erf, wide and deep, as the greatest historical examples of True Dragon Art.

"Oh, it's wonderful isn't it, Roj? It's the most wonderful place I've ever, ever been to, ever!" Mary cried ecstatically.

But before Roger could answer, Mavis came to a sudden halt, now hovering with them in mid-air, but still fairly high above the teeming Dragons' Cavern World. Her serious telepathic tones now cut into their excited and jumbled thoughts, as quietly, she again telepathed and explained to them her purpose for their journey into Under Erf.

"My dear children, there are certain things you must be made aware of, as I said before; while there is still time and while I am still able; There are lessons that you must learn; lessons in Dragon Erf Geography, lessons in Dragon History, and lessons in the three Dragon Magicks!"

Mavis now calmly told them how she had recently flown up from this, her very own home of the Dragon Cavern-World, in-order to lay her third and final Egg. She explained how a female Dragon could only ever lay three eggs in her entire lifetime and that each Egg must be brought to the surface of the Over-Erf to cool and then to be hatched in one of the assigned, magical nests, hidden in special locations there. The Forest of Lundun being one of the most special and magical of all.

She explained how a True Dragon's life was normally one that lasted for many, many thousands of years. However, a female Dragon never survived her third hatching. For once she had laid her third and her final Egg, then she always and without any exception, died.

But a female Dragon didn't just die; she exploded!

Mavis had finished her introductory journey and now everything in an instant went black. The visions of the Dragon's Cavern-World suddenly cleared, like smoke swept away by a gust of wind. They were once again sitting in the dim cavern, deep under the Smoking Tree.

They were back in their own space and time, and once more in their usual bodies. Mary was once again aching and hurting, and Roger, tired and weary. And they were still trapped, deep under the ground and far from home. And still all alone with a wounded Dragon!

Roger sat in stunned silence for a few moments and then gently asked the Lady Dragon.

"What do you m-m-mean, Mavis? They explode! Are you talking about yourself?"

Roger gulped and looked meaningfully at Mary, who now took his hand into hers.

"It's all true," Mary said aloud, now uncovering the object she'd been keeping carefully concealed for ages, wrapped up under her coat. "Yes. Mavis is about to self-combust too; She'll explode once this night is over, she thinks; But we have to help her, Roj - that's why, that's why we're here; we have to get her last Egg safely away before she explodes!"

There, in Mary's lap, softly glowing like a huge, beautiful gem, lay the Dragon's Egg.

"And it's going to happen very soon!" Mary cried, tears streaming down her cheeks.

"Yes, Children; Truly, I will meet my ancestors very soon, much sooner than I had planned for," Mavis rumbled somberly, but soothingly, deep within their minds. *"But my hatchling here, he must somehow be taken to the surface; I am unable to continue, as I ... I am damaged and I have a missing wing. Thus, I have been forced to turn to the Great Forest Powers for aid. And thus, you are both here... by the will of the venerable Tree-King of Lundun himself,"* she sighed heavily, now sounding very tired and world-weary indeed.

And she had a very good reason so to be. For there were yet further dark and evil forces gathering nearer, and fully intent on the destruction of herself, Queen Sivam-Sivad of the ancient Sivad Dynasty of ruling Dragons, as well as that of her unhatched son, the Royal Prince and the one and only Heir to the True Dragon's Under-Erf Kingdom. The last hope of all the worlds within the World... of all the Under-Erf and Over-Erf together!

The children sat quietly huddled together on the floor as Mavis explained her plight, and this time, Roger reached out for Mary's hand, and they sat, hand in hand, in somber silence, both enthralled and appalled, at the wonderful visions and the incredible knowledge that Mavis had brought to them, as their Spirits flew united with hers.

"My son will be named 'Regor Yram," Mavis continued, *"and he will eventually become the most powerful True Dragon in the History of all Dragon-kind!"* She finished, breathing more painfully now, as she rapidly blew gusts of blue-grey smoke from her flaring nostrils.

"Oh, it's just not fair!" Mary cried out, feeling very distressed. "Isn't there anything we can do, Mavis? Isn't there some way to save you, any way at all?" she asked desperately, looking longingly and sorrowfully up into the Dragon Queen's large and wise, amber eyes.

"My fate is sealed child. But my Eggs' is not! He must go to the surface and must be kept somewhere cool, damp and safe; far away from our enemies, as well as the all-consuming fires of my death and my re-birth!" She answered enigmatically.

"Wh-what do you m-m-mean?" Roger stammered out, startled and confounded as to what Mavis actually meant by that. "What d-d-do you mean your death and re-birth, are you coming b-b-back from your death, Mavis? Are you t-t-talking about some sort of reincarnation or something?"

"Yes, in a manner of speaking, I am Roger," sighed Mavis, *"but… only in a manner of speaking, for I will then be with my ancestors and I will be flying free forever, in the great Fire-Dance of the Dragon Souls. I will be re-born as pure potential of spirit, my wings as good as new, and my colors of magic as bright as ever; But, my dear, I will not be as you know me now,"* she sighed mysteriously, but with a bright gleam shining in her amber eyes.

"Ooh, I'd like to know more about the Fire-Dance of the Dragon Souls!" Mary told her.

"Yes, so would I!" Roger agreed, but also wondering what it all exactly meant.

"You will, oh, Human children of the endless sky, you will, but not for some while yet!" Mavis quietly replied, breathing a soft warm breath into the children's faces and somehow meaning much more than she was saying, with her penetrating, but gentle telepathic thought.

"Now attend to me," Mavis continued, *"we must now fulfill your basic education and you must speedily find a way from this Cavern to the surface with my Egg; I will show you what you....!"*

But then without warning, Mavis was suddenly cut off from any further communication as a huge explosion, along with much violent shuddering and shaking, resounded all around them. The whole of the cavern floor writhed and buckled like a storm-tossed sea.

Several more explosions occurred, each in rapid succession, and then great, gaping cracks started to appear across the cavern's floors and walls. The whole place was being shaken and seemed to be breaking into bits!

Several of the stalactites came spearing down through the dust, sending great billows of grey smoke high into the air. Clouds of choking smoke whirled about the noise-filled cavern, like crazy coils of cream, spinning in a huge coffee cup.

Roger clutched Mary tightly in his arms, as the sudden and mad vortex of dust and smoke swirled madly about them; Soon to suffocate them in its relentless stranglehold of death if it didn't quickly subside.

The cracks were splitting up the sides of the cavern walls and Roger could see that large chunks of jagged rock were sheering off from the cavern roof above them too, threatening to fall on them and crush them like little bugs under a large brick.

"Oh, my Saintly Sagan!" he cried out, aghast, "I think we're really done for now, Mary!"

CHAPTER 14:
ATTACK OF THE TRYDRA.

M avis however, had seen the danger they were in and had reacted as quickly as she could by at once unfurling her one, surviving wing and covering them from the very worst of the falling rocks and the swirling dust cloud. At the same time, she blew a torrent of blue flame from her flaring nostrils, enveloping them in a translucent bubble of pale blue flame.

"Keep close to my side," she ordered, *"as long as we are protected by the magic of the blue flame, we will not be harmed; But we must stand our ground and be ready to fight. The Minions of 'The Enemy' approach even now!"*

"Wh-wh-what Enemy; What m-m-Minions?" Roger cried out in alarm.

"That you will soon know, but first, you must arm yourself, with whatever rocks you can find; The Minions of 'The Enemy' are worms who will try to surprise us and steal away at least one of you humans, along with my precious Egg of course!"

The thunderous echoes of the explosions were now dying away, and the tremors of the quake were doing the same, too. The acrid smoke and the grinding dust still swirled about them. Roger saw that barely a foot away from him, just beyond the rippling surface of the bubble of blue fire, the Dragon's magical shield surrounding them all, the manic winds of dust and debris swirled and whirled about its globe of shimmering blue-safety.

And beyond that shimmering skin of pale blue light, Roger could barely see anything at all. Just the occasional blur of a rock rolling by or a spurt of pebbles hitting the bubble of flame and making it momentarily sparkle and spit. Even when all was stilled to an eerie silence, there seemed to be nothing but a bowl of featureless gloom beyond the bubble.

Then after but a few brief moments, he thought he saw something else, something out there in the haze of smoke; Something moving, something wriggling and getting steadily ever closer towards them.

In fact, several 'somethings' were approaching; all wriggling and writhing about in the dim murky depths of the smog-filled cavern; All of them, slowly approaching wriggle by wriggle, getting ever nearer and nearer.

"Ugh! What are those horrible things? Can you see them Roj?" Mary cried out.

"By Schrodinger's half-dead cat, yes, they're nasty looking creatures, aren't they now?" Roger hissed, agreeing with her.

"Look like a cross between fat slimy maggots and slithering green slugs!" Mary replied in heartfelt disgust.

"These are but The Enemy's mindless Minions," Mavis told them gravely, *"and they come here but to do his bidding; which is to destroy us all and particularly my Egg. Unfortunately, I have not had the time to complete your educations in such things, and now we must stand and fight them instead!"*

Roger saw that the cavern floor was teeming with the slithering, slimy Minion creatures, all faintly glowing with a sickly green luminescence in the cavernous gloom. And they were now totally surrounded.

The slimy Slug-worms were each about a foot long and were all the same pale green color, but also tinged and spotted with shades of vile yellow and with many red veins running the length of their bodies. They had no eyes but gaping maws for heads, and jaws edged with serrated teeth, like saws. Each worm dribbled a thick, acidic saliva.

This acidic slime oozed from them as they squirmed relentlessly across the rocky floor, their slime trails eating into the very rock itself.

"I will protect us as best I can with my blue flame shield, children, and I have tuned the flame so we can hurl whatever we can to keep these worms from us. The shield of blue flame will allow nothing to enter. You must throw what rocks you can find at them; we must, at all costs, keep them from breaching my shield with their foul acid spit!" Mavis ordered.

The children quickly scrabbled together suitable rocks and began pelting the advancing worms with them.

"You take the left side and I'll take the right," Roger shouted to Mary.

"O.K. I'll do my best," Mary answered.

She was actually a very good shot, but having cracked ribs and a bad ankle too didn't exactly help.

"These are Fire-worm Minions," Mavis mind-cast to them, *"do not let them near or they will burn you; their slime is like your Helladian fire; Naught but Dragon Magic can quench it! I will try to pick off as many as I can with my red battle flame, but it is very difficult to both attack and defend at the same time!"*

Mavis intermittently hurled her blasts of red flame, switching from red flame to blue; While Roger and Mary bombarded the Fire-worms as best they could. Roger was getting a hit every other throw, but Mary was having trouble getting her aim in. She could only really use the one arm, and each throw made her wince with pain from her hurting ribs.

"Ow! Hooray! I got one!" she cried. "But there's too many of 'em Roj, what are we going to do?"

Roger had knocked over and squashed several of the killer Slug-worms himself, but Mary was right, there were just too many of them. The acid spitting worms were now just madly hurling themselves at the Dragon's dome of blue flame that had, so far, kept them both safe. But they were now relentlessly swarming up its sides too, hissing and spitting their dreadful drool; causing several areas of the blue-fire-dome to dissolve and erode.

"Whatever happens, don't let them get through my blue-fire barrier," Mavis ordered, *"just concentrate your aim on any who are creating any holes!"*

"Why are they doing this?" screamed Mary. "What's wrong with them; They don't seem to care whether they live or die; they just want to kill us!"

"Yes, they don't care about their own lives, killing is all they live for!" Mavis told her grimly, as she spat another deadly fireball into the heaving mass of acid-spitting fire-worms.

The cavern floor was soon littered with writhing and blasted worm-bodies, but more and more soon replaced them. Mavis's protective blue-fire dome was still holding, but for how long? If they kept coming like this, then they'd eventually break through. Then there would be no escape!

Oh, by Galileo's Galloping Grasshoppers, what a horrible way to die! Roger thought to himself with horror.

But the hordes of mindless maggot-Minions were not without their limits. And whatever malevolent intelligence had been guiding and dictating their every move, now brought them to a sudden halt. For unknown to Roger and Mary, they were just the beginning of the hidden enemy's intended onslaught.

The Slug-worm army sat rooted to the cavern floor like a thousand wriggling, green fingers; Like a writhing sea of dead-men's hands, all reaching, groping and grasping at the grimy, putrid air; But not making any further moves forward at all.

Mavis and the children sat and waited within the bubble. Just what were these fiends up to now? They hadn't any idea. The seconds ticked slowly and agonizingly by, and then at last, they heard it; A distant scratching and scraping noise. Then another, and another.

Roger could dimly see three large scorpion-like creatures, coming ever closer towards them, but as yet, he couldn't see them clearly, the fog of surrounding dragon smoke badly obscuring his view. But he could see that one was coming from straight ahead and the two others, from each side. Their strange scraping noises sounded out in regular, repetitive beats, each punctuated by a loud and harsh, rattling sound.

"Shkkkrrrrrrr-brrrr! Shkkkrrrrrrr-brrrr! Shkkkrrrrrrr-brrrr!"

Then Roger saw the one in front, the leader, suddenly loom into full view and soon followed by its two fellow cohorts, one to the left and one to the right of him. The three vile creatures towered above him, being nearly as tall as the Dragon Queen Mavis herself.

There, right ahead of him, loomed a trio of huge, six-legged monsters, each three-headed and each head, three-eyed! And each, carrying a spiny tail with an evil-looking sting coiled behind it and held high over their cobra-like heads.

"Beware, children, these are the dreaded three-headed Trydra!" Mavis cried out.

"Oh, my Fernickity Ferkins! They look really nasty and very dangerous!" Mary gasped.

"The wh-wh-what, what's a Trydra?" asked Roger, open-mouthed with horror as the three Trydra stealthily and steadily approached them in their three-pronged attack, wending their way through the army of writhing minion worms.

"The three-headed Hydra are from the Core regions; They are themselves a form of giant fire-worm, half snake and half scorpion and usually only found in the fiery depths of the Erf. They always attack in threes; It is part of their magical natures. They are creatures of three and are deadly to all forms of life; At their worst, they can even damage dragons!" Mavis hissed urgently in their heads. *"If I lower my blue-flame defence I can concentrate enough red attack-flame to stop them; but if I do, then you children will no longer be protected!"*

"Well, if you don't do something, they'll get us anyway, won't they?" Mary pointed out.

"Very well, then you must retreat behind me best you can and I will try to protect you with my one good wing, at least. I just hope, by the eternal fires of my ancestral sky-spirits, I can summon enough attack-flame to take out all three at once."

"S-s-so d-d-do I!" Roger exclaimed.

Roger and Mary then quickly scuttled behind Mavis and sheltered as best they could, underneath her one golden wing. They lay as flat as they could and peered out from under the wing's bony edge. Mavis quickly positioning it just in time, as the three Trydra came within a dozen feet of her blue-flame shield.

The three deadly creatures loomed and swayed menacingly above them, like three gigantic cobras, but each with three heads and each head with its three glinting red eyes.

But they stayed there, now no longer moving forward at all, but just swaying side to side, hissing and repeatedly flicking out their forked tongues from their gaping, scaly mouths. Their venom-loaded fangs drooling and glistening with their own potent concoction of acids.

"The weakness of the Trydra is that it is invulnerable, but only if it at least retains one head!" Mavis telepathed to them urgently, *"I must therefore blast them and take out all heads at once and so utterly destroy 'nine heads for three beasts' and it must be done quickly and without one head left to function; or the Trydra will just regrow its head and fight on!"*

"O.K. We're ready, Mavis, do your best!" Mary told her, sounding braver than she felt.

"Or your worst—for them!" Roger added.

The leader of the triad of Trydra, flared his cobra-like hood and then raised the very end of his coiling tail and pointed it at Mavis, violently and noisily rattling it at her in an obvious show of hostility. Stony, ophidian eyes glinted coldly at the patiently waiting Dragon Queen; and then with a harsh, hissing sound as of a thousand pebbles, skittering over slippery rocks, the lead Trydra suddenly spoke:

"I am Trinimicusss and thessse two are my brothersss, Masterssss Trimorbisss and Tridissipantisss. Sssso, dear Missstresss Sssivad, we hear you are sssickly; we are ssso sssorry to hear thissss!"

"I am well enough, you Snake-worm!" Mavis retorted loudly. "And I know you have come but to do your Core Master's bidding. But be warned; no foul fiend of the slimespawned, such as you, can defeat me and keep me from my goal!"

The rearing Trydra leader hissed at this and lunged forward, momentarily stung to the quick by Mavis's taunting insults but then seemed to quickly hold himself in check.

Trinimicusss had pulled his head back with a jerk; As if some invisible rider was on his back and controlling him through invisible reins. Which was in fact very close to the case.

"Oh, ssso prrroud, are we not, eh? Oh, ssso very Queeenly! Then, very well, Missstresss Sssivad, my Massster asksss only thisss one sssimple requessst of you; Give usss your Egg!"

"Never!" cried Mavis. *"So, return to your sniveling, fat snake of a Master, or die!"*

At this, the triad of what Erf humans would more usually know of as the mythical Hydra, but known in the realms of Under-Erf, as The Trydra, all gathered in their snaking coils and reared their evil heads up even higher. Mavis could see they were intending to surround her; They knew that she couldn't attack in three different directions at once.

Trinimicusss took the lead, suddenly lunging forward and lashing at Mavis directly ahead. As he did so, Trimorbisss snaked to the left, while Tridissipantisss did likewise to the right. Splatters of foaming acid-venom struck at Mavis's protective dome of blue-flame, all at once. The blue, fire bubble rippled and blistered; soon showing patches of ashen-brown blotching, as the blue-flame shield was infected simultaneously by the three Trydra's foul spitballs.

Mavis saw that it was time to act, before the two flanking monsters had time to maneuver any further around and get behind her. She had to catch all three at once, directly in her blast.

She watched and judged for the exact right time to move, just as the foul Trydra spat their bombardment of venom and before they had any chance to recover and so repeat their attack; Thus, with deadly aim, she reared up and struck!

As she did, the dome of blue flame rapidly shrank away to nothingness, and in the split second of it doing so, she opened her jaws wide and let forth a tremendous blast of searing, orange flame. A gigantic burst of boiling fire enveloped the Trydra. All three of the hideous creatures were instantly set alight, shrieking out their agony; as twisting, living candles.

The three Trydra were now hissing and howling and spitting and spluttering as the ruby red Dragon flames ravaged up and down their writhing, lizard-like bodies.

Roger could see that over to his left, Trimorbisss had collapsed onto the cavern floor, and was thrashing about amongst the corpses of the crushed Fire-worm Minions there. And all three of his heads were burning brighter than Lucifer!

Meanwhile, out to Mary's right, Tridissipantisss was also in trouble, but unfortunately not all of his heads were alight. He was now desperately attacking two of his own burning heads! There was one burning head held tight in the jaws of his unharmed head, and as she watched in horror, he ripped the head from its neck and then did the same for the other flaming head, knowing that new heads would soon replace the burnt and damaged ones.

"Quick, Mavis, to your right, quickly, or it'll just grow new heads!" Mary screamed out.

Mavis reared to her right and saw Tridissipantisss was indeed already growing a second head and the third would follow fast. She filled her fire-lungs with attack flame and fired a great gout of sizzling flame. This one was a blast of yellow and orange and not quite as hot as her first rock-melting blast had been. But it was hot enough to do the job required.

Tridissipantisss crashed to the ground with all three of its heads now fully aflame.

Soon there was nothing but three smoking stumps, clogged with ash and smoke and all dribbling congealing venom. And so, the second of the three Trydra had been dealt with.

"But wha-wha-what about Trinimicusss?" Roger shouted to her in alarm.

The cavern was rapidly filling with smoke from the violent and heated battle and Roger could no longer see Trinimicusss, the evil leader of the Trydra.

"Where's it gone?" he yelled, scanning the billowing murk of the fog-filled cavern for any sign of the monstrous creature.

But then, the awful answer came.

Trinimicusss was behind them! He had managed to fling his scorched and flame-ravaged body away and had coiled and rolled himself behind Mavis. And he still proudly held high, three hooded cobra-like heads, still dripping venom and still intent on their total destruction.

"I am growing weaker, Egg-bearers, I don't know how long I can hold Trinimicusss off!" Mavis mind-cast to them. *"I have just enough attack-flame for one burst, but if that fails…"*

"Ssso, my ssso called Queeen, Ssssivam Sssivad, Oh, Mighty Missstresss of the so-called True Dragonsss, you and your lassst egg will sssoon be nothing but puddlesss of ssslime!" Trinimicusss hissed vengefully.

Roger saw that Mavis hadn't had time to turn and adequately defend her rear. So now, both Roger and Mary were dangerously exposed to the last Trydra's venomous attack.

"Quick Mary," he shouted to her, "get on the other side of the wing, before he spots us."

Mary hurled herself forward, scrabbling on her hands and knees, as did Roger, to get out of the line of the enraged Trydra's fire. They both did so, in the nick of time.

However, Trinimicusss saw the flicker of their sudden movement from the corner of his third eye, as they lunged for cover on the other side of Mavis's wing.

But what was worse, as Mary flung herself alongside Roger, rolling under Mavis's wing, her precious cargo, the dragon's last Egg, came tumbling out of her coat and went rolling away from her for several yards. And the precious Egg finally came to rest almost exactly half the distance between Mavis the Dragon Queen and Trinimicusss the Trydra.

"Oh, no! Oh, no!" she screamed out, totally aghast. "Oh, Mavis, I'm so sorry!"

Mary's eyes welled up with tears at the anguish she now felt from the accidental but awful exposure of the dragon's Egg to this hideous and hateful Trydra creature.

But as yet, Trinimicusss hadn't seen the Egg. He was still consumed with battling Mavis.

Mavis had seen it though and quickly maneuvered herself to turn Trinimicusss's view away from her precious Egg and now taunted him with her choicest insults.

"So, you coward of a three-chicken-headed fish-freak; You think yourself a match for me, do you?" she cried out to him scornfully. "Well, let's see how brave you can be, shall we? Come here and stand and fight me, you foul and filthy excuse for a slithering slime-ball-slug. Try standing against me instead of small, helpless Humdrum children for a change, eh!"

Trinimicusss was furious. His nine, stony eyes burnt with rage as he turned towards her. Mavis and Trinimicusss now glared at each other in a momentary stand-off; each deciding on what their next best move should be.

Meanwhile, Mary was in a state of near total despair, shame, and regret.

"I must get it back, I just have to get it back," she cried to herself and then started to get onto her knees, getting ready to spring forward and retrieve the lost Egg.

But Roger gripped hold of her tightly around the waist and pulled her back.

"Don't be an ass, Mary!" he hissed at her. "That thing's bound to spot you. That monster will pick you off like a bunny rabbit in a lion's den!"

Mary just crumpled into his arms, realizing that Roger was right. Her tears streamed down her cheeks; she felt utterly lost and defeated. How could she have let the Dragon's Egg slip away from her like that? And after she'd just sworn an oath to protect and save it too!

Seeing Mary like this affected Roger very much. He felt he had to help somehow.

"L-l-look Mary, we're not done for yet, you know. We'll get the Egg back, O.K? I know, we'll use a diversion; you know, we'll use the same tactic that the Trydra used against us."

"What do you mean?" Mary sniffed at him.

"Well, I mean, I'll run out and distract him, off to one side, and as soon as he's onto me, *then* you can dive out and scoop up the egg; then we meet back here, behind Mavis's wing, O.K.? You'll get Mavis's Egg back, Mary, I know you will."

"Oh, Roger, you really are an Ass, you know!" Mary said, smiling at him admiringly.

"Wha-wha-what do you mean?" Roger asked, feeling a bit perplexed, deflated and hurt.

But before Mary could offer any explanation as to the, to her, obvious idiocy of his plan, that would more than likely just get him killed, events quickly moved on.

Trinimicusss had, despite Mavis's bullbaiting, spotted the Egg. His beady eye gazed firmly on it and he now slithered his way slyly towards it, but still facing toward Mavis as he did so. He wasn't at all sure how hurt and damaged the Dragon Queen really was.

"Well, sssee here!" he said, eyeing the Egg. "The Massster will be ssso very pleasssed!"

Then Mavis urgently, mind-cast to them both, *"Lie flat, get down as low as you can get!"*

The children flung themselves flat on the ground as Mavis at the same time reared upward, high over the Trydra; her fire-lungs pumping, ready to burst forth with a final and ferocious fountain of red battle-flame.

Trinimicusss, seeing what the Dragon Queen intended, furiously snapped his gaze and his course of action away from the Egg and instead met Mavis head on in battle.

The irate Trydra spat out a sizzling-hot torrent of acid-venom, right towards Mavis's head; It hit her squarely on the left temple, just as she likewise managed her own bolt of red flame that enveloped Trinimicusss in a ferocious, red-hot fireball. Dragon and Trydra screamed out in pain together. Roger could see the three-headed snake was in very bad trouble indeed; two of its heads had burst into flames immediately, and it was now desperately attempting to tear off its burning heads as quickly as it could, so it could regenerate two new ones.

However, Mavis was also in great difficulty. She fell back heavily onto her hind legs and began clawing at the side of her head; urgently trying to remove the thick, acidic slime eating its way into her. She had one eye closed and badly swollen, and several sizzling wounds from where other globs of Trinimicusss's evil, acid-sludge had hit her as well.

Roger knew Mavis had little to no attack-flame left with which to defend herself, the Egg, or them either. It all looked completely hopeless.

The last Egg of the True Dragon's, lay exposed and helpless, awaiting the outcome of this titanic battle to the death, as did the two terrified human children, hiding and watching under the injured Dragon's wing.

Everything now depended on who was the worst off; the Dragon or the Trydra?

CHAPTER 15:
THE RETURN OF THE
MEGADRILES.

Mary though, had thoughts for only one thing. The Dragon's Egg.

"This is my only chance," she thought.

She scrambled to her feet and then sprinted the short distance across to where the Egg lay. She threw herself onto it, covering it with her body and clasping it to herself as tightly as she could. She looked up and realized Trinimicusss had, as she'd expected, spotted her; But she could see that he was also caught between the two urgent and conflicting needs of either getting the Dragon's Egg or of saving his own rotten life. He of course chose the latter.

Mary dived into the cover of the dragon's wing and breathlessly lay there clutching the Egg to her chest and was overjoyed at feeling its cool, leathery texture under her hands again.

"Oh, well done!" cried Roger, beaming at her.

But Trinimicusss now did something that none of them had expected.

Instead of hurling himself in another all-out attack on Mavis, he rolled himself into a loop, with his three heads tucked tightly inside of the hoops and then rolled himself right around Mavis with surprising speed. He had deftly gotten himself behind Mavis again, and was back in the position he'd originally come from. But his clever maneuvering didn't stop there.

Roger and Mary still clutching the Egg, lay exposed on the wrong side of Mavis's wing once more. But then they soon saw what the vicious monster's tactic was really all about.

He now commanded the remaining, worm-minion army to the attack again!

The Fire-worms had been lying quietly dormant in the background, while the three Trydra monsters had attacked. Many of them had been heedlessly squashed and burned in the battle; but there were still hundreds left for Trinimicusss to control and hurl into the fray.

Roger watched in horror as they now surged towards him and Mary.... and the Egg!

Trinimicusss though was intent on slaying the wounded Queen Dragon, while his Minions captured, or more likely, killed the children and captured the treasured Egg.

They attacked, mindlessly hurling themselves in a pincer movement, trying to cut off Roger and Mary from Mavis and so surround the Dragon's egg and gain that precious prize for their all-powerful Master.

Mavis though, heedless of her own peril, now turned and fired a broad, raking sweep of yellow-red attack-flame, clearing the area between the children and the attacking Minions. She had just enough firepower to have the desired effect. But more Minions were coming.

Trinimicusss had not stood idly by. He took his opportunity and lashed out at the valiant Dragon Queen, searing her exposed flank with another gout of his flaming venom.

Mavis screamed in agony, hissing and spitting and her broken wing now aflame with the venomous fire and literally, going up in smoke. The acrid smell of burnt flesh and singed leather filled the air with its noxious stink.

But Mavis somehow turned herself toward the Trydra and snapped at her own wing stub as she did, ripping it from her tortured torso. While doing this she somehow lifted her one good wing and slammed it down between the children and the advancing minion horde.

Mavis had been very badly wounded by Trinimicusss, and was expecting even more damage to come, both from the Minions advancing suicide mission, as well as the relentless assault of the deadly and persistent Trydra, Trinimicusss.

And although Mavis had managed to turn around, dragging her one wing behind her in such a way as to still give some protection to the children; She was now totally spent and exhausted.

And she well knew all their lives could be finished at any moment, if she now failed to defeat this vile Trydra monster. Mavis had blown a great gout of yellow-orange flame, which had hit Trinimicusss squarely in his trio of heads and two of these had immediately caught fire. But he had evaded the total destruction that Mavis had intended and hoped for and was even now re-growing those damaged heads.

"The potency of my attack-flame is weak," she sighed to them. *"Your only hope is to flee with my Egg and try to make it to the surface as best you can. I will stay and do my best to see to the end of this ophidian filth, even though it will cost me my rightful death tomorrow."*

The Trydra however, had already regenerated one head and was very close to gnawing away the second burning head; And if it managed to do so, then again, it would be at full power.

"Ssso, Queeen of Ssssluggs, you sssee, you and your ussselessss egg will sssoon be oursss after all!" he hissed at her, sensing his looming victory.

He tore away his second head-stump and immediately a new venom-filled, fanged skull began to form. The cavern was still full of swirling smoke and Trinimicusss used this to his advantage. He began to sidle nearer, towards the Egg, swaying in rhythmic time to the ever-swirling smoke as he came. Causing a strange, hypnotic effect on those who looked upon him, not knowing his insidious powers of mind control.

Normally, Mavis would be impervious to such a brash and, to her, primitive deceits of the mind, but she was much weakened now, both physically and mentally.

And the children were no longer protected by her blue-flame, they were once more choking and coughing, their eyes stinging and streaming from the churned-up smoke. Roger looked all around him, but peering through his tears, he could see no obvious and direct course of escape whatsoever. They now were at the mercy of the advancing Trydra.

"How in the Pesky Pascal can we get out of this murder hole?" Roger muttered grimly. "And that blasted three-headed giant-cobra monstrosity has somehow survived everything that Mavis can throw at it and will be on us any second!"

The gigantic, last surviving Trydra reared over them again, its charred and scarred body, smoking and glistening in the blood-red glow of the seething smoke-clouds all around them. Its rhythmic swaying form disappearing within the coils of grey smoke and then reappearing. Its three sets of venomous fangs once again poised and ready to strike triple, fatal, blows, raining poison down upon them all.

Mavis mustered the very last of her red attack fire from her bruised and aching lungs.

She brought her head around level with Trinimicusss, staring him steadfastly in his cold, soulless eyes, ready to blast him with her very last bolt of attack flame.

But then, without warning, a mighty crash and craaaak, resounded in the cavern and the rocky floor between Mavis and Trinimicusss, suddenly split asunder!

There, boring through the crumbling rock floor, came a bluely glowing, Giant Erf-Worm! Then came another and yet another until there were now three of the huge, tubular creatures, speedily undulating towards Mavis, the two children and the Egg.

They were gigantic but graceful beasts now flowing relentlessly across the cavern floor.

As they moved, they flattened the few remaining minion worms who had still somehow escaped Mavis's blasts of attack flame or had been crushed in the battle with the Trydra.

"They somehow remind me of Blue Whales, you know," Roger gasped, incredulously.

"Yes, I know what you mean," whispered Mary, replying in awe at the spectacular sight unfolding before them. "They're just fantastic and truly majestic, aren't they, Roj!"

The Giant Erf-Worms or Megadriles as Roger scientifically called them had once more come to his rescue. But not just his, this time they had saved them all.

Mavis acted instinctively at the sight of her swooping saviors. She immediately lowered her bulk to the floor and allowed the Giant Erf-Worms a distraction-free access to the Trydra, while at the same time ensuring the children and her Egg were still protected.

The three Erf-Worms headed directly at speed for Trinimicusss.

The lone Trydra leader stood momentarily stunned. Three Giant Erf-Worms plus, even a mortally wounded Dragon, were too much for him. He knew that he was done for. He now crumpled onto the cavern floor, cowering and squealing in terror like the coward he was.

"No, you mussstn't do thisss!" he hissed, pleadingly to the advancing Erf -Worms.

Roger could sense his terror and fleetingly felt a pang of compassion for the evil brute. But this soon passed, as he remembered how close it had come to slaughtering the noble Dragon Queen; And then no doubt, intending the very same for them.

The Giant Erf-Worms curled themselves around the Trydra's blistered and quivering torso, in ever-tightening, strangling coils. However hard Trinimicusss tried to spit his hot venom at them or bite them with his seething fangs; It was all to no avail. These Giant Erf-worms were some of the toughest creatures in all the many worlds of the Under-Erf.

Soon the wrecked body of the Trydra leader was crushed within the seething coils of the three, great Erf-Worms who worked together in perfect harmony, like three practiced street dancers, as they slithered and pulled the flesh-pulping noose of their vermicular coils tighter.

Roger knew it was all over for the Trydra now. All he could see was the occasional globs of green and grey, fleshy sludge, oozing out from between the Erf-Worms' coils.

Trinimicusss had been crushed and squashed to a jelly!

The Erf-Worms slowly uncoiled themselves from its limp length of seeping, pulped flesh, that lay squashed and oozing in steaming puddles of grey slime. Its lifeless, unrecognizable carcass now left on the cavern floor to rot away in its own putrid poisons.

Then they made their rippling, methodical ways toward Mavis and the two children.

Mavis lifted her wounded head towards them and gave out a final, weak blast of flame, setting alight the hideous remains of Trinimicusss they left behind them.

The Coup de grace had been delivered by the Dragon Queen herself.

"Thank you, oh, great brothers of the Under-Erf," she mind-cast to the three Erf-Worms, *"the illustrious line of the Sivads is forever in your debt."*

The three Worms said nothing in answer, not that Roger could hear, physically or even mentally; But he had the distinct impression they understood every word that Mavis had said.

"You know, I think these creatures are actually very intelligent, Mary," Roger whispered.

"Yes, just like Whales and Porpoises and such like, we have in our oceans," she replied.

Mavis and the Erf-Worms were now deep in conversation it seemed; Though neither Roger nor Mary could work out how or what was being said by either exactly. It wasn't the 'normal' sort of telepathy that Mavis had introduced them to. But then again, that had been in Inglishe, so maybe this was another type of telepathy, a giant Erf-Worm one, Roger thought.

The Worms raised their heads, one after the other, and gathered around the Dragon Queen, now encircling her with their long and massive bodies, as in some sort of vermicular homage. Then their telepathic conversation was at an end.

All three Trydras, the mightiest Minions of the Masters of the Core, had been defeated.

And now there were no more Minions, big or small, left at all. The cavern was littered with the smoking, burnt bodies of the thousands of smaller, Minion-worms, as well as the fuming carcasses of the three vanquished Trydra.

Mavis now sensed that the Enemy, the Fire-Worm Lords of the Erf's Core, had no more reserves ready, as yet, to send in for further battle in the attempt to destroy her and her Egg. But she knew her time was running out.

"Thanks to the Erf-Worms, we have some respite, for a while at least," she told them. *"However, we can waste no time, who knows what the Core Lords may have planned?"*

"And thanks to you too, Mavis! But what is this Enemy?" asked Roger. "You still haven't told us that, you know. What's going on here? Why are these vicious creatures attacking us?"

"Well, my young Sky Child, we now have some time for questions and time for answers, and Sky-Spirits willing, I will tell you more of what you need to know before I resume my imminent journey through the awaiting portals of my fiery death."

"Oh, Mavis, I forgot. I'm really sorry. But is there nothing to be done to save you at all?" Mary asked her, longingly.

"*No. Nothing, child, but it is just… well… nothing. For I am Spirit and I can never die!*" she replied, mysteriously.

There was a moment's awkward silence and then Mary piped up rather sheepishly.

"Well, before you do die, Mavis, is there anything you can do about all this smoke in here? It's really hurting my eyes, and it makes it very difficult to breathe too, you know."

For answer, Mavis turned her head toward the children and blew a cooling cloud of gentle blue-flame all about them. "*This will keep the worst of the smoke at bay awhile,*" she said.

The raw redness in their eyes at once eased and their chests also felt lighter too somehow; The magical properties of the blue-flame, was definitely making it easier for them to breathe. Roger also gallantly handed Mary one of his clean hankies and that helped too.

Being always the gentleman, he seemed to have an endless supply, Mary wryly observed.

"*Now, I require a little time to recuperate and re-energize my supply of red and blue flame; We may well need them again. And by my reckoning I am not due to combust until well after the Dawn tomorrow; as is traditional with the passing of all female Dragons. So, we now have some of tonight to rest and recover, and to attend to your educations regarding the Under-Erf. And then you may both, forewarned and forearmed, make your way up to the surface safely with my Egg, and with plenty of time to get home.*"

The two children were keen to learn more of the Under-Erf and the proper procedure for hatching a Dragon's Egg and the correct rearing and education of a baby Dragon too. But before doing this she felt they should rest awhile first. And before they did that, Mavis had them swear their allegiance to her cause and that of her Royal Egg.

She had already had some words on this with Mary before, but this was now the time for their official induction into the sacred bond of the Dragon-Blood and their heartfelt swearing of unbreakable oaths.

"Now children, I will breathe the soul-blood of my spirit into yours and you must then swear your oaths of allegiance to the True Dragons for all time!" she solemnly told them.

The children stood up and obediently waited hand in hand before her. Both fully realizing this was a major turning point in their lives - it was in fact a momentous occasion and one they could never, ever have imagined happening before.

"Do you hold forever true to the sacred Dragon Oath, to always seek for the path of truth and harmony and that you will now serve and do all you can to save and aid my son?"

"We will, and we do!" they told her in emphatic unison. "And we'll get Regor away to safety, somehow. We promise."

The Dragon Queen nodded her satisfaction. *"Well, that is done, and it is good, very good indeed, I would say; But now you must rest awhile, as I must do too, and you should nourish yourselves too with any provisions you may have brought with you,"* Mavis told them.

Roger heartily agreed - feeling pleased he'd brought the biscuits and water flask with him.

"I will wake you in but two of your sky-light hours children, do not worry. There is time enough and then we will commence teaching you what you need to know," Mavis told them, as she curled herself up to rest and recuperate as best she could.

Roger and Mary sat comfortably together, their backs against Mavis's flank and so drank some water and nibbled at their biscuits. So much had happened to them in such a short time; They hardly knew what to say about it to each other.

One thing though was for sure. The World of Planet Erf was absolutely nothing at all like what they had been told and taught in school!

But while they were resting and recovering, with Mavis gently smoking and snoring away behind them, Roger raised himself from his uneasy dozing and now prodded Mary in the ribs.

"Oh, what on Erf is it, Roger? I'm still hurting and tired you know!" she moaned.

Roger then piped up about his worry that had been stopping him from getting any sleep.

"There's just one thing." he told her, having had a scary realization about this particular problem. "I don't want to be bothersome or anything, b-b-but there's something we really haven't thought through properly, you know."

"Well, what's that?" Mary huffed at him, impatiently.

"Well, it's, err, well, it's just ..." Roger's thoughts trailed away, and then in a quick rush, he shouted out loud his unspoken fear, his voice echoing strangely in the cavernous darkness. "Well, just how in the Dizzying Dirac's are we going to get out of this c-c-cavern anyway, even if we were all as fit as f-f-fleas—which we're not" he inwardly groaned, thinking of his poor fleas, "and we d-d-didn't have to climb, crawl or jump or run with a D-d-dragon's Egg, as well!" he finished, with a pained, apologetic expression on his sooty, bespectacled face.

Mary looked at him, a bit shocked, but she kept her tongue. She wisely realized that Roger had been having just as bad and unnerving and testing a time of it as she had, even more so really, considering how so very unused to the wild and unruly ways of Mother Nature he was.

Also, he did in fact have a very good point. Despite magical Dragons, deadly Trydra's, Giant Rats and Erf-Worms, just how were they actually going to get back up to the surface, and then find their way through the Bad Wood at night and get home all in one piece?

Mavis then coughed and blew a big, grey cloud of smoke towards Roger's face, and then just before it totally enveloped him within its coiling, dense, grey fog, she blew once again, and it just vaporized, disappearing before his very eyes.

"There is always a way to find a path that is worth the taking," she thought to them both, very pointedly, but at Master Roger Briggs, in particular.

Mary got the gist as well though and piped up in Roger's defense. "Oh, we know, we really do Mavis. Roger's clever at working out solutions to problems, aren't you, Roger?"

Roger felt somewhat guilty, thankful and embarrassed, all at once. He had been having something of a crash course in the emotions this most fantastic and fateful day. He looked at Mary and he looked at Mavis and then he looked up at the wall of the cavern.

It was about twenty feet to the top and he thought he could probably climb it, but he didn't think that Mary could, and in fact, he wasn't that sure, on second thoughts, that he could, not while carrying a Dragon's Egg as well anyway, even if he could leave Mary all on her own, which he really couldn't do, he knew.

His logical brain seemed to have completely deserted him. His mind was in some turmoil and he felt he was beginning to panic again. He felt he could burst into tears at any moment, which was really not on, he knew. But just how were they going to escape from this terrible, smoke-filled cavern? There surely had to be a way somehow, but what way? And how?

As yet, the truth was, Roger just had no idea!

"All right," he said, "just give me a minute, will you? Let's just look at this scientifically."

Roger paced up and down the cavern floor. He looked to see if there were any stalagmites still standing, after all the confusions of the battle and the Erfquakes.

Maybe we can find one that we can use to climb up, he thought, but rapidly saw that there were none. The cavern was strewn with the rubble of the once towering stalagmites, all now lying in broken ruin along with the debris from the many fallen stalactites. There were still swirling, grey wreaths of smoke everywhere as well, giving the whole scene an eerie, gothic-church, cemetery look.

"How about building something from the rocks?" he then suggested. "Maybe you could lift some of these rocks, Mavis, and then sort of build a bridge up to the edge of the slope?"

"I am barely able to move myself, let alone build bridges of solid rock!" Mavis gently and mournfully murmured in his head. *"And I will need a little while to recuperate my powers; Meanwhile, we must use what time we have left as profitably as possible. But there will be a way out, do not fear."*

Roger was now feeling very under pressure. There must be some sort of a solution to this, he thought, banging the side of his head with one hand and biting the nails of the other.

Mavis, observing this, lowered her head next to his and calmly bathed him in a strangely cool and glowing blue flame once more. This had the immediate miraculous effect of calming and cooling his mind and thoughts.

"Remember, young Skyling," Mavis whispered, *"there is always a solution to a problem, the skill is usually only in the choosing of the solution which is truly the best!"*

Roger was about to reply but then without any warning the cavern once again shuddered. More rocks came crashing down about them and yet more clouds of dust billowed up from the cavern's floor, setting Roger and Mary to yet further bouts of coughing and spluttering.

After a few secondary, minor tremors, things soon finally settled down and became still and relatively peaceful again. Roger could still hear a distant rumbling, however, as the seismic waves from the tremors continued passing beneath them; reverberating away into the vast, rocky depths of the Under-Erf.

"If these Erfquakes carry on, then sooner or later they're going to get us!" Roger muttered.

"Oh, Ponging Pilchards! Not another bloomin' Erfquake!" Mary said aloud, sounding more exasperated than scared.

"*No, my innocent but courageous young Humans*," came Mavis's somber tones again; Calming them further, so they'd be ready to hear the alarming news she now had to tell them.

"*You must know this, my two trusted Egg bearers. It is not the Erf that is causing quakes, but something far worse, I fear. Something that I wish you did not have to face!*"

"W-w-what on Erf do you mean?" Roger asked, aghast. "What could possibly be worse than those horrific Trydra creatures?"

CHAPTER 16:
THE BATTLE OF THE BLACK CAVERN.

"*I will show you,*" Mavis stated matter-of-factly. "*You must now learn something of the true history of the Under Erf, or at least that of a thousand years ago, that is. We have no time for anymore I fear, and there are others on the surface who will be able to teach and guide you further too. First, you must learn of the catastrophe that began the long, slow decay of the True Dragon's power and rule of the Under-Erf.*"

Mavis closed her eyes and Roger immediately felt his mind gently enveloped, as with a soft, pearly light, pervading the very essence of his being.

"Oooh! What's happening?" gasped Mary, as she too felt the same strange sensation.

"*You must know of the Enemy we face. It is time I show you what I can,*" Mavis sighed, "*but you must both be very brave, although I'll never knowingly show you what you cannot fully confront. Come now and witness the tragedy within my Home World Cavern, nearly a thousand years ago!*"

The children all at once felt themselves dissolving into space and time and falling into its hidden depths. Their very beings seemed to mix, melding together and moving into the awareness of the Dragon Queen's.

This time, though they were sharing the unique viewpoint and ancient mind of Mavis; Slowly, her powerful mind became the benign host for the children's own individual minds. From there they would be able to safely share in the long history of her many dragon years. But not as separate phantoms this time, but cocooned safely within Mavis's mind. And now they were being drawn along with her, down the long, long centuries of her tortuous time-track; Back to her own tumultuous, Dragon-World past. A thousand years earlier.

Roger mentally gasped, as he once again saw the wonderful landscape of Mavis' home Cavern-World, but as it had been so long ago, deep beneath the surface a millennium before.

He again observed many happy Dragon families, gaily colored and busy and bustling, flying about in the pink-red sky. They swooped about their ornate, smoking Cone-homes or stomped across lava plains or through lush fields and jungles; or splashed and played together in the many steaming magma pools. It was a lovely, peaceful and well-organized world, and once again, he saw that it was full and teeming with creatures that no 'Humdrum' would recognize. Many of these creatures still being unknown to modern, 'Humdrum' science.

By Newton's Rusty Pen Nib, I'd love to explore this place. I wonder what sort of Insects they have here? He wondered to himself.

"Look down there," squealed Mary pointing excitedly as they swooped along over the colorful Cavern-World's landscape below them.

"Yes, yes, I see them! By Neil Bohr's Barmy Barnacles, they're fantastic!" Roger yelled.

Mavis took them down even closer, to where Mary had pointed. There they could see Dinosaurs of all sorts and sizes. There were thousands of them; great browsing herds of Brontosaurs and Brachiosaurs, and also several smaller groups like the Stegosaurs and the Triceratops. And they all seemed to live together in harmony.

Roger also spotted, splashing about in a shallow lake, several of the huge, Diplodocuses and the spiny Spinosaurs; The Diplo's unbelievably long, sinewy brown necks serenely swaying in slow motion, as they lifted their tiny heads up, peering into the pink-streaked skies above, sensing but not seeing the Spirit-Dragon passing over their heads.

Mavis flew in a wide, sweeping curve that soon brought the children toward a distant flock of dark and strangely shaped flying creatures, that Roger at first couldn't quite make out.

"They look like like a flight of black, hand-made kites from this distance," Roger thought. But as Mavis swooped ever closer towards them, he soon made out what they really were.

"Oh, by Nicks Copper Knickers!" Roger cried out. "I just never would have believed it!"

Suddenly, he was flying along amongst a squadron of bat-winged Pterodactyls, skimming above the rolling, lush plains and weaving in and out of all the towering volcanic cones there; all reveling in their recently evolved freedom of flight.

"This that you witness is a very early memory of mine," Mavis murmured soothingly but sadly too, "it is here, that my very first experience of the dreaded Un-kind, the vile spawn of the Core Lords, occurred!"

"The wh-wh-what?" gulped Mary and Roger together.

"Hush now children," said Mavis, in a firm but kindly manner, "Be brave and… well, just look, listen and learn."

Mavis flew steadily onwards, and along with her they saw all about them many beautiful dragons flying about singly or in groups. And there were also other sorts of flying creatures; Prehistoric birds of various varieties and not just the flying lizards like the Pterodactyl flock they'd already seen. Everywhere that Roger looked there was some new spectacle or species, some new fantastic creature or strange new feature of this incredible Under Erf world, that he very badly wanted to explore and investigate.

Mavis swept downwards now, skimming over a stretch of hot and humid, tropical jungle. Roger saw there were several

Archaeopteryx down there, adorned in bright plumage and flapping their brightly coloured wings and grand tail feathers. There were other birds too he just didn't have any name for. And this jungle seemed to be full of giant, Parrot-like birds, but at least five times larger than the normal South Amerigan Parrots he knew of.

There were also many strange-looking monkeys, great troops of them swinging along in the trees; Some even looked like little hairy men; Half pygmy, half ape! "Maybe they're tribes of early Humans!" Roger thought, his curiosity roused.

Now Mavis flew upwards once more, soon leaving the teeming jungles and the plains far below. She soared higher and higher, at last reaching the Dragon Cavern's vast arching ceiling once again. She then hovered there, just under its bright shimmering mesh of sparkling, crystalline lights.

"You must now understand, my Skylings, more of what brings the light to this world of mine, this my very own home Cavern-World; and as with so many of the worlds within worlds of the Under-Erf, it also has its own unique ecosystem."

Mavis took them up closer to the rocky ceiling, so they could see what gave light to these cavernous Under-Erf Worlds. There before her, and therefore 'their,' very own eyes, lay the ancient and intricate network of 'Light Rivers' that flowed across the high-arching dome of the cavern's vast ceiling. This wondrous network of luminescent crystal-threads glowed with a rosy-hued radiation; shimmering its life-giving light upon the flourishing flora and fauna, far below them.

"You see before you, this great mesh of interconnected veins, running like a million rivers of radioactive, molten-ore, covering our cavern's ceiling?" Mavis told them. "This net of opalescent light has shone down upon the Dragon World for eons untold, strengthening and weakening its brilliance in a daily cycle much as your daytime and nighttime does above. And this is where the Enemy attacked. Now you will witness the dark-time that heralded so much destruction and despair!"

Then, without warning, the lights began to dim. Mavis took them to a time just a little later, but in the exact same place. Here they could see the huge and seemingly endless ceiling-skies of the Cavern-World were slowly darkening.

Roger looked up, at first still awestruck, at the sight of the brilliantly lit Cavern ceiling; But then gasped in sudden horror. The rivers of Crystal light that had brightly shone like a billion, flaming, translucent bright rubies, casting a shimmering glow over the land below, were darkening and dying. And not by any natural means. They seemed to be sickening!

Somehow, this intricate network of beautiful light was being turned off!

"Wha-wha-what's going on, Mavis, why are all these lights going out?" Roger asked.

"This deed you now see was but the first sign of the invasion of the evil hordes of the Fire-Worm Minions; Sent by our direst Enemy, the Fire-Worm Lords of the Core themselves!" she gravely replied.

Roger now saw the lethal legions of Minion-worms that were swarming over the glowing, cavern's ceiling; Each minion much like those that had attacked them earlier. Though these worms each exuded a horrid black slime. This mighty and murderous army comprised thousands upon thousands of these slithering dark-red Fire-worms.

They spread like a deadly infection all over the cavern ceiling, leaving their thick trails of oily, congealing, black goo wherever they went. They flowed across the Cavern's ceiling in a relentless dark wave; Flowing like a tide of black death, the Cavern's life-giving light, gradually dulling and dying away to a dismal gloom in their wake.

Mavis swept downwards once more, now flying towards the teeming plains, that were still for the moment adorned with the Dragon Cavern's many wonderfully constructed and colorful Home-Cones. But Roger saw that the Fire-Worms were now invading everywhere and without warning. The Land of the Dragons was under attack from above and below!

The light of the Cavern-World was now reduced to a redly glowing gloom and through this hellish light, came the huge and mighty Fire-Worm Lords themselves, along with their marauding battalions of armored-centipedes and cockroaches, and many garish-colored and highly poisonous millipedes too. They came storming across the Cavern-World's landscape, spouting venom and flame, poisoning, pillaging and destroying everything in their paths.

"Oh, Mavis, this is horrible, it's just ghastly!" Mary cried out inside the Dragon Queen's head, the Erf children and Mavis still being conjoined, as one mind. What one thought or felt, then the other thought or felt. Through Mavis's dragon-mind-meld they were three-minds in one, observing the horror unfolding before them.

"The bulk of this army are but the Enemy's Minions, child; they are merely the mindless slaves of the Fire-Worm Lords of the Core. These lesser, worm-like creatures, being much the same as the creatures that attacked us before; but all of them, large or small, have been mercilessly mind-warped into being nothing but soldier-slaves; All members of a mindless and disposable army, existing only to fight for whatever evil purpose their Core Masters so decree - which in this time and in ours too, a millennium on, is nothing less than the Erf's conquest. For their master's desire dominion over all the Under-Erf and not just the Core." Mavis grimly told them, as they skimmed along above the embattled land below.

Mavis flew grimly onwards through the glowing, red gloom, as her Home Cavern-World increasingly became a chaotic and cataclysmic battleground. The True Dragons had been caught out and taken by complete surprise. There were now hundreds of skirmishes in the sky and on the land. Everywhere they looked the True Dragon's Home Cavern World was under deadly lethal and continued attack.

Most of these battles were occurring hidden away in the gloom now, but Roger and Mary could still hear the many cries and screams of death and destruction, echoing all around them.

Then Roger saw the Enemy himself. A huge, bloated Fire-Worm, a Lord of the Erf's Core. He was right below them and urging his mindless minion armies onwards to sacrifice their worthless lives by the many thousands for his war-crazed cause.

Then he noticed a small band of youthful, True Dragons, much smaller versions of Mavis, not yet fully grown, but who were valiant and steadfast. These were merely a troop of Dragon Cadets who were now bravely battling the Minion foes, despite their being vastly outnumbered. Their backs pressed up hard against their Cone-Academy's curving rocky wall; defending their home and their kin against the hopeless odds of advancing Minion-worms.

Roger cried out in horror, seeing they were being relentlessly harassed and surrounded, the Minion-worms hissing and spitting torrents of their vile acid poisons down upon them.

Then, in a great burst of burning slime, one of the Core Lord's huge Millipede Monsters, suddenly attacked them from one side, and slaughtered them all, with but a single blast.

Roger gaped in shocked disbelief, as he flew on by. The Dragon Cadet's melting corpses burning as one bright and gruesome bonfire below him and briefly lighting up similar scenes of horror going on all around him. This indeed was a bloody battle to the death; one for the total annihilation and extermination of all True Dragon-kind!

And these vile vermin, both the Masters and Slaves, these were all of the devil-spawned races of the Un-Kind, the cruel creatures of the Core. And all mindlessly committed to the utter destruction of their most hated ancient enemies, the True Dragons of the Dragon's Erf.

These Fire-Worm Lords of the Core, Roger could see, even in the deepening, red gloom, were easily spotted; they were huge lumbering, Pythonesque creatures; Or more accurately, elongated, armor-plated Crocodiles, hundreds of feet long. Each burning with a fierce, red glow in their chests; Their very hearts being but pumping cores of molten hate, much like their core-furnace homes, deep down within the hot and hellish realm of the Erf's Core.

"Their plan, as you can here see, children, was to douse the living veins of our light-producing crystal web with their vile, black slimes, thereby darkening our Dragon World," Mavis calmly explained, as they flew across the ravaged battle-scape that unfolded its ever-flickering, fiery horrors, below and above them.

The Dragon Queen grimly continued her narrative on the evils unfolding before their very eyes. "And so, with superior night-vision and vaster numbers, they would wreak havoc among all of Dragon-kind; and all other creatures of the Under-Erf kept under our Dragon Peace, from the Dinosaurs to Diatoms. They had planned well, luring our King away in defense of several other Under-Erf Cavern-Worlds. Only our Home Guard remained to defend the realm."

"The Core Lords knew that with the True Dragons gone, nothing could stand in their way, and they would be free to spread their evil reign throughout all the Under-Erf, just like an incurable disease. Spreading its rabid infection from Cavern-World to Cavern-World."

"Or just like an apple being rotted away by a worm from deep inside it!" Roger said.

"Yes. Exactly!" Mavis said.

The companions of the Egg continued onwards, skimming over the ever darkening and battle-scarred plain, and below them Roger now saw a Tyrannosaurus Rex. He felt scared out of his wits for a second, but then he realized that he wasn't actually there; Not physically, so he knew he really didn't have to feel scared at all. But somehow, he still felt very uneasy. Roger, from a very young age, had always had a strange fascination, as well as an admiring horror and fear, of the ruthless Tyrannosaurus Rex, the King of the Dinosaurs.

This courageous colossus of a Dinosaur was now busy battling a giant Centipede of the Core, twice the size of the Tyrannosaurus Rex. The giant, armored grub was built like a battering ram; But one that lumbered along on a hundred, skittering red legs. Its segmented green and black body glinted in scaly armor-plates. Its shiny and bulbous, black head, ending in red, fang-like mandibles that were snapping open and shut and viciously biting at the T. Rex's flanks, trying to gouge bloody chunks out of him.

The Tyrannosaurus Rex wasn't having any of it though. Its tiny, fierce eyes glowed red with raw rage, as it swung its great bludgeoning tail, like a giant's club and striking the ramming Giant Centipede in its side, toppling it over onto the ground. The Rex roared above its prey and thereby making its one deadly mistake. By such gleeful gloating, it delayed from seeing to the giant grub's final dispatch unto death, for just a second too long.

As the King of the Giant Lizards roared its boastful battlecry, a swarm of Fire-worm Minions poured in towards him too, and then crawling in a deadly, squirming mass, right up his legs, and along his ramp-like tail. Each worm was busily biting, stinging and poisoning as it went.

The Dinosaur King was momentarily distracted and in those precious moments the fallen Giant Centipede found its legs again and turned and lunged upwards, once more. This time its jaws found the flesh it craved; steel-like pincers tearing into and gripping the Rex's throat.

Between the marauding mass of malevolent Minions and the grim, gory grip of the Giant Centipede, it looked like the mighty Tyrannosaurus Rex's valiant battle was over for good.

However, the Minion worms and the Monster Grub hadn't counted on the one thing they had no knowledge of whatsoever; they hadn't planned for the intervention of... Love!

As the valiant King roared out in pain, bleeding from several wounds and staggering and desperately trying to release himself from his foe, his very irate mate, Madam Tyrannosaurus Rex, suddenly appeared, charging as if from nowhere, out of the hellish, smoky-red gloom.

She immediately struck at the Centipede, still firmly and stubbornly attached to her poor husband's throat. Her huge, dagger-like teeth slashed at the Centipede's blunt head, as she flung herself upon the mindlessly, murdering brute with the savage intensity that the female of the species rises to whenever their loved ones are being threatened or harmed.

Quickly, the Giant Centipede loosened its grip, now having half its head slashed away and spewing out a foul, steaming ichor from its terrible wound. In fact, it barely functioned at all, but its tiny brain, even tinier than the Tyrannosauruses' famously walnut-sized one, had also been sliced in two. The garish, giant grub slowly slithered to the ground and then quivered and quaked... and then went totally, raving mad; wildly thrashing about, convulsing and coiling uncontrollably... in its final, fearsome death-throes.

Meanwhile, the Dinosaur King of the prehistoric Lizards had recovered his balance and his dignity too, and voraciously set about lashing Minions from his blood-splattered body, clawing away the many Fire-worm Minions foolishly clinging to his torn and tattered hide.

As Mavis and the children continued on their way over the darkening plain, the last thing Roger saw of this touching vignette of mutual, marital bliss was the husband and wife team of Tyrannosaurus Rexes, bravely beating away at each other's flanks with their mighty tails, swatting away the very last of the verminous minion hordes.

They flew on in silence. Nothing could have prepared them for the carnage they were witnessing. The world about them was a hell-ridden rendition of a Devil's dream. There were now islands of flame where volcano Dragon homes had erupted, and it was by the light of these the children witnessed the continuing horrors of the battle of the Black Cavern.

The Core Lords, though, had prepared their onslaught well. Roger observed that all the larger warriors of the Enemy, all the generals and officers, were all creatures with enhanced night-vision. Besides all the Minion hordes, there were battalions of ogre-like giants running amok, butchering and bludgeoning anything they could get at with their huge clubs and axes. There were squadrons of spider-like men too, hairy and black, running about below them and wielding venom-dripping swords, at least four swords to each spider-warrior. And there were others there too, evil creatures of a kind that Roger couldn't even put a name to.

Then Roger's vision suddenly blurred and darkened, and he found he was flying amongst a cloud of inky, bat-like creatures. He stifled a short scream of alarm and ducked and again realized that he wasn't actually physically there at all. Feeling rather sheepish that he'd been scared out of his wits unnecessarily, he steeled himself to really look and confront what was happening all around him.

But the vicious-looking squadron, of what turned out to be a species of deadly Bat-hawks, soon flew onwards, leaving Mavis and the children to do the same. He looked behind him in horror as he saw the Bat-hawks dive-bombing down, one by one, like the Stuka bombers had done in the Great World War of the Thirties. The once peaceful volcano homes below were all being mercilessly bombarded, the Bat-hawks firing out ferocious blasts of incinerating flame, setting home after home and creature after creature on fire.

"The Fire-Worm Lords are well skilled in all the powerful arts of heat and fire. They can easily manipulate any flame and bend it to their wills." Mavis solemnly mind-cast to them. "Only they have the knowledge that is at least the equal to the True Dragons of Under-Erf. But they are creatures of pure and malicious evil who wish only for death and destruction or the slavery of all other forms of life."

Mavis continued in her flight for a moment in silence, as Roger and Mary gazed on the horrors below, in stunned disbelief at the sheer scale of the carnage. But then she continued, "And you must understand this, children: besides their great powers over all Heat and Fire, they also have great powers of Mind. This, along with their control of Fire and of Erf-quakes, makes them a formidable foe. It has only been the True Dragons who have stopped these foul creatures from dominating the whole of the Under-Erf, for many, many eons."

As Mavis flew along, skimming low over the land, Roger saw the last ruddy, red rays of light were being extinguished from the cavern's high ceiling. The only light left was that of the erupting volcanoes and the burning trees and animals.

About them they saw once beautiful fields and forests, as well as wild animals, all aflame. And although the Dragon Volcano homes had long ago been made secure and tamed by the True Dragons, these too had somehow been re-ignited by the Fire-Worm Lords.

Roger saw, here and there, the huge, distinctive form of a Fire-Worm Lord burrowing into the base of a Volcano and then causing it to erupt with a sudden and violent explosion.

Cone after cone exploded, belching out great pyroclastic flows of gas, rock, and colored flame, high into the black and blood-red sky. Many-tongued rivers of lava snaked across the shattered landscape, drowning all plants and creatures as they flowed relentlessly onwards, engulfing everything they found in their silent, sliding seas of dismal death.

Mavis spoke to them again, her words echoing loudly in their shocked, mind-shared heads.

"You children have witnessed the most hideous and heinous Battle of the Black Cavern, of nearly a thousand years ago. For this, not long after, is what this day came to be known as; The Dragon Kingdom and the Home Cavern-World was eventually saved, but at very great cost." She paused, obviously feeling the emotional pain of these ancient events but then continued on, "It was my future husband who saved us, Lord Commander Nevets Yelgnal, Sky Marshal and Dragon Minister for Peace and Security, at this particular time."

Mavis fell silent and Roger had the distinct impression she was controlling herself at the mere mention of her illustrious husband. He didn't want to intrude on her privacy, but Mary asked the burning question anyway.

"What happened to your husband Mavis? Is… is he still alive then?"

"In our true, present time… I, I don't really know… but I do hope so, Skyling child," Mavis answered hesitantly, obviously not wishing to say anything further on the subject.

They now swooped up towards the cavern ceiling. Roger was shocked at seeing how ugly it now looked. The black goo had congealed and doused every last beautiful glimmer from it. But he had no further time to reflect on such matters as Mavis flew straight through the rocky ceiling, just as if it wasn't there.

Then everything again went dark and still.

CHAPTER 17:
THE BEGINNING OF
THE END.

They flickered out of existence momentarily and then reappeared at a different part of the Dragon's Cavern-World. It was later in the day now, but the natural daily dimming-cycle the Cavern ceiling's lights usually went through was redundant. The only light left to illuminate the horrors of the landscape below came from the erupting volcanoes and the many areas where raging fires ravaged their way across forests and fields.

"There is now one last event of this day to show you and one I dread more than any other; But for our… our bonding, it is necessary," Mavis told them, sounding exhausted.

"Oh, I'm so sorry, Mavis," Mary replied, her own heart feeling as broken as the Dragon's, at witnessing all the death and destruction of that black day from the overwhelming forces of the Minion-armies of the Core Worm Lords.

"And we will do whatever we can to help you, Mavis. We promise," Roger added.

"I know you will dears," she replied, "but now I must show you the saddest day of my life and the most evil and terrible act that precipitated the long decline the High King, Divad Sivad, my Father, and from that, the slow decline of the True Dragon Empire too, these last thousand years. For where we go now, truly was… the Beginning of the End."

They spiraled down toward a particular volcanic Home-Cone thus far standing unscathed. This being where Mavis's very own, beloved Mother, the Dragon Queen, Anivad Sivad, had been flying resolutely towards, with her baby Dragon, Mavis, clutched tightly to her breast.

The three spirit-entities of the elder-Mavis, along with Roger and Mary, as part of her time-travelling consciousness, now mentally joined with the new-born and unique and inno-cent viewpoint of Mavis, as a baby Dragon.

The desperate Queen, Anivad Sivad, (now known to the children as Mavis's own mother) held her dragon baby tightly in one taloned claw, causing her to squeal and squirm in protest, as she flew onwards, frantically evading fireball after fireball and blast after blast of deadly venom-spit.

"Ow! I felt that!" Roger yelped. "My ribs feel bruised."

"So, did I!" Mary exclaimed. "Seems everything Baby Mavis sees and feels, then so do we!" She explained to him.

Queen Anivad battled on through the sooty, flame-licked sky, making her way towards the ever-nearing, relative shelter and safety of her eons-old, Dragon Home-Cone.

Roger felt the wind rush by his dragon scales and ruffling through his still feeble baby wings. For whatever baby Mavis felt or saw or heard, he did too. He could smell the cloying stink of Sulphur and soot and smoke, in the flame-streaked air. And he saw it through baby Mavis's new and innocent eyes; All the flaming fireballs streaking through the skies and all the thunderous explosions and the crackling cacophony of the many fiery infernos engulfing the ravaged land beneath him. But what was worse, he could also hear the horrific screams.

As her mother flew bravely on, trying to protect her baby as best she could, little baby Mavis was bombarded by the howls of despair and screams of death being wrung from the throats of so many innocent creatures. She didn't understand what was happening and was becoming increasingly scared, squealing her protests to her embattled mother.

"Try and control your telepathic volume, my dearest. We will soon be home and I will get us safe, hidden within the deepest parts of our volcano cellars," Queen Anivad telepathed to her frightened daughter.

Roger directly felt how absolutely terrified and confused the small baby Mavis was.

He could also see that the evil army of the night, the mind-controlled Fire-worm hordes, were still falling from the Cavern's ceiling like a relentlessly raging rainstorm of pure hate intent on only death and destruction, as they came hailing down in their thousands to join the fearsome fray.

As Anivad desperately flew through the dark smoke-wreaked skies, so full of embattled core creatures, all shrieking and screaming their war-cries of hate, she twisted and turned while also shooting torrents of Dragon flame at any enemy that came near her. Repeatedly, she dodged and avoided near-fatal collisions with the myriads of mad mindless marauders.

"As you know, my Skyling Children," Elder Mavis interjected, "all True Dragons are well versed in the skills of telepathy; however, here, I am very young, so I will now use the point of view and the direct experience of my desperate mother to relay to you the full horror of this terrible day."

"Oh, is that you down there, I can see beneath us now?" asked Mary. "That tiny, baby Dragon, who's just barely clutching hold of Queen Anivad... I mean... your mother? Oh, Mavis, that must have been terrifying for you!"

"Yes, child, it was. But now I will show you my first meeting with a Fire-Worm Lord," Mavis answered her somberly.

The baby Mavis hung on for dear life, as her mother swept and swooped through the sky, weaving and wending her way onwards, still avoiding incoming attacks from all directions. All she could do was cling tightly to her mother's stomach as she desperately dived and dodged her way towards their Cone-Home, looming ever nearer.

Then, a few moments later, just as they were about to land on one of their Home-Cone's balconies, her mother was suddenly and without warning, hit from high above, by yet another onslaught of dive-bombing Fire-worm creatures, that Queen Anivad hadn't seen in time.

These were spider-worm minions and had come, as if from nowhere, falling from the murky sky on sticky, red strings, like a deadly battalion of stinging, six-legged paratroopers. They fell and cascaded all around her, like a barrage of fiery, red-hot hailstones; Each, by itself, unable to inflict any real damage to a full-grown Dragon, but together, they definitely could. Just by sheer numbers, they could overwhelm her, and especially while she was desperately trying to protect her defenseless child and fight her enemies at the same time.

The children gaped in despair as they watched and understood how Mavis felt, realizing how it was not for herself that her mother Queen Anivad most feared, but for the life of her child. Even as a babe, Mavis had understood, that just by her presence alone, she had been unwittingly endangering her mother's life; And she felt deeply and dismally guilty about it.

"Oh Mavis, this is terrible," Mary gasped, "but it really isn't your fault, you know!"

Baby Mavis felt her mother's huge wide wings desperately beating the air and her strong, sinewy body stretching, with every muscle straining to its uttermost limits, as in her heroic acrobatics, she battled on to get them both to safety. But there was nothing baby Mavis could do. She felt terrified and useless and small.

More than anything else, despite being but a defenseless hatchling, she wanted to do something to help her mother. She innately sensed great harm was being caused by these demonic spider-worms, and to her Cavern-Home World too.

She was just a weak, unskilled Dragon Baby, who could barely fly, but her heart was of the illustrious and noble line of Sivad, and she would have given her own small life to help save her courageous mother.

It was now impossible for any True Dragons to see very far in the smoky, deep gloom of the Cavern at all. And Queen Anivad was having to rely on her sixth and her seventh senses. And all that baby Mavis could see and feel was the teeming Spider-worm-Army falling on them like a relentless swarm of stinging hornets.

Her mother continued blasting great gouts of deadly, red dragon flame at the worms, incinerating many of the mindless Minions. But, alas, this was too few of the deadly creatures. The Core Worm Lords had been breeding their Minion armies for many centuries and had a seemingly endless supply of such slaves.

The truth was there were just too many of them for one lone Dragon to vanquish all alone, and little by little, they were sapping the Dragon Queen's strength, and what was even worse, they had damaged her beautiful wings too, so now she could no longer properly fly.

Mavis softly spoke into the children's minds, as they shared her mother's ancient memory. "You must know and feel this as I have known and felt it, children; your oath will then be as an eternal bond of immortal Dragon-blood between us!"

The Queen couldn't get a firm hold upon the Home-Cone's ledge on which she desperately landed with a skidding jolt. She scrabbled at the rock, desperately trying to get a proper purchase on it, but no matter how hard she tried, she couldn't regain her balance. The spider-worm horde thronged gleefully about her and now pushed her backwards, step by step, until finally, she stumbled and fell, hurtling out of control, down to the fuming ground below.

Queen Anivad controlled her perilous fall as best she could, crashing in a tangle of wings, crushing many Minions under her, but clutching her child, the baby Mavis to her scaly breast.

She called out, trumpeting as long and as loud as she could, and mind-calling as well. Desperately needing her husband, Mavis's beloved Father, Divad Sivad, the long-ruling King of the True Dragons. Anivad knew, only he had the strength and power that could save them. But alas, he was too far away, and unknown to her, was furiously fighting for his own life.

The Spider-worms, and the scuttling scourge of the Core-World, some nearby Giant Centipedes, charged at her as one, all realizing she was weak and exposed, and being well informed of the importance of her as a prize to the Core Lords. They fell onto her, as one biting, stinging and spitting mass of hate; As one huge, hungry horde, of all-consuming evil.

Roger and Mary felt and saw, through baby Mavis's horror-filled eyes, the sudden flashes of red hot flame, illuminating the vicious attack upon her fallen mother. The courageous Queen did all she could to keep the foul and putrid Core vermin away from her youngest Dragon child.

But the baby Mavis still felt every drop of the splattering, golden-hot Dragon blood, and the viscous worm-venoms, hitting and hissing upon her mother's bruised and bloodied flanks.

Queen Anivad flamed and flared; Twisted and turned; Desperately trying to fight off the seething sea of Worm-Vermin, now scurrying all over her body. And at the same time, still trying to protect her precious dragon child from their frenzied, evil onslaughts. Knowing these deadly creatures would make short work of such a defenseless Dragon-babe as Mavis.

Baby Mavis could hear only the echoes of dread and horror and anguish from all around her. Her once so beautiful and peaceful Cavern home had now become a seething and chaotic Hell. As she clung to her mother's belly, she saw there were more Fire-Worm hordes pouring in for the kill, scuttling and scurrying around her Mother in ever-increasing numbers.

They slithered relentlessly on, over the corpse-littered ground, intent on finishing any wounded creature they found. Queen Anivad, unfortunately being just another hapless victim of their quest to inflict death wherever they could.

The children saw how the wounded Queen quickly and deftly took up her defenseless infant, between her pointed teeth and then lurched her bloodied bulk towards some nearby boulders. There, she took hold of baby Mavis and wedged her safely in between two large rocks. Then, turning defiantly to face her foes, she put the bulk of her mighty body between her whimpering, frightened babe and the Fire-worms, Spider-worms and Centipedes, all now converging on her.

Her majestic, blue and gold Dragon-form, reared up on high, as she unfurled her glorious, though torn and tattered wings, preparing to attack, with tooth, talon and a torrent of flame.

Her red-scaled chest pulsated and glowed ruby-red-hot; The ferocious furnace within her fiery lungs, readying itself for a final, flesh-frying blast of minion-melting flame.

But it came too late.

Baby Mavis, and the children too, saw, crawling in a silent slither from behind her Mother, a huge Fire-Worm Lord. Baby Mavis desperately tried to warn her; But her feeble mind-casts came as weak bleats of alarm, as from a lamb, lost and alone, in a field full of bleating sheep.

Her mother's attention was elsewhere, and she paid her no heed. But as Anivad was about to release her final bolt of flame upon the frenzied Worms, the cowardly Fire-Worm

Lord of the Core suddenly struck with a torrent of acid-flame.

Queen Anivad immediately recoiled and tried to twist herself around and defend herself, but it was all to no avail. The vicious, flesh-eating flames engulfed her even as she moved, the deadly acidic tongues of fire eating into her body. The Fire-Worm Lord's flames flickered and licked all about her torso in a sulfurous, yellowing haze of searing heat.

And all the crazed Worm Minions, seeing her fall, and writhing on the ground, in agony, quickly came slithering and slurping upon her, with eager, ghoulish appetites, all wanting to be in at the Dragon Queen's kill. They flooded over her body like a vile infestation of rancid, rabid rats, running riot over a barn, full of fuming, fouled grain.

But even as she died, Queen Anivad's final, brave and noble act was to fall purposefully, intentionally collapsing upon the two rocks where she had hidden her last, lone Dragonbabe, Mavis, the Dragon Queen to be.

Then the shocking vision, that Roger and Mary, with unspeakable and disbelieving horror had mind-shared with Mavis, abruptly went black. Their Mind-meld and their Vision-journey to Mavis's grisly past, was over.

And thus, was baby Mavis saved.

"That lowly, slimy, Fire-Worm Slug! That stinking, slinking creature of pusses and poison, he killed my Mother!" Mavis thought heatedly to them, and with much heart-felt venom that she momentarily could not control or contain.

"Who is this creature, this Enemy from the Core then Mavis, the one who just killed your mother… and what has he to do with you and your Egg right now?" Roger quietly asked her, realizing Mavis's reliving of her past had been a very great ordeal for her.

"It is one and the same foul, core-creature; Morgrave is his name, who has followed me here and now," she answered him, somberly.

"And still he seeks my death as well as my Egg; But that will never be; for I have out-witted that blighted, black-souled beast of a Worm.

And I have arrived here, as close to the Skylands as I can. Although, the truth be told, it would have suited me better to have made it to a far more central area of the Great Forest of Lundun. For it is deep within that ancient Wood that my Dragon hatchling must be born to achieve his full magical potential, you see. For all that remains is my death and my re-birth... but also a new glorious life for my son... with the help of you two children, by your ensuring my last, most precious Egg, is safely hatched!"

There was a long and meaningful silence in the dimly glowing Cavern that the children's consciousnesses had returned to. They had quietly re-entered their dormant bodies in their true present time and blinked their eyes awake in the smoky, red gloom. And there, together, hidden deep below the once enticing and mysterious Smoking Tree, their heart-wrenching and grief-stricken emotions, needed no magical telepathy, whatsoever.

"And thus, we have witnessed the beginning of the end," Mavis murmured, after a while.

Then, the stillness and silence of the smoky cavern was again shattered by an almighty, resounding roar; Quickly followed by a continual rumbling and shaking that built in intensity all about them. Further rock-falls crashed, clattered and echoed through the Dragon's Cavern and several hissing-hot fissures appeared, creating further cracks in the corpse-littered cavern.

"Is all this the work of your Arch Enemy, this King Morgrave, your Core Worm enemy?" asked Mary, "Is he the one causing all these Erfquakes that keep 'appening?"

"And they seem to be getting nearer... and stronger too!" Roger added, with some alarm.

"Do not worry, my dearest Skylings, I have barricaded all possible routes to this cavern. Morgrave is using his formidable power of mind only. That vile Worm even now but rages against the trap I have him in,

far below us, baited there by my own, sorely sacrificed wing. Even as we speak, he is entangled and engulfed within a mountain of enchanted rock and lies pinned beneath my hex-laden dragon wing, a magical hex from which even he will find it impossible to escape from for some while."

"B-b-but if he's from the Core I'd have thought these Core creatures can bore through any sort of rock, just like that, can't they?" piped up Roger, feeling unconvinced.

"My dear young Erfling, I am no longer the unlearned and innocent babe that you saw in our journey to the past who Morgrave did not find and kill so long ago," replied Mavis rather indignantly.

"Now children, please attend, our time must not be wasted. I hereby entrust the future of my line and the hope of all True Dragons and all Erf-kind, to your safe-keeping and to your bravery and sincerity in confronting all the horrors of the Un-Kind; all of those deadly and destructive creatures of the Erf's Core and their poor, weak-willed puppets; and thus for you to bring my final Egg to the Dragon's Nest, the place of his hatching."

"We understand, Mavis, really we do, and we will!" Mary replied, staunchly.

And Roger nodded his agreement. "Where do you want us to take the Egg exactly, Mavis? Is it very far at all?" he asked, politely curious as to just where they'd have to go.

The mortally wounded Dragon Queen sighed heavily.

"My Egg must be gotten to the surface and away from the Forest of Lundun, at least for a while, at first. No one will suspect the Dragon's Egg would be hidden amidst the Humdrums. You must briefly hide it; Then, when the time comes, you must take it to the hatching place. This will be at the Great Forest's heart, and will soon become known to you, I promise."

Mavis's eyes were now drooping with weariness and Roger could tell she was doing her level best to suppress the pain she was in. He had briefly got an insight into all the terrible turmoil and terror she had suffered through the last few days. He wondered though, that if such a marvelous and powerful creature could be hurt so much, then how on Erf were they, two insignificant human Erf children, going to manage? How were they supposed to survive such a deadly and determined enemy, like this Morgrave monster was?

"I appreciate your concern, my young Erfling. It is true, you have a dire task before you, but you will find you have powers and knowledge well beyond your current understanding," Mavis answered him, having clearly heard his worried thoughts. *"But you are now blood-kin to the ancient dynasty of Sivad, the Royal line of the True Dragons, and by your oath and by this sacred bond, all three of you will grow in power and wisdom of the True Dragon Lore."* Mavis confidently assured him.

"All three?" Mary queried her, puzzled. Then realized. "Oh, you mean your Egg here too, Prince Regor, as well as us two, right Mavis?"

But Roger couldn't keep quiet any more. He had to tell Mavis how he really truly felt.

"B-b-but there's so much that we still don't know yet!" Roger burst out in exasperation. "Can't you tell us more about what we're dealing with, so... you know... so we're better able to succeed? All of this stuff about Core Worms and... True Dragons and... everything, well, it's all totally new to us, isn't it? And I don't want you to die Mavis... or your Egg to either, but we really don't want to just get killed either, now do we?" He paused, feeling flustered, but then continued confessing his unvoiced concerns "And really, we don't know that much about the Under-Erf, other than what you've shown us in these time-trips to the past. And I... well, I just don't know... if we can do it all on our own!" he finished with a final gasp.

*"Roger, you must have faith! You can succeed, I do assure you, but you must trust... and not just me, but yourselves too. And you will not be alone. But you must learn to use your own 'knowing' to recognize what is really true. Follow your own hearts - your own observations - of what is really true for you - **not** what you are taught as just passed off as truth by others!"* Mavis answered him, sincerely and emphatically.

Roger's heart lifted and he and Mary immediately nodded, mind-casting their agreement and heart-felt understanding, with a mutual recognition of the simple truth of her words.

"Well, I trust you!" Mary piped up aloud. "We're in a totally different sort of a story now, aren't we? All those silly things we're told we have to learn all about… and must believe in, at school, well, what we're dealing with here, right now, this is the real reality, I think. All of that Psychonomy guff, that's the real fantasy that is. 'Science and Law - and nothing more' What a load of rot! Well, that's what I think, anyway!"

"Yes. I agree dear." Mavis answered her gently. *"And now, dear children, we must solve the immediate dilemma before us. How to get you and my Egg out of this Cavern and safely up to the surface."*

"Yes. That's what's been worrying me too," Roger muttered, frowning. "Just how on Erf do we manage to…?"

But then another even bigger Erfquake shook the Cavern, sending several more Stalactites crashing noisily to the ground and sending further clouds of boiling, grey smoke billowing up all about them. And along with the Erfquake, an enraged and booming voice suddenly came shattering its way into their stunned minds.

"You filthy, slow-brained, worthless, slime-mold of a measly Dragon!" the irate voice boomed telepathically.

Mavis immediately created a protective bubble of blue all around them. But even as she did so, the deep and reverberating voice, although now somewhat controlled and muffled, continued crashing telepathically into their minds.

"Your extinction draws close, you wretched winged-worm. Do you hear me, Queen Sssivam? For my brother, Morgrim, is coming to free me. I am Morgrave, the King of the Erf's Core, and a mere, magically booby-trapped dragon's wing will not defeat me. Do you hear me Sssivam, your death draws nigh!"

Roger and Mary reeled with the force of the Core King's angry words ripping through their human heads like lightning bolts. Their minds unused to such a telepathic assault.

"Your family is all but extinct Sssivam and I have your daughter, Princess Enilorac, captive too, and soon now we will have your third and final Egg as well. And you, oh, pitiful Queen of Winged Slugs, will not be able to stop us. I swear, I will see you before dawn arises in the Skylands above. Prepare to die, you overgrown fly!"

The mortal enemy of Mavis and of all True Dragons had reached out... telepathically... and had found them. And this enemy was adamant on only one thing. Killing them all.

CHAPTER 18:
STAIRWAY TO HEAVEN.

Mavis refused being goaded into reacting though. She knew Morgrave was still not free and was too far away to cause them any direct mortal harm, at least not till well into the next day, despite all his bluster and bravado. But she also knew his incredible mental powers were such he could easily hurt and influence the two human children, as well as mentally cause many more Erf quakes and rock-falls to hinder their escape.

But Mary with her usual empathy had realized something else; Exactly what Morgrave's words had really meant to Mavis, personally.

"Oh, no! Mavis, I–I–I had no idea. How horrible! You've lost most of your family now, and you never said," she choked, near tears herself. She had felt the emotion of barely suppressed grief bubbling from the Dragon Queen's broken heart. "You… you have a daughter and she's been captured… and you, you didn't say anything about her!"

"No, my child, it is only that I didn't want to distress you unnecessarily," Mavis answered morosely. *"But the rescuing of my last Egg here has far-reaching consequences and will save many millions of innocent lives on this, our unique Planet Erf, both Under Erf and Over Erf. That is what is important now. He must survive and so attain his true legacy, as rightful heir to the royal throne of the True Dragons."*

"Listen to me, you poor deluded Queen of Flies." Morgrave raged, again violently interrupting her. **"As I've offered before; I will return your daughter to you unharmed, but only if you give me your last Egg in ex-**

change. Now, how much fairer can I be, eh? One off-spring for another. Come on then, you old Winged-Snake. What do you say?" Morgrave telepathed insistently to her, trying to sound as reasonable in his offer as he could, but failing miserably.

"*I am not a fool.*" Mavis blasted back. "*You would not honor any such promise!*"

"Then, so be it; Await your doom. I will see you soon, and you will all die! For I now know that you are harboring and protecting two of those puny Humdrum children too. I don't know why, but I will find out... and they will die too!" Morgrave yelled manically.

"Oh, my Dizzy Dirac!" Roger exclaimed, aghast. "How long have we got then, Mavis?"

"We have no time to waste now," Mavis replied sadly. "Your educations, such as they are, will have to suffice. You must take my Egg and leave immediately. I suspect King Morgrave plans to surprise us in some devious way, and you will be much safer on the surface and will also find new friends up there who will help you. And the Core Worms cannot stand being on the surface for very long. Sunlight is deadly for them!"

But Roger was getting increasingly worried. In fact, if he was being fully honest, it wasn't just a matter of simply being worried. He was getting increasingly scared and was secretly very concerned his being scared would soon turn into a total and abject terror and panic.

He swallowed hard, looking all around the gloomy, smoke-filled cavern, full of the blasted corpses of the many hundreds of Minion Worms that had attacked them just a little while ago. The Dragon's cavern was dimly lit by the few burning corpses still smoldering, and from the occasional red flicker of flame that blew raggedly from out of Mavis's long muzzle.

He scanned the whole cavern in a slow 360-degree turn, desperately looking for any hint of a tiny clue as to just how they could get out of this infernal place. His best and only friend, Mary Maddam, in this unexpected adventure, now turned into a serious quest, was wounded and still in pain from her long fall down the underground slope. He gulped and felt even iller, realizing that without him she'd be done for.

And that led to but another concern becoming a deadly skin-crawling fear too. Just how was Mary expected to climb up the cliff and get through the blanket of cloud hanging above them and then make her way up the long dark, smoke-filled slope, that hopefully led them to eventual freedom and escape on the surface? How on Einstein's Erf was she going to do that?

Not to mention they had to do it with a monster of a Fire-Worm Lord, old Mad Morgrave, the King of the Core, literally hot on their tails, well, at least on Mavis's the Dragon Queen's. But Roger was pretty sure, that once Morgrave had caught up and dealt with wounded Mavis, it wouldn't be long before he'd be right after them too.

Roger had a zillion and one questions he wanted to ask but knew there was no time left. Mavis had made it clear, they had to get back up to the surface and take her last Dragon's Egg with them, with no ifs ands or buts; The fate of the whole of the Under-Erf and maybe even more, depended on it. Which meant… everything depended on him!

Mary looked over at Roger with concern on her strained and sooty face, she could tell Roger was getting more and more agitated, every relentless murky minute that passed on by.

"Can you see any way we can get out from here yet, Roger?" she asked him hopefully.

"Fraid not," he replied rather tersely, his brow knitted in concentration. "Look here, Mary, just how bad off are you?

Erm, well... what I mean to say is, you climbing that cliff there's going to be a tall order, you know ... and, well, what with your sprained ankle and... and..." His words faded away, drying up in his mouth. Mary was giving him a decidedly black frown of her very own.

"Oh, don't be all soft belly and boiled blather, Roger," she scolded him, "I'll do my best, O.K. And what choice do we have anyway, eh? We've got to figure a way out of here, right? Simple as that I'd say. Mavis reckons Morgrave will be here sometime during tomorrow and we need to be long gone by then, even if it is the middle of the night right now."

"*And also, do not forget, my dear children,*" Mavis calmly telepathed, interrupting their argument, "*this, my last Dragon's Egg, is the True Dragons only chance of ever redressing all the terrible wrongs perpetrated by these Core Lords for a thousand years. Therefore, somehow, a way must be devised for you return to the surface immediately.*"

"Sorry, I do understand Mavis, I really do," Roger replied. "But... what happens if... if... if Morgrave gets to you, then kills... I mean, then... goes after us... What do we do then?"

"*Do not fear, my young Skyling, I am not as defenseless as I seem,*" Mavis replied coolly. "*I will guard your rear and I will also monitor Morgrave's approach. I will do everything in my power to delay his arrival and aid your escape and so assist your rescuing of my last Egg. And you will find you have good friends, as soon as you reach the Tree King's roots that is. The Tree above us, you know of as the Smoking Tree.*"

"All right, Mavis. Fair enough; But that still leaves us with the tricky little problem of just how we go about this rescue, doesn't it? You haven't got any spare dragon's magick or such; you know... something up your sleeve... or... under your wing, have you?" Roger asked her, feeling increasingly frustrated and afraid.

"*My most powerful magick, right now, rests in yourself Roger... in you and in Mary here,*" Mavis answered him softly. "*Your courage, compassion, intelligence and humanity, these are what will rescue us all one day I believe. And these are the magicks you must use most now!"*

And with that said, it quite naturally and tacitly fell to Roger, once again, to somehow work out a clever scientific solution for their immediate seemingly insolvable problem.

Just exactly how were they getting out of this smoke-filled Cavern, with an injured girl and a Dragon's Egg as well, and do so before their brutal enemy, the Mad King Morgrave, es-caped and hunted them out for the final kill?

And, not to mention too, before the Egg's wounded mum, Mavis, a thousand years old Dragon Queen, imminently died, naturally exploding... and so killing them all, anyway!

Roger walked carefully around the dingy, minion-corpse-littered Cavern, while quietly, Mavis watched him from her heavily lidded eyes, very weary from all her recent exertions, but keeping a close eye on his movements and being ready to protect him with another blast of her blue flame if needed, just in case King Morgrave suddenly attacked again.

Roger walked and carefully studied some of the rock for-mations that were still standing here and there; Then he be-gan doing some intricate, tricky geometric calculations in his head. Raising his arm out and extending his thumb up to get a bead on various angles and distances. He then paused a while and then scratched at his head deep in thought, then he frowned some more and began quietly muttering to himself. Then he started pacing around the Cavern and then all around the reclining Dragon Queen again.

And then he suddenly stopped in his tracks, staring di-rectly up at Mavis, the now bemused Dragon Queen, who looked back at him with a dragonish smile of puzzlement on her noble face at all his strange and serious-faced antics.

"O.K. Mavis, you've said you're too weak to move any of these rocks, and any of these fallen stalagmites too, right?" he asked her, "but what about... well, are you strong enough... to move yourself, at all?"

"*Yes, Roger, I think I can just about manage that*!" Mavis replied, with a tinge of sarcasm.

A huge grin spread over Roger's soot-soiled, bespectacled face. "Then, Eureka!" he cried, yelling with joy at the top of his voice. "Eureka, Eureka, Eureka! By good old Dizzy, Dozy Diogenes, himself, EUREKA!"

"Oh, I think he's got it!" Mary laughed up at Mavis, then smiling at him admiringly said. "So, what is it?" she asked, "what do we do then, Roj? How do we get up the cliff an' up that slope an' back up to the surface? How?"

"We walk!" said Roger, grinning from ear to ear. "We walk up!"

Mary looked at him dumbfounded.

Then very patiently, he explained to Mavis and Mary, and telepathically too, as he did so, showing them exactly how he intended to get up to the slope above that led to their freedoms, both Roger and Mary - and the precious Dragon's Egg too!

"It's quite easy when you know how, you know!" he quipped, feeling extremely relieved, as Mary and Queen Mavis beamed at him, both mentally sending him their congratulatory and very admiring thoughts.

"*Very well done, Roger! That's an excellent idea*!" Mavis warmly telepathed to him.

"Oh, it's so simple, Roj! How clever you are!" Mary happily agreed.

He had found the way out. And truth be told, he felt proud of the sheer simplicity of it too. The answer had come to him in a flash of inspiration, as he'd been busy dithering, calculating and whimsically wishing for a set of stairs to just magically appear. They sort of had!

"Yes. It's like a sort of 'Stairway to Heaven'," he told them both, smiling proudly.

Roger then gave the instructions necessary to implement his ingenious solution, especially to Queen Mavis, as the enormous ridge-backed Dragon was crucial to this particular solution. And very soon they could safely climb up and so reach the beginnings of the slope at the top of the cliff; And all in just a few minutes of careful preparation.

"Just a bit more over to the left," he called up to Mavis. "O.K. That's it... just about right, I think, now just hold it there, O.K. That's good? We'll have to cover our faces and make our way up as quickly as we can up through the smoke cloud and then get onto the slope's edge." He told them. He then stepped over towards Mary, who stood waiting with the Dragon's egg, now wrapped up tightly and safely under her thick, school coat. "After you, Mademoiselle," he said, gallantly taking her arm.

They then proceeded to slowly walk, step by cautious step, up to the as-yet unknown... and incredible and unbelievable dangers... that awaited them - up the Dragon's back!

Mavis's back was broad, and her spine was well ridged with large bony scales giving the children a natural set of steps. They steadily made their way from her tail and onto her thick, well-scaled neck. And Roger had had the presence of mind to whip out a couple of his trusty hankies before they plunged their way up through the layered cloud of smog. With these tied around their mouths and noses, they ploughed onwards and upwards, through the smoke and at last climbed onto the top of Mavis's head, poking up through the smoke cloud.

By following Roger's directions, the Dragon Queen had maneuvered herself right up close against the cliff face and stretched her neck up through the bank of smoke, her long dragon's snout now resting on the ledge where the much sought-after slope to the surface began.

All they had to do now was slide down her nose onto the ledge and they'd be on their way.

But as Roger was helping Mary clamber down between Mavis's eyes and onto her muzzle, Mad King Morgrave now suddenly attacked again. His mental roar thundered in their heads, immediately causing them to wince and cry out in pain. Mary lost her balance and fell to one side and slid dangerously across Mavis's left cheek, still tightly clutching the Dragon's Egg, so, unable to stop herself from falling headlong into the swirling cloud of smoke below and therefore from plummeting to her certain death.

Roger stood aghast, frozen in shock and helpless with horror, upon Mavis's scaly brow, his stomach churning and clutching onto one of the Dragon's horns that sprouted from there. There was absolutely nothing he could do to save her.

But Mavis, the Dragon Queen could. As soon as she felt Mary slip from off of her cheek, Mavis blew out a great cloud of blue-grey smoke from her flared nostrils that immediately enveloped Mary and stopped her falling any further. Then she deftly dipped her head down into the smoke and using her Dragon's fangs, with the precision of a brilliant brain surgeon, she hooked and plucked Mary up through the cloud and safely deposited her on the cliff edge, right at the beginning of the much longed for slope.

"Oh, Mighty Merlin! Thank you, Mavis, oh, th-th-thank you very much." Mary exclaimed. "You saved my life there fer sure!" She lay there crying and breathing heavily on the cliff top and clutching the Egg to her. Even as she'd fallen, she'd refused to let go of it.

Roger quickly slid his way down Mavis's curving muzzle and joined her on the cliff ledge.

But… the murderous Morgrave hadn't finished with them yet!

"Whatever trickeries you're up to, Maggot Queen, they won't work. This Humdrum spawn seem to be important to you… so they will die with you. None shall escape me!"

"His enraged mental roar once again thundered through their heads, sending them both into spasms of mind-searing pain. Mavis though immediately countered this attack and once more mentally protected them both.

"You hear me, so-called, Queen Sivam, you broken down and crippled wreck of a False Dragon. I the Mighty Morgrave will not allow them to leave!" he raged madly on.

But Mavis's mental powers were easily a match for the Core Worm King's.

"You are just a bully and a coward, Morgrave. So, you would pick on children rather than confront me, would you? Well, you mentally retarded, cinder-hearted, slime-ball of a worthless Worm, I will not allow that!" the Dragon Queen retorted, and then transmitted a terrific mental pulse of pain herself, sizzling through the rocky miles that still separated them. The powerful pain-wave hit Morgrave hard and wracked his body with nerve-searing agony.

"Let that be a lesson to you, you arrogant, pea-brained fool!" Mavis mentally roared out. Then turning her attention to the awaiting children, she blew another cloud of blue smoke all around them. *"That will help protect you from further mental intrusion from Morgrave,"* she assured them, *"at least for a while, but you must now get to the surface as fast as you can."*

Roger stood on the sloping tunnel's ledge and looked up into the inky darkness up ahead. He was very well aware of the difficult route that lay before them. Yes, they'd managed to get to the start of the slope, but now, since all the Erf Quakes, there was the added threat of hidden crevices, not to mention other unknown hazards from the recent rockfalls.

He could see Mary was still limping and wincing from the pain in her ankle. So how in all of Heisenberg's Hell were they going to get up this slope? He thought anxiously to himself.

But Mavis had heard his every thought. The top of the Dragon Queen's head rested against the clifftop edge and her heavily lidded eyes now blinked wisely and reassuringly up at him.

"I fully understand your concern, Roger," Mavis's cool tones flowed gently into his mind, once again. *"But you are never alone, so do not fear. I will assist you now.. and others will follow. Now, if you and Mary will just step over to one side of the slope, we will proceed."*

Mavis raised her chin up over the slope's ledge and then flared her nostrils wide, and then blasted the stony floor with a long stream of strange, yellow-green flame. Roger saw this had the immediate effect of melting all of the slope's rocky surface, causing it to rumple and fold for quite some way up.

The molten, corrugated surface of the slope rapidly cooled, and the greenish glow faded, and soon, there before Roger and Mary's disbelieving eyes, was a newly created, undulating stairway, already hardening, and ready for the children to walk up by.

"My dragon-flame blast will have gone only a few hundred yards at the most, my skylings, so do be careful when you come to the parts higher up, there may well be cracks and crevices up there." Mavis mentally warned them.

"Well, another Stairway to Heaven was definitely what we needed!" Roger answered her, now feeling a bit more confident.

The children stepped carefully onto the first curved and springy step of their new stairway. But Mavis's magical fire-blast had also disturbed the slope's grey dust layer and smoke and this was snow pinning and roiling all about them. Roger thought it was like looking into the window of a giant spin-dryer, but one full of dirty looking rags.

Roger and Mary stood perched on the very start of the slope that would, all being well, take them up to their eventual freedom and much longed-for escape. Just as long as there were no more disasters that is; whether of mutant Monsters or of violent Erf-quakes!

Mary tearfully stooped and grasped Mavis by the tip of her snout and gave her a big hug, the best that she could manage. Mavis's snout was far too big to wrap her arms all the way around though, but Mavis understood her intent. She lovingly blinked her large, amber eyes, looking intently upon the Sky Child, (giving her a comical, cross-eyed look, Roger noticed, with some amusement), and in her noble and dragonish way, Mavis rumbled her mutually felt, fondest feelings for her. Much like a cat would do, purring with peaceful contentment. But the purring of a Dragon Queen was far, far louder and a lot more meaningful.

"Oh, Mavis, I am going to miss you when you die!" Mary sniffed, barely holding back her welling tears, as she lovingly hugged the injured, dragon mother and queen, fully realizing she would never see her again. "And I promise I'll look after Regor for you." She sniffed.

"Now hush, my child," said Mavis gently, "there's nothing in death for either of us to fear. My passing is as natural as the hatching of my Egg. And you and Roger are now of my blood. You will come to learn, the great heritage of the ancient Sivads is now yours to share, both in the bounties of our magicks and our knowledge. And as you grow, you will learn more of this and you will find you have your own powers to discover too. But as you both learn; you will increasingly share the many responsibilities that True Dragon knowledge brings."

"But, d-d-do you really have to die and explode?" Mary asked her, only really caring now about losing Mavis. "Is there nothing we can do for you, nothing at all?" she asked, pleading, her eyes now red and swollen and the tears rolling down her cheeks.

"Yes, Mavis, isn't there something we can do to save you? Roger interjected, near to tears himself. You've done so much for us... and anyway... isn't... isn't it you who always says...

I mean... says there's always a solution somewhere to any problem?"

"I will always be with you, dear children; remember, we have mind-melded and have been heart-bound too; And I only pass on to a new chapter in another story. Here and now, though, it requires we serve the current story the very best we can. And our own Stories never really end you know. For my passing, it is not a problem to be solved... but it is more like... well, yet another sort of a solution. Remember, I will be watching over you, always. Meanwhile, you must continue this story yourselves; it's an important one, so make it a worthwhile one... and ultimately, make it a happy one!"

Roger now stepped forward. He didn't know what to say and stood there biting on his lip and looking glumly down at his feet. But he then mustered up enough courage to put a hand onto Mavis's scaly head and say his own heartfelt goodbye.

"Well, g-g-goodbye then, Mavis. You've been... I mean, I'll miss you too... and without all your... well, we'd both be, well, you know... so th-th-thank you, Queen Mavis, it's been a great honour to know you. It really has!"

He stumbled to a faltering, embarrassed silence; surprised at having found all the words he'd needed to express his true feelings, despite being tongue-tied and feeling overwhelmed, having to leave this wonderful and wise Queen of the True Dragons behind to die.

Mavis looked Roger deeply and intently in the eyes and he felt himself momentarily lost within her large, lambent pools of wise and ancient intelligence; As if he was slowly sinking, swimming gently down into their warm and golden depths.

"For good or for ill it is you two who have been chosen. Mavis replied. *"Above all others, on or in this Erf, it is you, Roger, and Mary too, who we must now turn to."* Then Mavis fine-tuned her telepathic communication so only Roger could hear her. *"And at this very moment, Roger, you are particularly needed, for your*

friend Mary here, is hurt, and so I rely on you to defend and protect her as well as my precious Egg, from all the dangers and harms that may fall upon you. Are we agreed, my valiant Son of the Sky?"

"Yes. I understand, Mavis; I agree, and I promise, I'll do my best, after all, as you say, there is always a way... isn't there!" Roger telepathed back, as courageously as he could. *"We'll make it somehow. We'll find the way!"*

"Then, very good, my sky-child; You are learning but now I must rest and so rebuild my energies for what is soon to come. I must be prepared. Go now and also know that for a short while we will still be joined in thought. I will be with you both - up until the very last second of my final ascension to the Sky Spirits. And if I am needed, I will answer. Now fare you well - and may the Great Spirit of the Erf be your guide forever!"

Mavis then turned again to Mary. *"Farewell, my faithful young Egg Bearer. There will be further lessons and others above and below who will also teach you, as well as serve you too. Now, children, please stand together; I must give you my final gift."*

She opened her jaws wide and breathed out a long, billowing cloud of magical blue flame, this time engulfing them and permeating every cell of their aching bodies and giving them a faint, pale-blue aura. This glowed all around them and also lit the sloping stairway ahead, that disappeared up into the ever-deepening darkness. Their only route to freedom!

"You now have the protection of a much deeper Blue Dragon Flame. This will protect you as you climb the slope to the Skylands. Remember, trust in the power of the True Dragons - and in each other too; All three of you. As you do, you will each grow and will learn and will be of great comfort to the other; now, Goodbye and Fare Well."

Roger took hold of Mary's arm and gently helped her to get onto the first step. She had put the Egg safely and snugly up her jumper and tied her coat over it with Roger's scarf this time. She now did indeed look like a very fat woman or a very pregnant one, and was fully aware of that embarrassing fact.

"Don't you dare say a word!" she hissed to Roger, quickly stopping the witty remark that he was just about to make, dead in its boyish tracks.

"I didn't say a thing," he said, with a slight smirk. "Now keep right behind me, Mary, we've got this blue light for now and then only got my old torch to light our way and I don't know how long that will last."

"Well, at least we know the only direction we got to go is upwards," Mary smiled at him, "and look, there's one of your discarded hankies, Roj, we're right where you came down."

The two weary children made their way up the murky, stepped slope, cautiously stepping forwards and ever onwards and upwards. The dull, red glow of the Dragon's Cavern slowly dimming behind them, Mary still limping slightly and Roger's torch searching as a weak smudge of pale, yellow light in the all-enveloping darkness ahead.

"Goodbye my Sky Children… and Fare Well." came Mavis's thought, telepathing to them, as they made their way, step by step, up their Stairway to Heaven.

"Be your Selves… and you will find the way!"

THE END

Dragon's Erf is continued in Book Two – Dragon's Inferno!

EPILOGUE:

"*O*h, *Morgrave, Morgrave; by all the Ancient Demons of the Core. How did you get yourself so helplessly trapped? Don't you know, my royal brother, all True Dragons have powerful magicks and skills that rival even our own?*" Lord Morgrim disparagingly telepathed to his imprisoned twin brother King Morgrave.

"*Don't waste your breath or my time, scolding me, Morgrim,*" Lord Morgrave, the King of the Core, hissed back defiantly. He had been trapped beneath this mountain of rock for some days now. But ordinarily, this would have meant nothing. Hundreds of tons of Erf's mantle-rock, usually for him, would be much like a tadpole swimming about in a muddy pool.

But he had been surprised and encased in that damned Dragon Queen's wing. Just as he had triumphantly wrenched it away from her body, he had realized just too late. She had allowed him that small victory, in order for her hexed wing to enfold him within its magical and ever-tightening and un-breakable grip.

The wing's veins and leathery material had been trans-formed into a relentlessly expanding death-trap. It had grown and covered his full length and held him fast within its un-breakable glowing, blue-grey cocoon.

"*I will be with you within a day I do assure you, Morgrave. But I must first complete my mission here with Doctor Rab Idego here in my secret Cavern Laboratory under Lake Gnash, in Skiltland,*" Morgrim growled softly. "*Just try to be patient, brother, and await my arrival, then between us we will soon negate that Winged-Worm-Queen's vexa-tious Magick.*"

"Well, by the Devil-divine!" Morgrave cried. *"Isn't your King more important to you, Morgrim? You should be on your way right now, not tinkering around with your strange, un-Core-like obsessions, all these greedy Humdrum Scientists and weird Psychonomists of yours!"*

"Of course, of course, my dear brother," Lord Morgrim replied as soothingly as he could. *"But I am already here, and my task is very nearly done. So, please be patient. I promise you; I will definitely be with you on the morrow, at the very latest."*

"Aaaargh!" Morgave raged. *"Patient be patient, you say. That's just fine for you to say, dearest brother, isn't it? You're not caught in this infernal wing, are you? Whenever I move, it just gets even tighter, and it burns me, so hurry to me brother. I demand you, please hurry; The Dragon Queen must be caught and I must have my vengeance!"*

"Yes, your Majesty, I assure you, I will alert you when I am nearer to you. But for now, please believe me when I tell you these obsessions, as you call them, are purely for your benefit, my Laboratories are providing new and ever greater advances, and these are all in aid of your magnificent rule brother. For one day you will be King of the Erf – and not just the Core!" Morgrim earnestly replied, but with a slight tinge of sarcasm hidden within his bombast.

***

And it was but a day later that Lord Morgrim duly made his way southwards to see to the rescue of his brother, Morgave, the King of the Core. And as he burrowed through the butter-like rock, he ruminated darkly on the increasing irrationality of his over-emotional and far too-little-brained royal brother.

It has become even harder to control the dim fool of late, he thought, as he sped onwards, burrowing underneath the border between Skiltland and Inglande, lying far above him on the Erf's surface. *He has become ever more obsessed with the killing of every Sivad that breathes in Under Erf. And ever since our recent attack on the Dragon Cavern-world, where we killed the High King and captured his grandchildren, still Morgrave refuses to be satisfied.*

Lord Morgrim radiated his navigational psychic sense outwards, sweeping the rocks ahead for many miles, sensing the buried scar of a deep fault line there, away to his left. He shifted towards it, knowing it was going his way, and would make for a slightly faster passage.

Trouble is, I must keep my damn fool of a brother on the throne. I can do so much more with him there, taking all of the attention away from me. I must be free to execute my plans, but Morgrave has an incredible knack for getting himself into trouble. It has only been by my diligence that he's been kept alive this long at all! He continued to himself bitterly.

Now, by my reckoning, I should be within mind-meld reach of him this very night. Then I must try to persuade him against going off on a fool's errand chasing that Dragon Queen up to the surface and getting himself burnt to a crisp by the Sun God. If not, then I must at least persuade him to return quickly back to the Core. The other Fire-Worm Lords are already growing suspicious of his many absences. But I think I'll have a permanent solution for that particular problem too very soon now. Doctor Idego, in the Psychonomy Lab, in Under-Hell on the Umber, has come up with just the device I need.

Lord Morgrim gloated pleasantly at the wonderful thought of his being able to have complete and utter control of his dim-witted brother, very, very soon.

And shortly I will have the new Prime Councilor of Inglande in my pocket too. Such a shame that the last one died on me. But these Humdrums are much weaker than Minion worms. And they are so gullible. Even believing that things like gold and diamonds and radioactive ores from the core will make them happy and successful. They hardly deserve to be kept as slaves. And I must gather in the latest reports from my Spy Network. There should be news of interest from both the United States of Ameriga and the United States of Cathay, by now. Oh, dear me; But complete world domination does take such meticulous planning... and patience too, he added, as a wise afterthought.

***

King Morgave was beside himself with rage. It had been another whole Erf day gone by now, and still no word from his secretive and haughty brother, Morgrim.

Just wait until I get my jaws on him, he thought, distracting himself from the ceaseless web of pain that covered his entire body, with pleasurable thoughts of taking out his frustrations on his twin brother. *How dare he leave me like this? Doesn't he appreciate, I am the King, not him? I'll have him thrown in the Core Dungeons… I'll get him experimented on too, see how he likes that, eh? I'll get a host of his zombie humdrum slaves to operate on him, instead of the other way around. He'll pay for making me wait. I swear he will.*

Morgrave had long run out of the various insane ideas of horrible, drawn out tortures and grim and gruesome deaths he would inflict on that upstart brat of a Dragon Queen and her feeble and puny Egg. He had even mentally filed away several of the choicest and cruelest ideas that he'd been able to imagine. Some of them were so very disgusting and horrifying they had even brought tears of joy to his own inflamed and evil, red eyes.

But now it was his brother's turn to be the focus of his ferocious fantasies.

Every inch of his horny, armored skin and every steely scale and bony plate was enmeshed within the Dragon Queen's indestructible wing, and he had long ago learned not to move a muscle. But however hard it was to admit, he really knew, in the deepest, blackest wrinkle of his ebony heart, his only chance of escape lay in the timely arrival of his brother. It was therefore with some relief that he at last heard from the long-awaited Lord Morgrim.

"I am close now, brother. I have come as fast as I could and will be with you very soon," Lord Morgrim's voice now came booming into the King's seething mind. *"And please do be assured, your almighty and Magnificent Majesty, the Core Worm Conclave still have no idea of your current predicament at all. They have all been informed that you are with me and on a top-secret mission in order to further expand our Core Realm. And I have good news, brother. You will be able*

to tell them we now have new vassals in more Under-Erf realms. The domain of Dark Imps, beneath the Forest of Lundun itself, is now ours, as well as the long sought after, Goblin Kingdom of Yekrut. The Core Worm Conquests go well. You will surely return to the Core a Hero, my liege."

Lord Morgrim's words had been chosen most wisely and carefully, having been cunningly designed to mollify, as well as to further inflate Morgrave's massive mega-ego. That Skiltish Psychonomist, Dr. Rab Idego, had been very useful and quite clever, and had even given him a few hints on how to manage his brother's wildly erratic temper and bloated self-importance; Just temporarily, while the new Mind-Cap machine was being perfected in his Lab.

"Harrumph! Well, erm... yes... I see, Morgrim. All very good." King Morgrave coughed and telepathed hesitantly in reply. At once, reluctantly realizing he couldn't totally ignore the influence of the other Core Worm Lords, especially those of the Conclave.

He knew he needed their support, or at least some token of it, so he could fulfill his one, true burning desire, to rid the world of the Sivad Dragons. They were the only royal family of True Dragons with the power and influence to defeat the Core Worms. And they were the only Dragons who could wield all three Dragon Magicks for a start. Not all of them for sure, he knew, but all it took was just one Dragon that could... and then... well, it just didn't bear contemplating... nothing at all must be allowed to stand in the way of his own majestic and magnificent reign continuing, forever and ever. Therefore, all Sivads must be exterminated!

"Well, get on with it then, brother. We must join minds and turn this damned wing to ash, and you must be close enough by now to do so, but be careful, I don't want a hair on my hide touched, let alone scorched," Morgrave chided and raged.

"Don't worry, dearest brother, we will be methodical," Morgrim replied patiently. *"Now, as you say, let us Mind-meld and so formu-*

late and ferment the necessary psychic-acids to rid you of this infernal piece of magickal, dragon trickery."

King Morgrave mentally roared out his agreement, but momentarily forgot the urgent need to remain totally still and unmoving. Jolts of electric pain now shot through his flanks and he juddered and writhed with agony as the wing's magickal torment tore through him.

"You filthy, slow-brained, worthless, slime mold of a measly Dragon!" he screamed.

And, as he did, inadvertently, mentally reaching out in violent shock and telepathing his unbridled rage through the many layers of rock up above him, straight into the mind of the trapped and wounded Mavis. The bellows of anger, insult and frustration tore through the Dragon Queen's and children's minds, along with the sudden burst of seismic shock waves; Causing sudden Erfquakes to violently erupt and so tear the Dragon Queen's Cavern apart.

"Oh, Morgrave, Morgrave, what are you doing, brother? Be silent, please," Morgrim cried out in despair. *"You have only now forewarned your enemy of your imminent escape. You will have lost all element of surprise!"*

"I care not!" Morgrave mentally spat back, after finishing his telepathic tirade and threats to the hated Dragon Queen, ensconced in her Cavern high above him. *"Nothing will stop me now, do you hear me brother, nothing. I will only return to the Core when that overgrown fly of a Dragon has been exterminated, along with her unhatched, addled and putrid little Egg! Do you understand Morgrim? Only then!"*

"I understand, brother, I really do," Lord Morgrim replied very smoothly, but inwardly, heavily sighing, now realizing he had no chance at all of persuading Morgrave to return with him back to the Core. *"But you best be quick about it for the Core Conclave can only be kept cool and ignorant for so long. Your continued absence will eventually be noticed and your authority will be challenged."*

"Then do your duty Brother and return to the Core yourself." Morgrave sneered. *"Let the Core Conclave know that their King will soon return with news of yet another great victory."*

Morgrim cloaked his inner thoughts, seemingly agreeing to this royal command and proceeded to help free his brother from the hexed dragon wing, which they achieved together, in but a few moments.

But as he left his royal brother, free now to bore his way upwards and confront his long-awaited destiny, to do final and deadly battle with the Queen of the True Dragons, Morgrim's hidden thoughts were now ones of a rigid steely anger and a cold and cunning calculation.

He needed the solution to the mind control of Morgrave right now. Not a moment longer should be allowed to pass. He must get that new-fangled Hypno-Cap gizmo, that's what the Doctor of Neural Implantations and Conditioning had called it. Let his brother believe he was returning on his behalf to the Core. What was of the utmost importance, right now, was to get hold of that newfangled Gizmo... and quickly... and get King Morgrave under control.

"Farewell, dear Brother. Enjoy your victory to come. I shall see you again soon." He telepathed, as Morgrave's massive armored bulk disappeared from view above him.

And then... once again my own well-laid plans will all flow as smoothly as red-hot lava! He added, as a hidden and satisfying afterthought.

***

A NOTE: FROM YOUR FUN-LOVING AUTHOR:

One of the great things I love about writing is … getting to know my readers …

So - Join my Newsletter now for all sorts of information, fun facts and fictional frolics!

You will receive all the latest news, releases and info on the many Worlds of Dragon's Erf.

JOIN HERE: https://www.srlangleywriter.com

(THE TEMPTATIONS: - (No! Not the 60's Motown Soul Group!) But the valuable Benefits you will Receive!

1: A Free Short Story. 2: A Monthly Newsletter. 3: New Releases and Special Offers. 4: Bonus Content. etc.)

A FURTHER WORD … OR SIXTY-SIX … FROM YOUR AUTHOR …

A POLITE REQUEST FOR REVIEWS …It would be a great help to me as an Indie Author, setting out on this wild and as yet uncharted exploration of blah, blah, blah …

OK. I'll cut to the chase!

If you can spare some time, please consider leaving an honest review for DRAGON'S EGG.

It really does help new readers to find me and me find them. Thanking you in advance.

***

INTRODUCTION TO THE NEXT BOOK IN THE EXCITING DRAGON'S ERF SERIES: BOOK TWO ~ DRAGON'S INFERNO…

EXCERPT FROM CHAPTER 1: MAGMA RISING.

After a few minutes, Roger had laboriously progressed some way up the rocky stairway; But Mary was feeling decidedly and increasingly queasy and out of breath. She hadn't wanted to say anything to Roger, but her long fall and then all their subsequent underground battles had really shaken her up, a lot.

The truth was though, that despite the Dragon Queen's help, the non-stop, nagging pains from her bruised ribs and swollen ankle were slowly draining her energy, if not her resolve.

Roger noticed that Mary was flagging and falling behind. He was growing more and more worried. Just how in the Dizzy Darwin was he going to get Mary and the Dragon's Egg, back safely up to the surface, let alone having to cross the Bad Wood, in the middle of the night?

Just as Mary hadn't wanted to admit to how weak and in pain she'd felt, Roger didn't want to confess to how inadequate he felt in actually achieving this momentous task; And also, just how hopeless it all seemed. Trying to keep brave and positive was one thing, but facing the harsh reality of their situation was another. The further they went, stepping wearily onwards and upwards, the more Roger's ill-ease and foreboding grew.

"O.K. if we have a quick break now?" Roger asked Mary gallantly, secretly thinking she would really need one but would be too stubborn to ask herself.

"Yes, erm, o.k. thanks, I could do with a bit of a rest, Roj," Mary sighed with some relief. "There's nothing like having a nice nap when yer deep underground and with a

Dragon's Egg stuffed under your coat and a wounded Dragon Queen, not far away and about to explode!" She laughed, doing her best to put a brave face on things.

"Well, at least you've still got your sense of humor!" Roger laughed back. "But Mavis won't be exploding anytime soon, Mary; she said she'll guard the entrance to the slope and ensure we have plenty of time to get up to the surface first."

Then they heard it; Just ahead of them, the sudden and terrifying roaring and rumbling of an Erf-quake. But it differed from the sounds all the earlier Erf-quakes had made, it seemed more directed and intense, Roger thought; But as to why exactly, he couldn't yet tell.

Roger saw several large boulders coming, tumbling and rolling out of the inky fog ahead, crashing down the slope and heading towards them. He pulled Mary off to one side as they rolled on by. He then realized that just a little further on up, the floor of the slope had erupted, and pools of seething red-hot magma were now bubbling and flowing from out the hole there. The initial force of the eruption had also tossed big chunks of rock and debris up into the air, and it was these boulders that had come rolling down upon them. And there were still more boulders coming their way.

Roger realized that if he didn't move fast, they'd be crushed before their journey home had hardly started. He took hold of Mary's arm and pulled her to him, just in time, as yet another large boulder crashed on by, just where she'd been standing.

"Quick, Mary, roll right over to the side wall and squeeze into any crack you find there!" Roger cried, as he too threw himself on the ground and rolled over to the side of the slope and squeezed himself into a narrow fissure there.

Luckily, most of the boulders were careening right down the middle of the slope, like giant bowling balls bouncing down a bumpy bowling alley. A couple though hit the side walls and cracked into smaller pieces, missing them both but showering them with pebbles and dust.

And one of the larger chunks went hurtling right over their heads, barely inches from their scalps, as they lay huddled face down and squeezed tightly into the crack in the wall that had accommodated them both. Soon, the rock-fall was over, almost as quickly as it had started. The last shower of pebbles went skittering by and just dust and darkness remained.

"Whew, that was close!" Roger exclaimed, peeling himself out from the tight crack.

But there was no answer. Mary just lay by his side in total silence.

"Are y-y-you, all right?" Roger anxiously asked, grabbing her shoulder and giving her a quick but gentle shake. But she just rolled over and lay unmoving on her back next to him.

Roger's heart froze, his breath caught and choked in his throat, and his stomach tightened to a cold hard knot. It terrified him beyond words that Mary had been hit by a rock and may have even been killed. He couldn't bear the thought that he could be left totally alone now with his only friend dead, or at the best, desperately needing his help, and him not able to do a thing about it.

***

BIOGRAPHY:

S R Langley is a… Writer and Poet.

Born last Century in the year of the Rabbit, he was raised in the Warrens of South Lundun, but after 18 years in the leafy suburbs, set out to seek his fame and fortune on the High Seas.

After some years circumnavigating Planet Erf, getting dizzy and then bored, he eventually returned home to his beloved Inglande where he finally caught a girl, settled down and after several years had gone by, discovered he had a family of five children, two cats and a dog!

He now lives in the vibrant Capital of the North West – and yes – he does of course support the greatest Football Club ever!

***

And don't forget …

Check out his Author Website at:
https://www.srlangleywriter.com

And you can follow him on Facebook at: @SRLangley.Writer

Or on Instagram at:
SoRoLangley or Twitter at: @LangleyWriter

Or you can email him at info@srlangley.com

And he will always be very pleased to hear from you and will do his very best to reply!*

(* Doesn't apply to Anti-Social Twits though!)

***